# STONE GUARDIAN

## Danielle Monsch

Enjoy the
Entwined Realms

Dalle Monsch

Romantic Geek Publishing

STONE GUARDIAN (ENTWINED REALMS, BOOK 1)
Copyright © 2013 Danielle Monsch
Print Book ISBN 978-1-938593-10-9

Publication Date: July 2013

Content Editor: Gwen Hayes
Line Editor: Jessa Slade
Copy Editor: Eilis Flynn

All rights reserved under International and Pan-American
Copyright Conventions

By payment of required fees, you have been granted the *non*-exclusive, *non*-transferable right to access and read the text of
this book. No part of this text may be reproduced, transmitted,
downloaded, decompiled, reverse engineered, or stored in or
introduced into any information storage and retrieval system,
in any form or by any means, whether electronic or
mechanical, now known or hereinafter invented without the
express written permission of copyright owner.

All characters and events in this book are fictitious. Any
resemblance to actual persons – living or dead – is purely
coincidental.

Cover Design Nathalia Suellen
Interior format by The Killion Group
http://thekilliongroupinc.com

# DEDICATION

It has been a long journey from the first moment I got the idea to write this book to that happy point when I became a good-enough writer I could pull it off.

It's not a journey I've taken alone.

This book is dedicated to all the people who have helped me become the writer I needed to be to make this book a reality.

My special thanks to Mary Buckham, Dianna Love, Margie Lawson, Laurie Schnebly Campbell, Grace Bradley, Mallory Braus, Rhonda Helms, Jennifer Haymore, Victoria Janssen, Gwen Hayes, and Jessa Slade.

And, as always, Mr. Jim Garner.

# OTHER BOOKS BY DANIELLE MONSCH

**Fairy Tales & Ever Afters Series**
(Slightly Twisted and Very Sexy takes on Fairy Tales)

**Loving a Fairy Godmother**
**Loving an Ugly Beast**
**Loving a Prince Charming**

And want to know whenever a
New Book is Released?

**DANIELLE MONSCH ANNOUNCEMENT LIST!**
http://www.daniellemonsch.com/dani/signup/

# TABLE OF CONTENTS

# CHAPTER ONE

Jack Miller aimed his shotgun at the monster's grey-skinned head and pulled the trigger. Green sludge and bits of bone and flesh splattered through the air to land on the street, the gory aftermath releasing a noxious, sulfurous odor.

*Shit!* His head whipped around, on search for others. He'd hoped to avoid these creatures, but his luck was overall fucked today. The noise would bring more monsters, more death. There was no further advantage to keep creeping around in shadows. It was time to haul ass.

After the earthquake an hour earlier, the streets now resembled pieces of a jigsaw puzzle strewn around. A car wouldn't make it three feet. Shotgun reloaded, he took off through the jagged mess, years of trail running keeping him upright.

A low undertone of anguish surrounded him, cries from people needing help, unable to escape their stone prisons. He didn't pause. *I'm getting my wife. I'm sorry, but you're on your own.*

His Lauren, who he had last seen rubbing her nine months pregnant belly, giving him that crooked smile at his panicked question, "Is it time to go to the hospital? Should we call Ana to get the boys?"

She had waved him out the door in the peaceful morning light saying there was still time, she would start to take care of things, now go be a good cop and let the captain know paternity leave was about to take their best detective away.

Six hours after she kissed him goodbye, Jack stepped into his standard public-servant-worn office, on return from a jail run. His own cell phone out of commission due to a run-in with a perp, he reached for the desk phone to call Lauren and see how she was feeling when the phone rang. He picked it up. "Detective Miller."

"Yes, is this the husband of Lauren Miller?"

Jack's skin goose-bumped at the detachment in that voice, as practiced as any cop who worked homicide for twenty years. It took two tries to swallow and relax his throat enough to speak. "I'm Lauren's husband."

"Detective, this is County General. Your wife has been admitted, and I'm afraid that an emergency situation has devel-"

The ground buckled and twisted and threw him against the wall. The building creaked and groaned, the high-pitched crack of shattering glass sharp in his ears.

The floor still moved. He struggled to regain his footing and watched the earthquake tear through the city from his third-story view. Buildings wrenched from the earth, cars tossed through the air, glass shattered in visible streams. Outside a maelstrom of loud, crashing noise accompanied by the acrid smell of smoke and burning gasoline.

As the destruction continued outside another change took place. Nothing physical signaled this wreckage, but against his skin was scraping, surging, scratching, a changing of air and atmosphere – something shaking up his guts, fucking with him down to the bone and beyond.

*Wrongness.* Jack locked his knees and leaned against the scarred-wooden desk. Acid surged up his throat and he kept swallowing hard against the urge to keel over and vomit.

"CODE 999! CODE 999!"

Moments later a volley of gunfire sounded outside. A stampede of footsteps pounded past his door. The precinct charged into crisis mode.

Jack stepped into the swarm of cops heading for the munitions locker. The sergeant handed out weapons, only taking enough notice to make sure he was handing to a cop. "Don't forget the sting grenades," Sarge called out as officers suited up in Kevlar, riot gear, and automatic weapons.

Running to the front of the station, Jack heard screams, then a horrified *"What the fuck are those?"*

Disbelief stopped Jack dead as he exited the station and looked what was coming down the road.

*Dear God...*

The rookie behind him plowed hard into his back. It didn't knock him over, but it shook him out of the daze.

Training took over, and as he drew his gun and began firing, he catalogued the monsters descriptions. Humanoid features, heights 6'5" to 7'5", built like weightlifters. Grey-green skin, with overlarge heads and features misshapen like they'd been pummeled thirteen rounds in the ring. Jaws shoved forward with tusks protruding upward like ivory knives.

They were every nightmare had by every little boy made flesh.

They carried swords and axes and bows as though they had stepped out of a medieval exhibit. The metal surfaces gleamed in the late afternoon sun, the glint menace personified as it shone in his eyes.

The bullets of the .45s weren't doing enough damage. Jack shouted behind him, "Get me a shotgun!"

Cops fired while several monsters broke into a run and ran at them in a full-frontal assault.

Gun empty, Jack looked around for a weapon. A sword lay on the ground. Not seeing any other options, he picked it up.

The fucker was heavier than any bat he'd ever swung. One creature ran to mow him down, and at the last moment Jack went down to his knees, swinging the sword at the creature's thigh.

The sword sliced clean through, severing leg from body. The creature fell forward and hit the ground with a hard thud. Before it could move, Jack drove the sword straight down into the creature's chest where a human's heart would be.

It worked. The creature exhaled in a death gasp. Jack pulled the sword out and again faced the fray.

"Detective, here!" called a voice, a shotgun thrust into Jack's hands the moment he turned toward it. The gun settled against him in familiar comfort.

With several officers now firing shotguns and automatics the monsters were taking damage at a good rate. As their body count rose the largest of the monsters – who stayed toward the rear during the attack – threw his head back and released a high-pitched primal scream. The monsters turned from the station and retreated deeper into the city.

Retreated toward the hospital.

*Oh God...*

The bark of the captain's voice overwhelmed the confusion. He took charge and centered the group of cops, breaking them into large teams to start search and rescue.

Jack stormed to the older man's side. "Captain, my wife's at the hospital, I've got to get to her."

The older man shook his head, dismissing Jack without even bothering to look at him. "Not happening. In case you failed to notice, we are in a state of emergency. We have a disaster plan to follow, and we're sticking to it."

Jack's hands curled into fists. Fear and anger and worry urged him to strike out against anything that stood between him and Lauren. This man was an obstacle to be eliminated. "My wife needs me."

As if he could sense the younger man's thoughts, the captain took a protective step back. "Those things ran into the city, straight in the direction of the hospital. It is unsafe to go there when we have no idea what the hell we are facing." Turning toward other officers, the captain continued, "We need to start canvassing the surrounding areas, get survivors out and to safety. Miller, I want you to take your men and scour zone D. Direct everyone back to the safe haven."

A firm hand on his shoulder prevented Jack from damaging both the captain and his career, a hand that belonged to his partner Hector Torres. Jack nodded at Hector's unspoken command, saying nothing as the plans were finalized. Weapons were distributed, boundaries were gone over, and one by one the groups went.

After his group had cleared the precinct, Jack turned to Hector. "Torres-" he began, but the older Hispanic man shook his head, stopping the words.

"I know, Miller, you're heading to the hospital. I'm surprised you lasted this long. Ana called me, she has the boys and they're heading to safety now. Lauren asked her to come get them before she went to the hospital. You worry about your wife."

"Thanks, man."

Hector shrugged, black humor that spoke of long years on the force coming out as he responded, "Hope you make it back alive."

"Just take care of my boys." And Jack left to face the nightmares between him and Lauren.

The bite of autumn air froze his lungs as Jack continued his jog, shotgun at his side. Several monsters appeared, searching the area.

Damn, they heard that last gunshot.

One monster spotted him, pointing in his direction and leading the other creatures toward him.

Jack started shooting. He was hitting his targets with the accuracy born out of long hours at the gun range, but too soon the last round was fired.

Dropping the useless shotgun to the ground, he pulled out the large bowie knife from his waistband.

A howl rolled through the darkening night – deeper and fiercer than any howl he'd ever encountered on the ranch growing up. Jack should have been pissing his pants in terror, but right now was only numbness, too much seen and felt and dealt with today.

Bursting from the ruined buildings came the biggest wolves he had ever seen, big as shit. Except they weren't wolves, they looked like wolves mixed with human. Some ran on two legs, some on all four. Broad barrel chests and long arms and legs thick with muscle, fur stuck out in stiff tufts, ears pointed and alert atop their skulls, short snouts that gleamed white, sharp teeth.

*Werewolves? Are these werewolves?*

They ran at the grey-skinned monsters, jumping from great distances to snap at the monsters faces and throats, claws leaving deep gouges and drawing out more green blood and viscous matter.

Creatures that only should exist in big-budget horror films fought each other. Even as blood and bodies marked the streets, he could only look on with a detached fascination.

Three of the wolven creatures broke away from the back and ran for Jack, and the numbness fled before a spike of adrenaline. Sweat beaded at the base of his neck and marked a trail down his back. He brought his blade up.

The werewolf in front was much larger than the other two. The closer they got the clearer the details were. Jack could start marking where they must have sustained wounds. The smallest one had the worst, a deep gouge on its face that still bled.

They stopped, all upright. Dark brown fur was absorbed by skin, snouts shortened to form a humanoid nose and mouth, claws became hands. In moments, a human man with shaggy dark blond hair and yellow eyes stood before him. The two smaller ones were both male, a teen and a prepubescent, with features so similar to the adult they had to be family.

The adult stared him down, those yellow eyes unwavering as they appraised Jack. "I would appreciate it if you lowered your blade," the now man said, motioning with his chin to the knife in Jack's hand.

These creatures could kill him with little difficulty. As loath as he was to give up any weapon, it would be nothing but stupidity to keep it out and antagonize the creature. Jack opened his mouth, and words he didn't plan tumbled out. "How is this real?"

Battle cries sounded in the background as the werewolf spoke. "I do not know. What I have been told is our realms have collided."

"*Collided*? What do you mean, *realms*?"

"I mean your world is not my world. Yet somehow, they have become one."

Jack looked to the battle still waging, the werewolves winning over the other monsters. "What are those things?"

"Orcs. They are our enemies."

"And humans?"

The werewolf studied him with the palest yellow eyes he had ever seen. "Humans exist on my world. Most were allies. We will see if the humans on this world will be considered the same. For the moment

I am willing to give you the benefit of the doubt. We will fight the orcs so the humans of this area will be safe."

The orcs were retreating. The werewolves still in battle followed, and all the monsters dispersed toward the city's edge.

Jack wasn't going to follow to see how it played out. Right now only Lauren mattered. "Thank you for saving me."

The werewolf nodded. "Perhaps in the future, you will return the favor," he said, turning back into his other form, the young ones following his lead. All three took off in the direction of the sounds of battle, and Jack went the opposite way, toward his wife.

The double doors of the hospital entrance were in sight when a great flapping sounded overhead, air gusting around him like a mini-tornado, whipping up debris in great chunks.

Around him the late afternoon sun disappeared, leaving shadow and darkness. Jack looked up.

*Fucking hell.*
*This can't be.*
*Am I...?*
*Crazy. Have to be crazy.*
*Dra-*
*Dear Lord, please,*
*Dragon?*
*Help us...*

It was straight from every fairy tale ever told. Enormous enough to block the sun. A wingspan easily three times that of the largest plane he'd ever seen. A long neck and an even longer tail.

It passed over him, lost to his sight within moments.

Sensation returned to his limbs. Only then did the throb of his palms and the ache in his knees make themselves known, where concrete shards sliced into his hands and ripped out the knees of his trousers to bloody the skin underneath. His legs throbbed as he rose.

No. Compartmentalize. Later. He'd think on it later. Now he had to get into that fucking hospital.

Ignoring shouts to keep out, he bounded up the steps to the sixth-floor maternity ward, leaping over rock and broken steps that littered his path.

The front desk of the maternity ward was empty and the automatic doors were open. Here the earthquake had done enough damage to twist walls and leave chunks of tile lying about. Power was on, but it was dim – back-up generator only. It was safe enough to keep the patients here, but it was clear the ward was in crisis mode. With no one to stop him, he ran down the hall. "Lauren! Lauren!"

A nurse ran out of one of the rooms in front of him. "Sir, you need to stop! We are trying to keep everyone calm."

"I'm looking for my wife. What room is Lauren Miller in?"

A stillness stole over the nurse's form except her shoulders, which pushed back in quick movement. "Lauren Miller?" she asked, but it was stalling disguised as a question, something a cop saw and heard on a daily basis. Tendrils of fear Jack had not experienced even when faced with those monsters only minutes before uncurled from his belly, his skin growing chilled as they wormed their way to the surface.

"Where is my wife?" he asked, advancing on the younger woman.

The nurse would not look him in the eye, her throat working in nervousness, and his skin went from chilled to sub-zero. "Sir, you need to wait here. I need to get my supervisor…"

*"Where's my wife?"* he screamed, grabbing the young woman by the shoulders and shaking her.

"That's enough." The voice was a whip, cracking through the air. He turned to behold a battle-axe of a woman, late sixties, built broad and strong with a face that told she had seen much and overcame it all. "Let the girl go."

"I want my wife! *Where is Lauren Miller?*"

The older woman walked to him, no fear in her as she grabbed his hands and peeled them away from the girl's shoulders, her focus such he could not look away from her. She said to no one in particular, "Bring Mr. Miller a wet cloth to wipe down and a scrub shirt."

The squeak of shoes at his side told him someone was following her orders. Wet cloth was thrust into his hands and habit had his body moving even as his thoughts were centered on his wife. As soon as he pulled the clean top over his head, he said, "Please, my wife, where is she?"

There. That flash of compassion in her eyes, that fucking flash that every cop and doctor and nurse displayed when they were about to tell you your life was over. He backed away from her, shaking his head. "No. No, no, no."

She was ruthless in her efficiency. "Mr. Miller, I'm sorry to tell you that your wife died today. There were complications. The baby was born as the earthquake started and we lost power, and in the chaos we couldn't do what was necessary to save her life."

*No.*

*No        no        no        nononono nonononononononononononononononono*

It was the hand on his cheek, the living warmth of another human that brought him to awareness, the realization the litany was not in his head but coming out of his mouth. He grabbed her wrist. "Let me see my wife. Take me to my wife!"

"No Mr. Miller." The nurse's eyes were steady on him. Not breaking eye contact, she called out, "Sarah, bring the baby."

A young woman approached, sidling up to the older woman and angling her body away from his. With unhurried movement, the nurse disentangled her wrist from his grasp, twisting to take the bundled infant from Sarah.

She put the baby to his chest. Long practice had him grabbing the precious bundle before his brain caught the significance of the moment. "This is your daughter, Mr. Miller."

*Daughter.* He had wanted a baby girl so badly, had prayed for her every night. *Lord, you've blessed me with my boys and I'm grateful for them. But if you could, I'd love a little girl. I want her to be like my Lauren.*

"Daughter…"

"Did you know you were having a little girl, Mr. Miller?"

He shook his head. "No. Lauren wanted it to be a surprise, Lauren..." and he choked, because Lauren should be here answering these questions, about how she refused to find out, because she said, *I'm not going to let anyone make a big deal if this baby is a girl or act all sad for us if it's another boy. You and me, Jack Miller, we make the best babies in this world, and boy or girl, that's how it is.*

"How many other children do you have, Mr. Miller?"

The question brought his attention back to the battle-axe, and he blinked several times to focus on her.

"I know you have others. The way you hold that baby speaks of a lot of experience."

"Four. Four boys."

"So you have four boys, and now you have a little girl to protect as well. I'm sorry about your loss, but you can't be carrying on any more. You've got too much responsibility on your shoulders and you need to be strong for them."

An electric current passed between them, empathy between two survivors who knew there was a path ahead they needed to take, and their loved ones would have to wait a little while before they were reunited. He straightened his back and brought his daughter up to his chest, laying her little head over his heart. "Yes, ma'am."

The nurse gave a decisive nod and turned back to the hospital personnel behind her, issuing orders as she marched down the hall.

His daughter started to snuffle, so he brought her head up higher onto his shoulder, bouncing lightly to calm her. He looked down, seeing the curve of baby cheek, smelling the baby soft smell only newborns possessed, bringing peace even when the world around them was falling apart. "Don't worry, baby. You're safe now. Daddy is here and will always protect you, I promise."

His little girl. He hoped she would have her mother's coloring, especially those cornflower blue eyes. He hoped she had her mother's kind heart and strong spirit and loving compassion...

He squeezed his eyes shut, holding the tears back. None of that now. There were other things to do.

Like a name. He and Lauren hadn't chosen one for a girl. Mostly because Lauren didn't really believe they were going to have a girl, but also because she hadn't wanted to use his choice.

*We can't name our daughter that, Jack. I know you love it, but it sounds too much like my name. I don't want people thinking I'm so egotistical I need my little girl to remind everyone who her momma is.*

*Lauren, my love, my life, your little girl will be as amazing as you are, and she'll be proud to let everyone know who her momma is.*

*Jack Miller, don't try to sweet talk me. Jack... - stop that! You letch!*

*Jack... Jack... I love you...*

He rubbed his cheek over the downy soft skin of his little girl's head. "Your name is Larissa, little girl. I know it fits you, and I think your momma would agree."

Later, and soon, he'd have the outside to deal with. Later was telling four boys they no longer had a momma who would love and care for them. Later was dealing with a world that went to hell and figuring out how to bring it back. Later. But now,

there was only this moment with his precious baby girl.

*Welcome to our family, Larissa Joy.*

# CHAPTER TWO

*26 years later*

*She is connected to the future of your Clan. Guard her well.*

Three months.

Three months he stood sentry, crouched in the shadows of the building across from her.

Three months he watched, waiting for her importance to become clear, to explain why she was brought into his life.

Three months she consumed his every waking moment.

She was in the living room, picking up the clutter which accumulated over the day. She danced as she went about her task, her hips moving in sinuous rhythm to the song heard through the open door of her balcony – the beat heavy, the female singer's voice soft and alluring and darkly sexual.

The fingers of his right hand curled, claws raking over his palm.

The autumn night had taken on the crispness that spoke of winter arriving soon. Humans were more sensitive to temperature than his kind, but the cold seemed not to bother her. After finishing her task, she walked out on the balcony and sat on the metal chair that stood flush with the outside wall. The thin sweater she wore offered little protection from the chill but she made no move to go back inside. She wrapped her arms around her waist and stretched long legs in front of her, crossing them at the ankles.

He burrowed deeper into the shadows, more habit than fear she would notice him.

Her long hair spilled behind her, a color he had only seen once before when he flew over a wheat field on a blinding summer day. Her face contained no harsh lines. It was all soft curves, heart-shaped with the fullest mouth, one that made her appear to always be on the verge of pouting. Her body was ripe, her sweater and jeans tight over lush curves.

She was so innocent to the dangers of this world, so unprepared to deal with any danger. Why did her Clan let her live away from them? They must know how exposed she left herself, what a tempting target she made. Her father had been a fool to let her leave the safety of his house.

Her phone rang. She took it from her pants pocket. Her side of the conversation was loud in the still evening. "Hello? Dad, hi."

After several moments her laughter rang out, light and airy and free. Tension eased from him, the bunched muscles in his back loosening. Her face was animated, enjoyment evident as she talked with her father. She confused him, but in this one thing they were the same – absolute loyalty to their Clan.

Then she groaned. "I'm going to be grading papers. I told you Mrs. Wajkowski's appendix burst, right? Well, the substitute they brought in is overwhelmed and I volunteered to help her out."

She would never refuse anything her family asked of her, so she tried to get them to rescind their invitations when she didn't like the request. What now was her father asking of her?

She rubbed the back of her neck, the motion causing her chest to thrust out, bringing the neckline of her sweater a fraction lower. "No, I don't think I've had the pleasure of meeting Nick yet, and I'm sure he's a very nice guy."

Now the reason for the invitation became clear. Her father often tried to match her with suitable mates, though without success thus far. They were too forward in their attentions. None crossed the line with her, but one had frightened her with his disregard for her words and the way he towered over her. That man would never go near her again.

"Can't any of the brothers fill out the poker game? Make it all precinct guys?" she asked, but her defeated tone told him she would be going to her father's home tonight. She snorted at something her father said, saying in return, "Are you trying to tell me you happened to schedule all four on the Friday night shift and not a soul said anything to you?"

Whatever her father said caused her to roll her eyes, but she responded as expected. "Okay, Dad, I'll be over a little later. I have a few things to do first, so you'll have to survive a little while without me." A beat of time. "I'm always cute, and no, I'm not changing into a skirt." A few more moments of her father speaking, then with exasperation on her features, she said, "Love you Dad, buh-bye."

She hung up the phone, a long sigh escaping. She stood up and stretched her arms, the movement lifting the sweater so the silky skin of her stomach was visible and the material bunched in such a way that it showed a generous expanse of breast.

He ran his palm over his mouth, the bite of fang on flesh hard enough to draw a thin line of blood.

She lowered her arms and leaned on the railing, her gaze coming to meet his.

Discomposure thrilled through him, alighting down his spine. Could she see him? Time hung for a moment, his puff of visible breath going still in the air as though it too waited for the answer.

She gave a final sigh and entered her apartment to get ready for her journey.

Relief and an odd disappointment skittered through his mind before sense reasserted itself. Of course she could not see him. No one as unobservant as she could ever hope to glimpse one of his kind.

The odd ache in his chest was back. The ache that started the night he realized he had only one more week with her, and it was time to get back to his life, his responsibilities, his Clan. Three months he had sworn to watch over her, and now he was free to never again take up this sentry, never again place her safety before his Clan, never again look upon her face.

*Never see her again...*

She finished her preparations and left her apartment.

He would now need to follow her to her father's house. It was harder to hide there, more chance of discovery, but there was no choice. She would not be allowed to leave his protection as long as he watched, not even to exchange it for the protection of her family. They were human guardians, yes, but he trusted her to no one else.

He watched the front entrance for her exit. It took only moments before she emerged from the building and went toward the side street where her car waited for her.

The wind changed. With the shift the smell assailed him. Decomposition, death, rotting flesh and decay.

Zombies.

*Larissa…*

This hard pit in his stomach, this weakness in his limbs, this ice in his veins that threatened to stop his heart – this was unknown. Never, not even as a fledgling warrior, had he been so powerless.

Rage, though, rage was a familiar companion, and the rage he welcomed, let it engulf these other sensations and bury them deep. A white and blinding wave overwhelmed all in its path and directed itself at those that would hurt what was his to protect.

They dare come after her?

*They dare?*

A bellow clawed its way from his throat. He ran the length of the roof and with a snap of his wings, he plummeted toward his enemies.

Her brothers were going to kill her. No way around it, she was a marked woman.

Subtle Dad wasn't. Sad thing was, her father wasn't the hairiest matchmaker she had ever seen. That honor belonged to her third-grade teacher, Mrs. Donovan, who had tried to match up every single father in her class with her unmarried daughter. Even her widowed father hadn't been able to escape the madness.

But Dad could scheme with the best of them. Would he really force all her brothers to work the despised Friday night shift so he could set up his daughter on a blind date?

Why yes, yes he would.

Larissa gave a loud exhale as she left the safety of her building and marched forth to yet another set-up. The coffee shop across the street was still open and Larissa faltered, a hot chocolate calling her name. No, better not. If she didn't hurry, her brothers would come to carry her bodily to wherever this Nick was, not unlike the traditional virgin sacrifice.

They really hated working the Friday night shifts.

Not that she wanted to go. It had been tough to leave the little haven of her apartment tonight. The night was crystal clear with a moon so bright and big she might have had a chance of touching it. The air was crisp and fragrant with the scent of the dampened oak leaves carpeting all the once-green, grassy areas.

And there was the presence of her phantom companion. It had to be her family's paranoia about her living alone catching up to her, but these last couple months she had been living with a constant presence. Maybe if the feeling scared her she would be more wary, but she was comfortable with this companion. It was protective in its watchfulness, a dark energy against those who would hurt her while it wrapped her in safety. She felt safer these last months than she had even when she had lived at home.

A snort of laughter spilled out as she imagined Dad's indignant expression if she ever told him that. Maybe a hint or two she should rethink the whole coming-back-home-to-live thing.

Enough with the flights of fancy. There were plans to make. Okay, poker. Another set-up sure, but maybe Nick would be nice. He couldn't be worse than Anthony, he of the love obsession with his abs, who pulled up his shirt four separate times to try to convince her to touch the muscle mass. Or there was Ben, who took her to the steak and seafood restaurant and ate and drank everything in sight while she ordered salad, then proceeded to split the check with her.

And then there was Leonard.

Yeah, Dad didn't do too well with choosing Leonard.

Still, he hadn't been *so* horrific, and she was a tad ashamed of the momentary glee that rushed through hers the next day when Dad told her Leonard's car had been mysteriously crushed.

Besides, if it worked out with Nick, she would be spared her brothers' accusing glares during Saturday dinner when she told them that, once again, there had been no spark and no chance for further romance.

So, reframe this whole set-up situation. She didn't want to go over to Dad's, but there was always a chance it could turn out to be a real blessing.

Larissa breathed in the autumn night air, taking in great lungfuls as she moved toward her car. There were no better nights than these, when the leaves were changing colors and the bite in the air made every breath a pleasure-pain mix.

And then her breath stopped, frozen in her chest as every muscle in her body froze when a roar sounded through the empty streets, the unholy sound moving ever closer.

# CHAPTER THREE

Larissa's mouth went dry, her palms dampening in spite of the chilled night. She looked up to find the source of that inhuman sound.

What was that? This was a protected area – humans-only. The magical wards had been recast only last month with the specific purpose to fend off any non-human race or species.

The low hum of voices brought her attention back down to the street. Three bodies moved toward her. Probably male, judging by the taller height and broader shoulders, but she couldn't be sure. They wore hoods to hide their faces, and their jackets hid any shape of the upper torso. She had seen similar groupings many times at the high school she taught at. Still, they seemed... -wrong. Their bodies were at odd angles, their steps uneven, more akin to a series of lurches rather than the awkward gaits of adolescents or the surer steps of adult males.

*If it feels wrong, run.* Even before the echo of Dad's oft-repeated advice faded, she had turned away from the group and was sprinting back to her car.

Their steps quickened behind her, faster than their shuffling led her to believe. It took mere seconds for her to feel a brush of fingertips against the back of her coat. Adrenaline surged, fueling her muscles, and she shot forward.

She turned the corner to see three other men in front of her. Skidding to a stop she swiveled on the ball of her foot, turning to go the opposite direction, but found that the three who had been trailing her had already come out of the side street and now surrounded her.

Her heart beat double-time, a staccato that urged flight, but no avenue was open. The men had formed a loose circle, blocking any escape, and several more beings coming from various directions. All she could do was stand there.

The wash of tears clouded her vision. Images of Dad, of her brothers, of school and Olivia and even her damned stuffed giraffe she had since kindergarten.

They bore down on her, their heads still covered by hoods. Thin hands with a skeletal appearance reached out for her, the faint whiff of decay around them, like meat that had been left out.

She wrapped her arms around herself, hunched over, bracing against that first touch.

The primal scream ripped through the air again, closer this time. A mountain of a man with wings descended from the sky.

He landed on the street before her with such force the pavement under her feet shook. No, he wasn't a man. Stone-grey skin, black hair, and those huge wings, but before she could get a better look, the creature advanced on the things that surrounded her.

The hooded men turned their attention to the creature. One of them rushed forward, but the creature picked him up by the front of the hoodie with one hand and threw the man against the building, the impact causing the hood to fall away and reveal his face.

One eye bounced against its cheek, only a ligament keeping the eye attached, while on the opposite side of the face the skin of its jaw was gone and the white bone underneath visible. Its nose was half chewed away and the remaining skin was bloated and pus filled.

Larissa screamed, covering her eyes in against the *wrongness*.

Zombies? Zombies here? No, not in the protected zone, it couldn't be. Things like these weren't allowed to be here.

Zombies meant…

Zombies meant…

"This is not happening, this is not happening, this is not happening…" But it was, and Larissa clenched her jaw hard to stop the flow of unconscious words. What would Dad say, what would Dad say?

*Always be aware of your surroundings, kiddo.*

Larissa forced her hands away from her face and watched as the zombies brought out knives and flung themselves at the creature. He towered over the zombies, but for something as big as he was, the creature was graceful, dodging the weapons while he used his wings, hands, and tail to fight off his enemies.

The creature ripped off one zombie's arm and threw him against the wall. The zombie hit hard and tumbled to the ground, the severed arm landing a few feet away. The zombie rose and grabbed the arm, pushing it back against the socket. As Larissa watched, the flesh mended together, and once again the zombie had use of the arm.

It flung itself back into the battle. This time the winged creature tore off its head before he threw the body away. There was no more movement after that.

There had to be at least fifty zombies swarming the creature. They were so engrossed in their fight they had forgotten about her.

*Move! Run away!*

A sharp zing raced through her body and broke the frozen panic that engulfed her. Let the monsters fight between themselves – she needed to get to her car.

Her car was on the other side of a nearby alleyway, and after a quick look around confirmed nothing was near her, she ran full speed toward the alley. As she neared the entrance something grabbed her ankle.

Larissa put her hands out to protect her face as she fell. Her wrist throbbed and the pressure she put on it to push herself up caused it to give way under her. She flipped over onto her back, but before she could try to stand again a zombie loomed above, milky eyes intent on her.

She used the heels of her hands and feet in an effort to push herself away from the zombie, but it reached down and grabbed the front of her jacket. He lifted her as if she weighed nothing and she dangled a good foot above the street. Larissa punched his arm, but for something disintegrating before her eyes, she couldn't make him move even a millimeter.

She looked for a weapon, anything that would help, but instead caught sight of movement out of the corner of her eye. Shadows moved like spilled ink over the ground toward the wall. They crept up the wall, fanning out. From the middle of this darkness, from the solid wall of the alleyway, a new man emerged.

He was shadow made flesh, his eyes and hair purest black, his body fuzzy as if the shadows still clung to his skin like a dark cloud. In each hand he held a curved sword.

The zombie jerked its head to look back, but before he could complete the action the shadow man moved and held up his hand, the streetlight glittering on the metal of the blade as it arced down and beheaded the zombie holding her.

With the loss of its head, the zombie crashed to the ground. Larissa fell those inches she had been held aloft but managed to keep her feet under her and stumbled against the building for support.

The shadow warrior came toward her. His eyes met hers for the briefest moment before commotion at the alleyway's entrance drew his gaze. With both swords aloft, he went to meet the zombies coming after her.

Sudden pressure on her arm. She turned, screaming and slapping her hands at whatever was behind her.

It was a woman, long red hair vibrant under the street lights. She blocked Larissa's flailing arms and ineffectual swats. "We're getting you out of here," she said, and grabbed Larissa's wrist to lead her out of the alleyway.

Before they could do so, the other end of the alleyway was crowded by more zombies. "Keep back," the woman ordered, pushing Larissa to the side.

The woman reached behind her shoulder and pulled free the longest sword Larissa had ever seen. It looked as tall as the woman and half as wide, but she hefted it in her hand as though it weighed no more than a kitchen knife.

The large sword took on a red glow. As though in response, scrolls of fire appeared on the woman's bare arm. They settled into her skin, winding their way up to her shoulder to disappear underneath the black leather vest she wore, muted flame under flesh. Sword in hand, she ran toward the zombies blocking the path.

Trapped. But across the alley was a door on that building's side. If by some luck it was unlocked maybe Larissa could get away from all this madness. She took one step forward when something fell from the sky in front of her.

The winged creature stood before her, his massive body blocking her exit. He reached down and grabbed her around the waist.

*No, no, I was so close!*

"Let me go!" she screamed, raking her nails against his bare chest in an effort to wound him, his skin so hard it was as though her nails slid against stone. If she hurt him he gave no sign. He put one arm under her knees and held her bridal style tight against him. He spread his wings, the wingspan massive.

She looked back at the shadow warrior. He had finished with the zombies, swords still in the air as if he had swung his last killing strokes. His head turned toward her as she was pulled into the air, the creature taking flight with her.

Soft words were spoken into her ear. "I will not harm you, little human. Hold onto me. I will protect you."

The creature could speak. His voice was deep and soothing and gentle and so at odds with his appearance. That voice, combined with her fear of falling, overrode any other considerations. She circled her arms around his thick neck for some semblance of stability and safety and held tight as the creature flew her into the waiting night.

# CHAPTER FOUR

They had been flying – what... thirty minutes? Three hours? – when they arrived at an expansive keep nestled within a jagged mountain range. From this angle she noticed several multi-story towers rising from the stone, but the design was so clever the keep had to be near invisible most of the time.

They set down on the top of the highest tower, the landing so skilled only the slightest bounce let her know they were on solid ground.

She was in shock – she had to be. It was the only explanation for why she was not crying or cursing her luck, the creature, her father, card games, and anything else that led her to leave her apartment in the first place. The calmness infusing her now felt unnatural, ready to shatter with the first application of force.

Still, she'd take whatever advantage she could get right now. Maybe the calm would hold, at least long enough to discover why she had been taken.

Be reasonable. Friendly. The first rule of negotiation her dad taught her was to find out what the other person wanted and figure out a way you could convince them you'd be able to supply it.

That, and always be realistic about what was going on.

Well, here were the ugly facts. She had no mad-ninja-skillz to rely on and her family didn't know where she was. *She* didn't know where she was. The only way she was leaving was if this creature allowed it.

The creature was looking at her and made no move to put her down. Should she look at him? Would he take that as aggression? During the flight she hadn't looked at him and instead kept her gaze fixed on the hollow at the base of his throat. His neck was thick and led into heavily muscled shoulders, and his body gave off so much heat he might be able to be substitute for the furnace of a small home. She hadn't gotten cold as they flew.

There was no other option. She needed to try to communicate, and communication couldn't happen if she didn't look at him.

She muttered a quick prayer in case any gods were wandering around. None appeared, so what choice but to get on with this? *Steady on, girl*. One deep breath, two, and then her gaze met his.

Midnight black eyes under a prominent brow bone. The planes of his face were nothing but hard angles, his chin a square slab. It was as if he had been chiseled out of stone, his face displaying none of the roundness of flesh.

He was studying her as much as she was studying him. He didn't have any eyebrows, but his brow bone came together to form a little furrow between his eyes.

He seemed approachable, no negative emotion on his face she could detect. No time like the present to find out her fate. "Why have you brought me here?"

Those eyebrows drew even closer together at her question. Did her words confuse him? Unless she had been hallucinating, he had spoken English to her.

Before he made any sign that he would answer she heard movement behind her, the same *thwup* that had marked his landing. She turned to see a good dozen creatures like him, every single gaze locked on her as though she was wearing a homing beacon.

*Calm, I need you to hang on. Don't leave me now.*

A female pushed away from the others and walked until inches from Larissa, one clawed hand coming to rest on her hip. Her features were a fraction softer than the male's, her body the stuff of comic books – outrageous curves framed with sleek muscle. About her she had an aura Larissa recognized from every cop she had ever met. It was confidence and authority mixed with a good dose of *Don't fuck with me.*

This female would never be pathetic enough to huddle in an alleyway screaming or freeze in terror. Larissa's eyes flicked away.

"Terak, what is this?" asked the female, in an offhand way that was supposed to indicate you really weren't interested in the answer.

*Terak, huh? Always good to know your kidnapper's name.*

Larissa's attention went back to the female, but as she met those eyes her throat tightened. Her earlier tone was a lie, because the female creature in front of her looked as though she were debating on how many strips of flesh she could cut from Larissa with those claws.

What had she done to earn this ire? None of the others displayed hostility.

Earlier she hadn't wanted to be taken for an impromptu flying trip, but her kidnapper wouldn't let her out of his grasp. Now when she had a psycho female in front of her and really didn't want leave the relative safety of his arms, of course Terak chose to put her down. His wings folded in, settling over his shoulders like the fall of a cape.

"What should we do with her?" the female creature continued. "Shall I take her to the dungeon?"

A dungeon? Whips and chains and iron maidens dungeon? That was what Terak planned for her? Bile rose in her throat when he answered from behind her, "No Valry, she is not a prisoner."

Valry was not happy with that, if the further flattening of her already non-existent lips was any indication. Nope, nope, no matter what, Larissa was not going to ever be alone with this female.

Valry's anger radiated off her in waves while the other Clan members showed only curiosity. The mood was not censorious but Terak hated that he had no answers to give. They might be uncertain on what happened to bring about this unprecedented incident, but their confusion could not match his own.

He had turned from his fight with the zombies to see his little human in the grasp of the female Guild member. He knew the Guild would not harm her, but they would take her somewhere he could not follow. A haze settled over his vision.

Once she was in his arms instinct took over. He brought her to where none would dare touch her without his permission.

She took a step back to put distance between herself and Valry, a move that illustrated his little human was no fool. She came close enough that her hair brushed across his wings. His gaze slid over her form. Small but constant tremors were shaking her frame, and his chest went concave.

She was unused to battle, and not only had she faced zombies this night but had been taken from her home against her will. Fear, tension, and fatigue were riding her hard.

And instead of sheltering her, he placed her in front of his people with no explanation, making her unsure if her fight was over.

Though he knew his Clan – Valry – was studying his every move, he could not let her suffer any further. He picked her up, hearing her small gasp from his unexpected movement. His mouth to her ear, his words meant for her alone, he said, "You are safe here, little human. I vow it. None will harm you."

He pulled back enough to study her eyes. The cornflower blue absorbed him, drowning out the knowledge that his Clan standing feet away or the words of the Oracle that had brought them together. All these months watching her, the one question he could not answer was the color of her eyes.

Terak thought he had imagined every shade possible, but he had been wrong. This shade of blue

– soft and warm, the color pure throughout – he had not conceived of, but now that he beheld them, he could think of no more perfect color for her.

The rustling of wings brought his attention back to his people. Valry's hands were clenched into tight fists. He would have to deal with her later, but for now his first responsibility lay in providing for the woman in his arms.

His gaze on his Clan, Terak said, "This woman is guest, not enemy." Ignoring the questioning eyes of his people, he continued, "Are all patrols back?"

Malek, his second-in-command, came forward. "All but two."

"Which patrols?"

"Over the vampire stronghold."

Terak nodded. "We will speak of it later," he said. With no further words of explanation and the human held tight in his arms again, he turned to descend the stairway that led into the tower.


Everything was grey – walls, stairs, ceilings. Maybe the creatures kept it that way so they could camouflage themselves if something attacked them here. If it weren't for his hair and the black pants he wore, the creature holding her would have disappeared into his surroundings.

The creature took her through the tower and into the body of the castle. After a lot of stairs, twists, and turns with nothing to look at but miles of utilitarian grey stone, they came to a room that held the biggest collection of books Larissa had ever seen.

The room was two, maybe three stories tall, and from floor to ceiling were nothing but shelves lined with books. Rich splashes of blue, burgundy, brown and green delighted her color-starved eyes. Several couches in a muted tan fabric and a large fireplace in the middle of the back wall were the only other decorations in the room.

The creature set her on her feet again. She stepped back a few paces, gauging his reaction as she moved away.

He did not try to keep her near and let her roam as she wished. With the speed of the night's events, Larissa hadn't had the chance to study him. She took advantage of this quiet interlude to do so now.

His wings appeared leathery, and though they were currently draped over his shoulders, she remembered the full wingspan well enough that she was sure it equaled his nearly seven feet in height. He had a tail, the tip of which currently rested beside his booted foot. He was thick with muscle, every part of his body defined. His arms seemed the size of support beams, his legs thick as oaks, and his clawed hands looked as if he could encircle her waist in them.

Outside of the wings, tail, and claws that tipped his fingers, his features overall were almost human, just a little – *more*. A little sharper, a little harder, a little bigger.

And almost...*beautiful*, in a rough-hewn, alien way.

He called her a guest and hadn't yet tried to harm her. She owed him an acknowledgment of what he had done for her. "Thank you for saving my life."

His eyes widened in surprise at her words, as if gratitude was the last thing he ever expected to receive. He inclined his head a fraction. "You are welcome," he said in those deep tones that relaxed her against her will.

"Your name is Terak?"

"Yes."

"I assume from your conversation-" Larissa waved her hand toward the ceiling, "-with the others, you are the leader here?"

"I am."

"So can you tell me what you are?"

His head tilted as he studied her. "You do not know?"

"I'm a human who lives in a human-only city. I know elves have pointy ears and dwarves are easy to trip over. Too much beyond that, I'm at a loss."

The question unsettled him, if the way he broke off from her gaze and stared into the blazing fire was any indication. "I am a gargoyle," he said at last, tension in the rigid set of his shoulders.

There was a time when Larissa had wanted to learn about the other races, before she realized why her father carried such stress at the mention of any creature that had appeared since the Great Collision and set aside any curiosity in favor of pleasing her father. She only knew the big ones – dwarves, elves, werewolves… vampires. Still, for the first time since she was little, Larissa wished she had read some books on the sly and spent a little more time learning about the new races.

Terak's tension had not abated, so he must be expecting a negative reaction. She could understand why. Gargoyles were a fearsome race if tonight was anything to go by. What human wouldn't be terrified of them?

"What were you doing in the city?" *And why didn't the wards keep you out?* she mentally added.

His body relaxed, maybe because she didn't react to the gargoyle revelation by screaming or something. He turned to face her. "My Clan is... friendless... in this world. We rely only on ourselves for survival. To that end, we patrol all areas to keep aware of the happenings of this world, even those places that are forbidden to us."

It made sense. She could see her father doing the exact same thing under similar circumstances. The whole *friendless* business, though, *not* a good omen. Was it because they feared other races, or other races feared them? From tonight's goings-on, she was a firm follower of the second camp. Still didn't explain the wards, but she wasn't stupid enough to bring that up to him. That was a question purely for when she was safe back at home.

"So why did you save me? Why did you bring me here?" The next question stuck in her throat. Swallowing a few times to work saliva into her mouth, she formed the question she dreaded asking. "Am I going to be allowed to go home?"

Her voice cracked on the last word. Terak made a brief move toward her before seeming to reconsider. "You will be returned home. I swear it."

Damn tears. She didn't want them to fall, not now, not when she wasn't sure she could stop them once they started. Larissa scrubbed her eyes with the back of her hand. "Please take me home then."

"Not yet. We have much to discuss."

"Discuss what?" Her voice rose several decibels. Larissa stopped for a moment, taking several deep breaths. He said he was going to take her home, but that didn't mean she was home yet. Best to remember that. "Sorry. I don't understand what we need to talk about. I thank you for saving me, but what else is there?"

Terak made a motion to one of the couches, an order to sit disguised as polite concern. Larissa obeyed.

He opened his mouth, then hesitated. "May I know your name?"

"Oh." Surprise at his words lit through her, the normalcy of the question releasing some of the tension pitted in her stomach. "Larissa. Larissa Miller."

"Larissa," he said, and she wanted to close her eyes and listen to him repeat those three syllables on an endless loop. "Why were you attacked by the zombies?"

"I don't know."

"You don't know?"

There wasn't any disbelief in his voice – none that she could detect, anyway – but there was still something in the spacing of the words that made it clear he didn't fully believe her. "No, I don't know. It was probably some random occurrence, though they shouldn't have been able to get into the city." *Like you* was added in her head, but once again, self-preservation kept her from speaking those words aloud.

"It wasn't a random occurrence." His voice carried absolute conviction.

"And how would you know?"

Once again that small hesitation before he spoke. "In the past, my Clan has had dealings with necromancers."

*Zombies meant...*

*Necromancers.* The word she been avoiding all night was now spoken, drifting through the air on icy currents. The sound alone had her rubbing her arms for warmth. "Dealings, huh?" she asked, more in avoidance than actual interest. She didn't want to talk about them, didn't even want to *think* about their existence, not while an image of one eyeball hanging out of its socket waited behind her eyelids.

"While I claim no intimate knowledge, I know enough to say the zombies I fought tonight were created by a master necromancer. Masters of that level do not make mistakes." He crouched before her then, so close she could reach out and stroke his face. "Are you involved with the necromancers?"

"What? No! Gods no, never!" She jumped up from the couch as though she could run away from the words. "*Necromancers?* They're... no, just no."

"Then why did the zombies target you?"

Maybe that was why he brought her here, thinking she was somehow connected with necromancers. "Listen, I don't deal with anything like that. I'm a history teacher. I work, tutor kids, and the most exciting thing I do is play card games with my dad on the weekend – that's where I was headed tonight when all this started. I was in the wrong place at the wrong time. Somehow those things got past the city's security and went after me."

She shook her head. It couldn't be real, zombies attacking her. Her? She was always the good kid.

While her brothers had given their dad many grey hairs over the years, she never got into fights or broke curfew or lied about who she was hanging around with. How does someone like that get attacked by zombies? Why would they come after her?

Why would they touch her?

Hold her?

Trap her?

*An eye hanging out of its socket...*

From far away a long, keening sob.

And Larissa realized...

...the sob came from her.

Her body betrayed her, legs giving out, limbs trembling and twisting and the hard inward jerk of torso to protect her, the curl that would shelter from the outside world, outside pain. Teeth chattered with an echo that resonated through skull, through bone, through marrow.

Weightless. A second of air. A second of vulnerability. A second of alone.

Then warmth seeped into her skin, burrowing into damaged spaces, replacing danger with safety, shame with forgiveness. She was immobile against an immovable surface, but as long as she could bask in that warmth she didn't fear her imprisonment. The smell of newly cracked stone washed over her, an unknown language sounded, spoken in a deep, resonant tone that promised protection.

The shaking eased, the sobs stuttered and hiccupped their last, and she opened her eyes to find her fingers digging into Terak's chest, his leathery wings curled around her, holding her close to him.

The hard planes and grey tone to his skin gave the impression of cold, but his body was a furnace, a warm blanket on a winter day. His skin was firm but supple, the texture inviting her to stroke where her fingers lay against him.

She nuzzled deeper into him when awareness of her situation slammed through her. Cloaking herself with the trailing ends of her dignity she straightened and leaned back.

The first attempt to get away from him was unsuccessful, his arms still tight around her. Clearing her throat, she looked up at him, glancing at his wings when his gaze met hers. "Thank you, but I'm fine now. You can let go."

He followed her gaze, his brows coming together once again. The wings opened and he set her down.

# CHAPTER FIVE

He had wrapped her in his wings.

Disbelief coursed through Terak's system as the little human stepped away and went to look over the books.

He had wrapped her in his wings.

Her hair was tangled, its usual smoothness lost to the exertions of the night. She appeared so defenseless at that moment he wanted to cradle her against him again, tell her that nothing like this night would ever touch her in the future.

He had wrapped her in his wings.

She was so soft, so fragile, she could never be a true threat to him. With no threat, there was no consequence to keeping her close. That could be the only reason his wings had come around her. That and no other.

He settled his wings around his shoulders, the softness of her lingering on the membranes.

She glanced at him, a faint tremble still on her lips. Pushing her hair behind her ear, she went to sit back down on the couch.

*She is connected to the future of your Clan. Guard her well.*

Three months ago the Oracle had come to them unannounced as few beings would dare. She had given little more than that cryptic message. Any questions were ignored, and she left their stronghold unconcerned how her words would be taken.

He was unused to taking orders from anyone, but he could not shake the need to discover why the Oracle had sought him out and placed this human woman into his care.

Larissa Miller was nothing like he expected. She was as ill-suited to his world as any being in existence. Instead of a woman wielding magic or sword, he beheld a woman who was petted and protected by her family. She was uninterested in the world outside of the safe confines of the human-only city. Nothing about her spoke of darkness or subterfuge.

All these months watching her, and before this night he had come to believe the Oracle had made a mistake.

Why had she been attacked? It was not a mistake, no matter what she claimed. He needed to unravel this mystery. Somehow she was connected to his Clan, and until he understood the reason for the Oracle's intervention he would not separate from her.

Before he could speak her voice rang out. "I need to call my father."

"Why?"

The line of her mouth turned mulish, her look equal parts confusion and annoyance. "He's expecting me, and I need to tell him what happened. He's a cop. He'll want to investigate."

That could not happen. If her father interfered, she would be lost to him. "He is human."

Her arms crossed over her chest. "My father is a good cop, human or not. You shouldn't be so quick to dismiss his abilities just because he doesn't have wings."

She was insulted on behalf of her Clan and would not let him say anything to degrade them. The last of the trembling stopped as her chin went high, and he much preferred the fire that lit her eyes to the trembling that engulfed her earlier.

Diplomacy had never been one of his strengths, but he must tread carefully here. He needed her to accept her family could not protect her but not feel as though he were dismissing their abilities. "It matters not how skilled your father is in solving human matters. These are enemies he has no hope of prevailing against. Has he ever fought a necromancer?"

Her lips tightened, but she answered honest. "No."

He stopped himself from pursuing the conversation and let her think on those words. He asked, "You truly do not know why the zombies attacked you?"

Defiance crossed her features, and for one moment he thought she would once again ask to talk to her father. Instead she seemed to reconsider, because she drew a deep breath and answered instead, "I understand what you are saying about how the necromancers work, but there is some mistake. There is nothing about me that would interest anyone. I'm as ordinary as they come and *I know nothing.* All I want is to go back to my life."

She was either the most accomplished liar he had ever encountered or she was telling the truth. He wasn't sure which of those options he wanted to believe. "Your wants do not change reality. A necromancer is after you. Yes, one is," he repeated, adding volume in case she tried to voice her denial, but while she did not vocalize her disagreement she did start shaking her head. "You do not know why, but you have caught the attention of a necromancer. This is an enemy you can in no way fight."

"My dad…"

She would not listen to reason, so bluntness was his only hope of convincing her. "If you involve your father, you will be responsible for his death. Are you prepared to bury him in hopes of proving me wrong?"

All color leeched out of her face, his words penetrating her stubbornness. If anything could change her mind, it would be the protection of her Clan.

She rose from the couch, her movements stiff and jerky. She walked over to the fireplace and stood in front of it, staring down at the flames. The firelight illuminated her hair, creating a glow around her soft face. "What are you suggesting?"

He walked to her until he stood an arm's distance away, not crowding her, but forcing her to deal with his presence. "Let me and my Clan protect you while we discover why you have been targeted. We can fight this enemy, your father cannot."

Her head jerked toward him, eyebrows furrowing together and a suspicious cast crossing her features. "Why would you want to do that? Even if you're right, why do you care I'm being targeted?"

This question he was not prepared for. Of course she would want details. She was naïve and protected, but his little human was not stupid or blindly trusting.

A heavy knock interrupted the moment. Never had he been more grateful for one of the constant interruptions on his time. He opened the door to see Malek. "Yes?"

Malek spoke in low tones. "The Council requires your presence."

News of the human's arrival had spread quickly it seemed. He said, "I will be out momentarily," and shut the door.

Larissa was watching him with undisguised interest. He said, "I find I must go and talk with my Council."

"Can I go home now?"

"I wish to finish our discussion first. This will only be a few minutes. I will not let it take any longer than that." He gave a small bow. "Excuse me."

"Wait." She held out her hand to him. "My father is expecting me. If I'm not there soon, he'll start searching for me. I promise I won't say anything about tonight. I don't want him to worry."

It was a reasonable request. "I will have a phone brought so you may contact him."

With those words, she smiled at him. "Thank you."

He had seen her smile many times, but never like this, never so close. Worry and tiredness still lined her features, but the smile created a radiance the firelight could never replicate.

Another knock brought Terak back to awareness. "Excuse me," he repeated and left the room.

Malek was waiting, along with another warrior. "Have a phone waiting for me when I get back," he told the younger warrior. As he and Malek turned and walked down the corridor to the Council Chamber, he asked Malek, "What news?"

"Word of your guest has spread throughout the Clan and not all are happy she is here. She is the one the Oracle told you of, is she not?"

"Who else would she be?"

The displeasure Terak was feeling must have announced itself in his voice, for Malek lowered his head. "I live and die for you, *Mennak*. Please do not mistake my observations for censure."

Malek did not deserve misplaced ire heaped upon him. Terak said, "Forgive me. I find I do not like being summoned like a youngling."

Malek nodded, accepting the apology. "Your absences these last months have emboldened the Council."

"They are my councillors, not my wardens." That they assumed they could summon him with a moment's notice meant they were bolder than Terak had suspected. That would be put to rights tonight. "Who is fueling tonight's displeasure?"

"Valry."

Of course. His future *Meyla* had hated his watching over the human from the first, had fought against the Clan acting on the Oracle's prediction. And now she presumed she could openly go against his decisions.

That also needed to be put to rights.

Terak entered the Council Chamber, a large room with a round table and thirteen seats surrounding it. He did not bother to go to his seat. Krikus, the eldest member of the Council, rose and spoke. "*Mennak-*"

"I have only a few moments, so all here will listen well," Terak interrupted, projecting his authority and banked anger into the tone. The members quieted in their seats. "You seem to forget who is leader here, though you still call me *Mennak*. Let me remind you. You do not summon me. You may seek my presence, you may ask for my decision, but never again shall you summon me. Is this understood, or are any here demanding challenge?"

Most lowered their heads and refused to look at Terak. Krikus held his hand up in apology. "We never wish to insult you, *Mennak*. But this news about the human was so unexpected, we needed to know the situation."

"You only need know your *Mennak* has the situation under control. Any explanations will come when I deem them necessary."

Krikus lowered his head. "If you wish for our counsel, we are always at your service."

"And I do wish your counsel," Terak said. His point had been made, now peace had to be restored. He did not want seeds of resentment and suspicion taking root because of this night. "There is a new development with the human. She was attacked by zombies tonight."

An explosion of sound circled the table as the Council talked among themselves. Terak held up his hand for silence. "I do not yet know what it means, but I do know we cannot leave the human unguarded. We must remain with her."

"Is she in league with necromancers?"

"No." Of that Terak was sure. "All of the information we have collected on her both by watching her and by other means, nothing hints at that. They hunt her for an unknown reason, and we must protect her until all these threads are untangled and the reason of her importance is clear."

Nalith rose. He was new to the Council, joining after the death of his father. While Terak had enjoyed the father's counsel, Nalith was discord and whispered poison in the shadows of the night. "*Mennak*," he began, his tone as far from respectful as it could be while still remaining civil. "This is foolish. We had agreed to three months of guarding the human, long enough to decide how she could be of interest to the Clan. It is clear she has no importance to us. The Oracle's pronouncement is nothing more than a powerful being bored enough that she wishes to cause mayhem among other races. It is not an unknown situation."

A couple Council members gave half-nods at Nalith's words, though none would speak aloud after Terak's earlier rebuke.

"While I do not disagree about the chaos the gods cause, it matters little in this situation. She was attacked in the agreed-upon time frame, and we will determine if this is what the Oracle alluded to before we leave the human." Nalith's jaw clenched and he sat. Terak continued, "We will watch the human. We will meet tomorrow at first light and continue this discussion. Now, I must go. Until the morrow."

Krikus nodded. "Agreed." The other Council members nodded, though Terak could not tell those who were displaying their true feelings from those who did not wish to anger him any further.

Terak left and headed back to Larissa. He needed to speak to Valry as well, but that he would leave to later. Larissa had been alone long enough.

The young warrior was holding a phone when Terak approached the door. He took the phone and entered the room.

Larissa was still by the fire, looking into the flame as though all answers could be found there. She looked up when the door, first focusing on his face, then on the small black phone held in his hand.

He held it out to her and she walked as fast as she could without running to grab the phone from him.

While she dialed the number and said, "Dad," into the receiver, Terak pondered the schism within his Clan, the one even now Nalith and Valry were working to exploit – between those who wished to have contact with the outside world versus those who wished to remain as they had always been, self-sufficient and without any outside encumbrances save for favors owed them.

Encumbrances this one human woman exemplified.

And as she said, "Yes, Dad, I owe you big. Promise, next time I'm there… Yes, Dad, with a skirt and make-up," Terak knew how to answer her question and convince her that he should be allowed to stay at her side.

# CHAPTER SIX

It hadn't been this hard to part with a phone since she was fourteen and had been waiting for Jared Thompson to ask her to junior prom, but as Terak held out a massive hand, Larissa placed the shiny black rectangle there without any outward sign of her struggle.

"I was able to convince Dad not to send out a search party by promising to be there for brunch tomorrow," she said, aware even as the words were leaving her mouth that such a blatant warning would do nothing more than amuse the gargoyle in front of her.

Thankfully he didn't laugh, though she could swear a ghost of a smile played on his lips. Instead he said, "You will be there, do not worry."

The reassurance beat back the fear that had begun creeping through her while he was gone. She nodded toward the door. "It must be hard to be in charge, people always needing you for something."

"It is my duty and my role to fulfill."

He said that without any boast or pridefulness. It was a statement of fact, his calling made into words. "How are you the leader? Were you elected?"

"My father was leader. At his death, I took his place."

"So you are a king?"

"Not quite." He went to the couch in front of the fireplace and sat down. There was a natural elegance about him, so at odds with the warrior exterior. His wings folded around him with enough of an opening to allow her to still see his hands and chest. "While leadership is passed down through a bloodline, the *Mennak* must also be the strongest. Any gargoyle may issue challenge to claim the title."

"*Mennak?*"

"The title of the leader."

"What kind of challenge?"

He didn't answer, not in words, but the way the question made his eyes flicker from hers answered it anyway. Before the Collision, the Magic Realm was closely related to Earth's medieval feudal societies. She knew that as a fact found in books and as lectures written in chalk, but it never impressed itself upon her as deeply as right now.

Terak rose then. He motioned around the room. "These books contain histories created by gargoyles of all the races, dating back tens of thousands of years from the Magic Realm, information that can only be found in this one room. They are observations, studies of outsiders looking in. There are very few interactions between my people and those of the outside world. Gargoyles have long kept ourselves apart from the other races. But with the Great Collision, many of my people wish to experience the New Realm not as outsiders, but as part of the fabric of this new world."

"It's a worthy goal," Larissa said, not sure where he was going with this.

"It is hard to let go of millennia of suspicions – on both sides – but it must start somewhere. Perhaps the first step needed is a gargoyle helping a human woman escape from necromancers. Let us watch over you as a first step."

So he was back to talking about guarding her. "You did that tonight. Why take it further?"

"Necromancers are an enemy of my people as well. Whatever plan you are part of can bring no good to anyone of this world. Not your people, nor mine."

*What if he was right?* As terrifying as the night had been, there was comfort in the knowledge it was a case of horrific timing, an event that would never be repeated.

But if she had been targeted? If it was not some random woman on the street, but *her* they had been waiting for?

She plopped onto the couch, no strength left in her legs to hold her up. She looked at Terak, his sculpted face taking on a pinched expression of worry as he watched her. "You're wrong," she said, the tiny voice coming from her mouth sounding nothing like her.

He came to kneel before her. "I hope I am," he said, putting one hand on the couch beside her leg. "But if I am not, I want to be there to protect you."

Memory struck her, bringing to mind another question. "The woman and man from tonight, the ones who were also fighting the zombies – do you know who they are?"

"Yes. They are members of the Guild."

The Guild. She had never heard of them. "Are they good guys?"

There was a considering pause before he answered. "They are protectors."

"Of humans?"

"Of anyone the necromancers target."

His words were very measured, and no way she was getting the whole story here. "You sound like you don't like them."

"Our history together is too complex to explore this late at night. Though we are not enemies, there have been clashes."

Probably not the only moment in gargoyle history where a personality conflict occurred. "Fair enough. But you said they were protectors. What about going to them and letting them protect me? They're supposed to protect humans, right?" And they seemed to be human themselves. Well, at least one of them did. Sorta.

Onyx eyes locked on to her, not allowing Larissa to look away. "They will protect you. They will protect you by locking you up in a room and allowing no one to come near you until they discover what use the necromancers have for you."

His eyes were too dark, too direct. Larissa looked away, the flickering shadows over a millennia of knowledge drawing her attention.

Did this night have to keep getting worse? What were her options here?

If he was telling the truth, then trying to contact the Guild would amount to jail time. Any self-respecting cop's kid had a healthy loathing at the thought of jail. And really, did she know anything more about them than she did the gargoyles?

Nope, she knew exactly the same about both groups – a big old zilch.

She should have... she should have learned. She could have done it without upsetting dad, and if she had bothered, and maybe she would know what decision to make. She had wanted to once, why didn't it occur to her she was allowed to change her mind and go back to it?

Hindsight and all that. It didn't change the now, and in the now, the only organization she could trust would be the police.

But she didn't want her father involved in this. He could not know what was going on, not yet.

He would disagree with her, in loud and vehement tones. If he ever found out she was hiding tonight from him, he'd ream her up one side of the block and down the other, then proceed to tan her hide as he hadn't done since she was a little girl.

He wouldn't understand. He would be hurt that she didn't come to him.

*But*... Larissa clenched her teeth hard against the image of the zombie that pushed itself to the front of her mind. She wouldn't cry again. That was done with.

But she didn't want him pitted against those creatures and that magic, that strength. He was a fighter through and through, but he wasn't a young man anymore, and Dad had already gone through one war with the creatures brought here by the Great Collision, a battle that had cost him dearly. She never wanted him to go through that again.

Besides, if she was right – *and I am right* – this was a mistake. This was random. Bringing her father in on it would only cause problems for her.

Dad would move her back to the family house in two seconds flat, the brothers carting her back kicking and screaming if that was what it took.

As much as she loved her father, she didn't want that. She'd been gone from home not even a year. She didn't want to lose her hard-won freedom.

Larissa focused again on Terak. His eyes were still steady on her, his jaw set as he waited to counter her next argument.

What she needed was time, time to figure out what was going on and somehow come up with a solution.

"How would you protect me?"

That jaw relaxed a fraction at her words. No doubt he considered the battle won. "You will go about your life and we will be near."

"You expect me to go into the grocery store with my gargoyle bodyguard?"

And there it was again, that tiny curl to his lips that disappeared almost before it registered. She seemed to amuse him. "You will never know we are there. You will only see us should another attack occur."

She didn't see how it was possible something as big and alien as a gargoyle could hide in the city, but Terak radiated conviction. He absolutely believed she would never know they were near.

Which meant entering the city was not a one-time event or something he thought of as dangerous.

Which meant the wards – those magical barriers in which she had placed absolute trust and belief in for all these years – were worthless.

She got up, walking past the bookshelves, trying to ease the unsettled sensation in her stomach. All her life the wards had been an absolute – never worry about the outside races, the wards will keep them out. Had it always been a lie?

With a delicate touch she stroked the spine of a very old binding, breathing deep the scent of wondrous decay that always accompanied large libraries. The familiar and much-loved perfume helped release some of the tension holding fast in her shoulders, her arms, her back. One worry at a time. Right now, it was getting back home. "I won't know you're there?" she verified, taking up their conversation.

He leaned forward a fraction. "No, you will not."

Larissa gave a small laugh, rubbing the back of her neck as she returned to the couch. "It has to be the exhaustion, but I'm going to agree to this." Before he could say anything she added, "As long as we have a few ground rules."

While his face remained impassive, Larissa noticed the tip of his tail twitched. *Interesting.* She filed that away for future reference and went on. "First, we need a time limit. I don't want to be an eighty-year-old granny wondering if a gargoyle is following me."

"A year," said Terak.

"I was thinking more along the lines of a month."

Terak shook his head. "Necromancers are immortal. They can afford patience. One month is nothing to them. They will want to give you time to forget this and let down your guard."

She sighed. He had a point. "Two months."

"A year."

"Three months."

"A year."

"You haven't had much experience with negotiation, have you?"

His head tilted, as though even the thought was foreign and without precedent. "Most follow my orders without question."

That's right. He was the leader here. "Then let me be clear," she said. "There is no way I'm agreeing to a year. Six months you can follow me around. After that, when there are no more attacks and you see how boring my life is, no more bodyguards. Agreed?"

There it was, another tail twitch, but his voice was steady when he replied, "Agreed. Six months. But when another attack does happen, we will renegotiate the time frame."

"I'm beginning to think you're kind of hoping I get jumped."

"Not at all. I know this enemy and am preparing for battle instead of living in a dream world."

Was that snark? Did he just snark at her? With that theater-actor voice and impassive face it was hard to tell, but she'd lay odds it was snark. Still, he was agreeing so far, so she didn't comment and pressed on. "Rule two, I don't want Valry to be one of my bodyguards."

Forget his former impassiveness. Shock was now writ large across his face. "Valry?"

"Yes, the female gargoyle from the roof. I do not want her ever to guard me. Never ever. If it's a choice between her and no one, you go with no one. Agreed?"

"Agreed," he said quickly. Too quickly. Her gut was right then. Joy.

"Third and final. If you're right about all this –
and that's a big if – and you find something out
about why I was targeted, you have to share with
me. No handling things on your own. No plans
without me knowing about them."

"Why do you desire this?"

One thing this night taught her beyond all doubt
– all males were lunkheads, all of them. She
recognized that *protect the poor helpless girl and
don't worry her little wee head* tone. "I'm not
stupid. I'm not going to run into a situation I have
no business being in to show no one can boss me
around. I'm not a warrior and tonight made that
clear in large neon signage. But I deserve to know
about events that concern me and help make the
decisions on how to handle them."

His jaw tightened as he considered her words. He
really didn't want to agree, she knew that like she
knew her own name. But this was a deal-breaker.

He must have seen that determination in her face
because he exhaled deeply. "Agreed. I will share all
knowledge with you. *However*, if we find ourselves
in battle, my words are absolute. You may not
question my orders, you will obey."

"That's fair." Larissa rose from the couch,
holding her hand out to him. "I think we have a deal
then."

He rose as well, looking at her hand as if he had
never seen the appendage before. "This is what
humans call a *handshake*?"

"Oh, I'm sorry." It had been pure reflex to hold
out her hand. She hadn't considered it an unusual
motion. Then again, not like she had much

experience with any other race. "I wasn't thinking…"

She started to pull her hand away, but before it moved even an inch Terak engulfed her hand with his.

His skin was warm, callouses and scars marking every inch resting against her palm. Up close his claws were more like mini-curved daggers.

"This is how humans become allies?" His voice had softened, the timbre dropping a few registers until it was a rough brush against her spine, and she fought the unexpected shiver, the first of the night that had nothing to do with fear.

"Yes."

"Then make no mistake, little human. You are under my protection now, and I protect what is mine."

# CHAPTER SEVEN

The *whoosh* of students running past her in the hallways, the slamming of lockers, the girls talking about their hair and clothes and make-up and the boys talking about the girls – all welcome signs of normalcy to Larissa as she made her way to the first class of the morning.

The bell rang moments before she entered the door. "Okay everyone. Settle down and take your seats," Larissa said as she headed toward her desk, placing her messenger bag on the chair and taking out graded papers and lesson plans.

Juvenile grumbling, paper rustling, and feet shuffling met Larissa's words. The mood was not a shiny happy one.

Ah yes, what senior in high school didn't love being up this early, especially on a Monday morning with only a few weeks until vacation. It was about time to petition for hazard pay.

Larissa handed out papers and accepted homework, answered some questions and shushed Jason Evans after he let out a wolf whistle when she passed. All in all, a normal Monday, making the events of this weekend seem even more surreal.

Necromancers after her? No, no.

A gargoyle protector? What an insane notion.

"Now," said Larissa, coming to stand in front of the room. "We are going to get into a favorite topic for most. We are going to discuss the Great Collision."

As expected, a hush fell over the room. No student could keep up the façade of indifference when the topic of the Great Collision came up, reason *numero uno* she always saved it for Mondays. "Twenty-six years ago, probably the most momentous moment in history outside of the actual creation of life occurred. I'll let your science teachers explain the theories behind why it happened, parallel dimensions and quarks and neutrons and all that good stuff. That's not for my discussion here."

"You trying to tell us you weren't a science genius, Miss Miller?"

Ah, Jason Evans, star quarterback and all around smart-ass. Class would not be the same if he didn't inject his *too cool for school* attitude into her lectures at least once a day. "Science is wonderful, Mr. Evans. I do admit, though, I never had the head for it. That doesn't mean you shouldn't ask Mr. Patel to go into details for you. Anyway, the Great Collision. In layman's terms…"

"Dummy terms!" Jason interjected.

"Layman's terms," Larissa continued on, not bothering to waste breath to engage him. "Our universe is composed of multiple dimensions, also sometimes called realms. How many is still a question the scientific community is grappling with, but that has no bearing here. What matters for our discussion is two of these realms collided. One realm was very similar to what you see around you every day – skyscrapers, cars, computers, cell phones – but humans were the only sentient race and no magic existed. I'm sure many of your parents have already told you stories about the good old days."

Groans sounded then, followed by tales of parental misconduct. Larissa let it go for a few moments before bringing attention back to her. "The other realm was a realm of sword and sorcery. Elves and dwarves existed there, as well as countless other races and magical creatures. For simplicity, we have come to label these dimensions the Human Realm and the Magic Realm, though humans did exist in the Magic Realm. The difference is they weren't the only sentient race."

A hand rose at the back of the class. "Miss Miller, my mom told me we used to use oil and electricity for power, not magic."

Larissa nodded. "That is true. In the Great Collision, the Human Realm absorbed the Magic Realm. Earth is the same physically as it was before the collision. What changed is now Earth can sustain magic, which was not possible before. Once the chaos from the collision began to settle, wizards and mages were able to figure out how to supply our energy needs magically."

"What's the difference between a wizard and a mage?" a female voice interrupted. Taneasha Jackson reminded Larissa of herself at a younger age, too smart by half and surrounded by family who protected her to the point of suffocation. The young woman was more likely to be found in a library than at any of the school events.

"Good question," said Larissa. "A wizard is someone who channels magic through spells and items. A mage is someone with an inborn gift for magic and channels magic from themselves. Mages are much rarer and more powerful, but they usually are more limited. They have a gift for a certain type of magic and can only create spells that use that classification of magic. Different classifications include transmutation, illusion, conjuration-"

"Necromancy. Are we going to talk about necromancers?" asked Jason, in a sly voice with a little too much enthusiasm backing it.

"Not as much as you probably want," Larissa said. Not at all, if she had a choice. *An eye hanging out of its socket*, and she rubbed the heel of her palm against her forehead as if the motion could erase the image. "Why are you not supposed to be so excited over necromancers?"

In the tone of someone who is humoring you and wants you to know it, Jason said, "They derive their power from death."

"Exactly," said Larissa.

"But all the girls love vampires, and I'd look hot with red eyes," Jason said, causing some girls to giggle and smile in his direction.

"Yes, well, while all vampires are necromancers, not every necromancer is a vampire. Only the strongest of necromancers become true vampires."

Jason leaned back in his seat, a satisfied smirk on his face. "Gives me something to work for, then I'd have an eternity with the ladies." The guys all started high-fiving amid themselves, and Larissa shushed them before the words got too far out of hand.

Taneasha spoke again. "I want to learn more about the fantastical creatures that we thought were myths until they appeared after the Collision. I really want to see a unicorn one day."

"Ever see any, Miss Miller?" asked a voice from the back.

*Not until three days ago.* "No, I've lived in the city all my life and never traveled outside of it." Maybe it was time for that to change, though.

Another male voice from the back said, "Unicorns are too girly. I want to see gryphons, basilisks, dragons, stuff like that."

And from the doorway came the response, the voice a smooth feminine growl. "There are no dragons."

Larissa hadn't heard the door open and turned to question why someone was interrupting her class.

The textbook Larissa was holding slipped from nerveless fingers, causing a sharp crack as the second silence of the morning fell over the classroom.

In the open doorway stood the redheaded woman from Friday night, her gaze locked on Larissa as she leaned against the frame, her arms and legs crossed in what would have been a relaxed posture for anyone else, but on this woman it seemed more akin to leashed watchfulness.

The woman continued, "Dragons were as much myth in the Magic Realm as in ours, disappointing as that seems." She smiled then, the barest trace of a dimple in her grin. "Or maybe not. Having a dragon fly overhead would not be my idea of a good time."

She was the very definition of an Amazon – taller than some men with broad shoulders and long limbs displaying muscle, but her evident strength only highlighted how very feminine she was. She had classic features most women would kill for and hourglass curves her musculature enhanced.

A higher-pitched feminine grunt came from behind the redhead, and the redhead shifted as she glanced behind her. "Move your ass, Fallon. I want to see her. I missed all the excitement, remember?"

"If you quit poking me, I will," the redheaded woman said to whoever was back there, and took several steps into the room.

Larissa gaped as she beheld the person coming in behind the amazon.

The other woman was short. Very short. So short even the platform heels on her shoes only brought her to average height. She was wearing an elaborate jade green kimono – except unlike a traditional kimono, this woman's skirt ended mid-thigh – with matching jade hair styled in three rolls and piled so high it added an extra half-foot of height to the woman.

It was hard to tell what age or ethnicity the woman was under her dramatic kabuki make-up. Best guess, early-to-mid-twenties, and Asian but mixed with some European ancestry.

The unnatural quiet the class had been under broke. With one voice, her students started calling out questions – about the women, what they were doing here, why did they want to talk to Miss Miller?

"Quiet," the woman called Fallon said, her voice level but her tone absolute, and in a situation

Larissa had never before experienced, her class shut up as they were told. "Miss Miller, I have some questions for you. Please step outside with me."

The small Asian woman sat on Larissa's desk, crossing her legs once she was settled. "It might have sounded like a request, but it really wasn't." She flicked her fingers at Larissa in a dismissive gesture. "You need to go. I'll stay with the kiddies."

Sure enough, the redhead didn't look like she was moving, and Larissa didn't want to have this conversation in front of her students. Stifling a sigh, she said, "Class, talk quietly among yourselves for a few minutes. I'll be right back."

There was an empty classroom a few rooms down. Larissa went in, not bothering with politeness to allow Fallon to enter first. The redhead followed, though not before her eyes scanned the room. Classic tactical maneuver. No cop in the world ever entered anywhere before getting the lay of the land.

The woman didn't crowd Larissa, but her unwavering gaze and unvoiced suspicions made breathing a tad difficult, like wearing a shirt with a constrictive collar. It was so different from how she felt with the gargoyle, where toward the end their interactions edged into the companionable.

Larissa cleared her throat, ready to start this inquisition. "How did you know where to find me, or who I am? Who are you, for that matter?"

"Me? I'm Fallon, and the monochromatic midget currently alone with your students is Laire. We're part of a group that protects the city."

Larissa crossed her arms. "If that's true, why didn't I know you existed before today? If you know about me, then you know my dad's the chief of police, and he's never mentioned you."

Fallon's lips twitched, though if the tic was irritation or amusement Larissa couldn't guess. The woman's features were neutral as she studied Larissa. "Why would you expect *daddy* to tell you? From what we can gather, it would be the opposite."

The *zing* brought a flush of heat to the back of Larissa's neck, but she pressed her lips together to keep from responding. This woman wasn't going to provoke her into anything, if that was indeed her plan. And the bit of embarrassment didn't mask the fact Fallon neither confirmed nor denied that Dad knew about them. If this whole protection business was the truth, that meant either her dad had kept this from her – and given his standard *modus operandi* that wouldn't be a shock – or this group was very, very secret.

And if a very, very secret group told you about their existence…

"Oh gods, you're going to kidnap me now, aren't you?"

The corner of Fallon's lip quirked at Larissa's outburst, that shadow of a dimple again emerging. "Your students saw you walk out of a room with me. It would be kind of stupid for me to grab you and run."

"You could make them forget. Who knows what kind of magic you can perform."

"I don't do magic. I turn your attention back to Friday night and the big-ass sword I was carrying. My job is to run and swing."

Larissa wanted nothing more than to lay her head on the desk and close her eyes until the woman disappeared. Unfortunately, there was no chance Fallon would cooperate. "What do you want from me?"

Fallon walked over and crouched in front of her, bringing them to eye level. "What happened Friday?"

"I don't know. You tell me. You were there so you obviously knew what was going to happen."

Annoyance reflected in Fallon's features. "You would think I should have been told the reason I was there, but no, the meddling bitch who sent me doesn't believe in giving anyone details. She thinks it's enough to send you on your way." By the end Fallon's eyes were narrow slits and murder was written over her face.

Not anxious to step on this particular minefield, Larissa still had to ask. "What about afterward? Couldn't you get any information from the zombies?"

"No. No information from that path." Fallon's tone was a stop sign, telling Larissa no questions asked would be answered.

Larissa swiveled in the chair and stood, needing space. "I don't know why the zombies were there. I wasn't even supposed to go out that night. It was a spur of the moment decision to join my dad's poker game. I think it was a coincidence, nothing more."

Fallon stood as well, and Larissa conceded that Fallon rising to her full height was a much more impressive movement than she could ever pull off. "What about the gargoyle?" Fallon asked.

"What about him?" Good, no cracks in her vocals. Learning to deflect her father's questions was paying off in unexpected ways.

Fallon's eyebrow arched. "He flew away with you. You were gone for a considerable length of time. Are you telling me that happens to you every day?"

"Of course not. I don't know why he was there either. He flew me away, and I guess when he decided it was safe, he brought me back?"

"That simple?"

"Well, at the time it wasn't! At the time I was scared to death. Actually, I'm still sleeping with my lights on. But I don't know what to tell you when I have no clue why what happened on Friday night... happened. Zombies attacked, you appeared, the gargoyle appeared. The more time that passes, the more it becomes a blur in my head, which is good, because I want to forget it!"

Fallon stared at her as though she were a bug under a microscope. Breathing as she did in her yoga class, Larissa quieted her mind, quieted her body. She would not give away anything. No matter what assurances Fallon gave, the little warning bell in the back of her skull was still sounding an alert.

Fallon's body relaxed, the signal to Larissa that she won this round. At least she wouldn't be kidnapped again right now, but Larissa didn't need the thinning of Fallon's mouth to tell her that the amazon was not yet finished with her. "By all means, you know nothing and the gargoyle flew you around for a couple hours before taking you home. Why, it almost sounds romantic."

"I need to get back to my class now."

"Of course Who am I to deprive those poor children of their education? Then again, Laire is probably educating them beyond their wildest dreams." Fallon went to the door and opened it, then turned and motioned for Larissa to precede her out.

Larissa entered her classroom to find her students scribbling notes with a frenetic intensity, their expressions sharpened as they seldom were for any of her lectures.

Then she heard the Asian woman speak.

"Yes, I do realize men who have an orc ancestor tend to be really ugly, but that's why they invented paper bags. Trust me, as long as a guy knows he's getting some, he'll wear a pink bunny costume if that's what's needed to seal the deal. What matters here and what you need to remember is guys who have some orc in them are hung like nobody's business. If you like your men large and dominating, make a beeline for them."

"What about elves?" called a male student.

"Elves are ridiculously high maintenance. If that's fine with you, the key to elves is the ears and the back. Sure, they like the other areas fine, but if you want to make one a little puddle of goo, spend ten minutes massaging their back. It's practically a sure thing after that."

"What are you telling my students?" While Larissa's squeaky tone may not have been what one would call commanding, it did stop the small woman from talking.

"I was answering questions. They are woefully unprepared to enter the real world," Laire said, turning back to a student in the front with her hand up.

"I think that's enough question and answer. Let's go," said Fallon, a quick movement of her head signaling the other woman to get off the desk.

"But Fallon, they need educated. You wouldn't believe the misconceptions they had about how to have sex with a shifter."

Fallon walked over to the desk and grabbed the woman's ear, walking toward the door without waiting to see if Laire was on her feet yet. "Ow, Fallon, ow! Let go, I'm coming, I'm coming!"

"Goodbye, Miss Miller," Fallon said. Larissa didn't have to be a mind reader to see the *for now* Fallon mentally added onto the end of that sentence.

Fallon walked toward the door, pulling the smaller woman behind her. "I knew I should have brought Aislynn," Fallon said as they left the classroom.

Laire's snort was loud and clear, though her voice was fading as they walked away from the classroom. "Good idea to bring an elf among hormonal high school seniors. Do you really think Ais wants to be the jerk-off fantasy of the graduating class... OWWWWWWW!"

"So I hear there was much excitement in your class this morning." Olivia Berry took her usual seat across from Larissa in the teacher's lounge, leaning forward as though she'd be able to get the full scoop faster that way.

"That's one way to put it," Larissa agreed, not looking up from the book she was reading. It was always nice when Olivia went crazy over good gossip, a situation not to be rushed.

Olivia didn't even try at uninterested. "Tell me all or I'll seduce one of your brothers and give you the play by play."

The full body shudder overtook Larissa before she could stop it. "Eww. Don't even talk about that."

"Michael is seriously hot…"

"Fine, I'll talk! Just stay away from the male members of my family."

Olivia settled down, smug radiating from every pore. "So who were your guests? I won't even tell you the official version of the story, it's too much BS to believe."

"Why are you such a conspiracy theorist? Maybe the official story is the real story." Olivia said nothing, just blinked once, twice, three times. Larissa sighed. "So here's what happened. I was attacked over the weekend…"

Olivia's face lost its maniacal interest, replaced by pure concern. She grabbed Larissa's hand. "Are you okay?"

"Yeah, I am, I am," Larissa reassured her, squeezing Olivia's hand. "I was attacked by zombies."

"Zombies!" Olivia's voice ricocheted in the empty room.

"Shh!" Larissa admonished, looking around to verify they were indeed alone. "I'd rather not everyone know, thank you."

Olivia leaned closer, her voice lowering. "Are you kidding me? Zombies?"

"Yeah, zombies. And those two who visited me wanted to know why."

Olivia's body shook as if in preparation for the answer. "And why were you?"

"I have no idea."

Disbelief was as evident on Olivia's face as it had been on both Terak's and Fallon's. "You have no idea?"

"None. I think it was an accident and they attacked the wrong woman, but everyone around me seems determined to believe I was attacked on purpose."

Olivia pulled back then, angling away from Larissa, her hand smoothing her brown curls back. "It seems likely that attack was on purpose. Necromancers don't make many mistakes."

"And what would you know about necromancers?" This was new. Olivia had never expressed any personal knowledge of the other races before.

Olivia shrugged, the movement the height of nonchalance. "Only what everyone else knows. Mages that powerful probably don't make mistakes." Changing the subject, she motioned to the book Larissa had open. "What's that? Going to teach gargoyles?"

It was Larissa's turn to shrug. This part she didn't want to mention to Olivia. "After my attack, I thought it would be a good idea to be a little more concerned with the other races. They seemed interesting."

Olivia studied the picture, tapping the gargoyle illustration with one long red nail. "I would have chosen another race to start with. Outside of necromancers, I can't think of any creature I'd want to meet less."

"Why do you say that?"

"Because, if they had nothing to hide, they'd be part of the world among all the other creatures. Hell, you can even find necromancer clubs in certain areas."

Which was disturbing, but considering how vampires had been romanticized and fetishized in the Human Realm before the collision, the fact those clubs existed wasn't as shocking as it should have been. "Maybe they're afraid. It can't be easy to enter the world when you've always shunned it before."

"Well, yeah, or maybe they are as evil as the necromancers but don't have that dark, sexy-charm swagger to cover their deviousness."

*Deviousness.* There was no word she could think of less right to describe Terak. No, he wasn't telling her everything, but it seemed to come from a place of protection, not slyness.

Then again, she could be fooling herself.

"Olivia, have you ever left the city?"

"Why, are you thinking of taking a long weekend or something? Your dad would flip."

"No, it's just..." Larissa looked down at the picture again. "I'm starting to think about what I don't know. It never occurred to me before, but the attack has me thinking about things."

The bell rang, and Olivia stood. "I have class next period, so I've got to get going. If you need to talk, I'll be free tonight."

Larissa shook her head. "I'm fine. Really."

Olivia looked dubious, but nodded. "If you change your mind, give me a call."

When she left, Larissa stared at the drawing in the book, at the large wings and sharp claws. The picture was terrifying, yet it was not nearly as impressive as seeing the creatures in moving flesh.

Emulating Olivia, she stroked the snarling face on the picture. Terrifying, yes, but she couldn't quite remember ever feeling so warm as when she had been enfolded in Terak's wings.

Larissa looked out the window. Was a gargoyle nearby, watching her? The sun was shining, a light wind whipping the occasional leaf past the glass. How could a gargoyle exist on a day like today? They belonged to the night, to full moons and dark clouds and the wind howling through trees.

They certainly didn't get involved with people like her, boring people with a too-stifling family and a regular job. She had no money problems, no social life... hell, she hadn't even had a steady boyfriend yet. Growing up, the brothers had scared off anyone who they didn't think was good enough for their baby sister, and then Dad took over with the matchmaking. Her big weekend plans involved playing cards with her family.

How sad was that?

How could someone like her attract the attention of necromancers? Or gargoyles?

Stubborn gargoyles who don't listen to reason and take over your life even though they may be next in line for the *Ultimate Evil* award.

Why couldn't she have been saved by an elf?

# CHAPTER EIGHT

When going back to your childhood home, there is that one perfect moment. It's the moment where, as you grab the door knob and start turning, memories jumble across your mind like the spill of photographs from a box, quick and cluttered and all of them so damned good you wish you could crawl inside one.

"Baby sister! Get your ass in here, you're letting the cold air in."

And then a male member of the family opens his mouth and reminds you why you moved out.

"Bite me there, Steven. How can you pretend to be this big, bad cop if two seconds in the wind has you whining?"

Her third oldest brother came over from the couch and enveloped her in a hug, which he used to maneuver her out of the doorway and then closed the door with his foot. "So, you missed Friday night, huh?"

Leave it to Steven to bulldoze over any pleasantries and get straight to what concerned him.

"I do have a life outside of this house."

"You were tutoring a student."

After he let go, she shrugged out of her coat and hung it in the closet. Larissa said, "Teaching is not a job, it's my life's calling. I read that on a greeting card somewhere."

She walked toward the kitchen, the hub of activity in their house, with Steven following. "Your life's calling is condemning us to the crap shifts."

"Don't blame me. I don't set your schedule."

"You're right, the chief does."

"Do I hear you complaining out there again, boy?" came the call from the kitchen.

Larissa stepped into the kitchen to see her father at the stove and her other brothers Gary, Michael, and Christopher sitting at the black granite island. She crossed the wood floor and gave her father a kiss on the cheek. "Hi Daddy."

"Pumpkin." Going grey dark-brown hair and a non-ironic mustache on a slightly chubby but still very handsome face, Jack Miller was in his element, stirring a pot of simmering chili and surrounded by his kids. "How was work?"

"Went fine. You didn't tell me we were having chili, I would have made some salsa and cornbread."

"I had Michael bring some. You can set the table."

The brothers jumped up and began their respective chores. Before her stomach had the chance to start growling, the table was set and everyone dug into their food, her dad on one end, her on the other, and two brothers on each side.

"So, baby sis, your television still on the fritz?" asked Gary, youngest of all the boys and the one who tortured her most while they were growing up.

Larissa sighed. "I haven't had a chance to bring it in to the shop yet."

"How did you manage to break this one?" asked Steven.

Jack snorted before taking a long drink from his bottle of beer. "Why is it I have four boys but whenever anything broke around here, it was always the fault of my baby girl?"

She couldn't help it she had a black thumb, only instead of killing plants, she killed all their electronics. Four rambunctious older brothers, but when something broke in the house, all eyes turned to her. "I had to do something to stand out from the pack. At least I never almost burned the house down, or snuck boys in by having them climb in the third-story window."

This time Michael snorted. The oldest, Michael was the only one who inherited their father's coloring of dark brown hair and eyes while she and the other brothers favored their mom. He also inherited their father's stubborn streak and overdeveloped sense of responsibility, leading to the nickname *Dad Two* while they were growing up. "No boy would ever have dared climb through your window, Ris. Remember when you hit puberty? Dad started to clean his guns on the front porch."

"Hell yes, I did. You look like your mother, who was only the most beautiful woman to ever be born. I saw her for the first time when she was sixteen and I was seventeen and I remember exactly what I wished I could be doing to her. No way any little punk was going to think those things about my daughter."

*"Dad!"* Larissa protested.

"Well, it's true."

Any parent could embarrass their kids during the teenage years, but only a true virtuoso could embarrass them into their twenties and beyond.

She opened her mouth to force out some sort of retort – what, she didn't know – but her dad's focus wasn't on her. He was looking to the left of her, where a picture of Lauren Miller hung on the wall, frozen forever in the prime of her life.

Guilt, thick and familiar, churned through her body and soured every cell it enveloped. Even after all these years her father's love for her mother was undimmed. It was the stuff of fairy tales, but because of her the fairy tale was cut short.

Her, and the Great Collision.

And now she was going to stir up bad memories, talk about things they avoided in this house. Gods knew she didn't want to hurt him, but she couldn't think of who else to talk to.

Larissa kept her head down and mouth full for the rest of the meal, letting the brothers talk. The meal was winding down; spoons clinked against flatware and a good portion of the side dishes were gone. It was now or never to start asking questions.

She wiped her damp palms against the legs of her jeans and began. "Dad, do you know what would happen if the city was ever attacked?"

Her father paused in bringing the cornbread to his mouth. "What do you mean?"

"Attacked. Like by a group of wizards, or some magical creature, or whatever."

Jack waved his spoon in the air, dismissing the possibility without words. "We've got wards to protect us."

*If only you knew the folly of that statement.* "But what if the wards failed?"

"They wouldn't. Believe me, we go through a lot every year to get them renewed."

Had she really been this complacent that she never thought to think beyond these answers before? Why did it take getting attacked to ask these questions? A five-year-old wouldn't accept these types of simplistic answers, but she had, all of her life. "Isn't there a back-up plan?"

The lines bracketing Jack's mouth went from charming to hardened as his lips thinned. "Baby girl, what's this about?"

Her father's tone roughened, taking on that edge that said to anyone who knew Jack Miller they should back off.

Dad hated talking about anything to do with the New Realms, and Larissa hated to bring this up to him. In any other situation, she'd be shutting her mouth right now.

But the wards had failed, and there was a secret group of protectors of the city. Would this info be a surprise to Dad, or was withholding this information another of the ways Jack Miller protected his family, most specifically her? Larissa's hands went up in supplication and she continued. "I'm curious. I got asked in class today about it and I realized I had no idea what the answer was. I figured it was something I should probably know."

"Well, there's nothing to worry about. The wards have held for over twenty years. They're not going to fail."

Her father dug into what was left of his chili, his signal that this discussion was at an end. Larissa rubbed the back of her neck. "Are there any exceptions to who can get past the wards or when?"

The spoon dropped from Jack's hand, a loud *clank* resounding through the room, and the tension from the brothers was now palpable as they looked between her and Dad. "Larissa Joy, where is this coming from?"

His anger kindled a similar blaze in her. She wasn't being unfair in her questions, and he needed to stop treating her as though she were eight. "I'm asking reasonable questions and you aren't giving me any answers. Wards are magical barriers. So what happens if the wizard who set them is incompetent, or has been blackmailed or bought off? And magic is dispelled all the time. But you sit there and act like none of these are a possibility, that I shouldn't concern myself over it."

Her dad gripped the edge of the table with one hand, the knuckles white. "It's several wizards casting several layers of spells that takes months out of every year to renew and strengthen. It's not someone showing up and waving a wand. And in my house I'll be shown respect, young lady."

"Then don't treat my questions as annoyances. You're the chief of police, Dad. You need to have some back-up plans in place, unless you want to find yourself in the middle of another disaster and have more people die…" Her voice trailed off as her brain caught up to her words. "Dad, I'm sorry."

Jack Miller took a deep breath. He pushed himself away from the table and stood. He was every day his age at this moment, older than Larissa had ever seen him. Without a word he left the dining room.

Awkward silence hung over the table for a beat of time, then by wordless agreement Gary, Steven, and Christopher got up and left to follow their father, leaving her alone with Michael.

Michael's eyes were narrowed on her, the deep brown burning with laser intensity. "Michael-"

"What was that about, Ris?"

The words hit her ear, but the vibration was wrong, unexpected. This wasn't Michael chiding her about upsetting Dad, at least not completely. Michael was in cop-mode, and he was *never* in cop-mode with her.

*Does he know about Friday?*

Her fingers went icy. *No. He can't. Dad doesn't know.*

Because if Dad knew, he would have been on her doorstep dragging her out of the apartment. No way around that. Dad didn't know, and he was the guy in charge.

So why was Michael looking at her as he would a suspect at the station?

It wasn't until right now, when the half-formed thought of telling Michael was discarded, that she realized she was even thinking of it. She deflected. "I went a little far, Michael, but I'm teaching the Great Collision and it came up and it's a valid point. The question stuck with me."

"Are you sure that's it? Anything else bothering you?"

His eyes didn't lose their laser focus, and she really needed to leave and think things through. "I'm-" she licked her lips, buying herself a few seconds. "I'm sorry I upset Dad. I think I need to go home. Things have somehow derailed, and me leaving is a good idea."

He placed his hands on the table, readying himself to get up. "I'll drive you."

She placed her hand over his, stopping him. "That's silly, Michael. My car is here, I haven't drunk any alcohol. A little fresh air and I'll be fine."

Michael looked dubious but didn't stop her as she grabbed up her coat and bag. She opened the door, slinging her purse over her shoulder, "Tell Dad I'll give him a call tomorrow and I love him." Without waiting for an answer, she went outside.

This was more complicated by the minute. Dad didn't know anything but Michael might? Impossible.

Impossible.

Just as impossible as a gargoyle protector.

Just as impossible as zombies coming after her.

Just as impossible as necromancers waiting for the chance to grab her again.

Instead of taking her usual back-alley shortcut home, Larissa kept to the well-travelled streets.

# CHAPTER NINE

Once again, Terak was on the roof of the opposite building and watched the little human through her glass doors. This time, though, she was aware of him, or aware someone was watching her. She kept pacing to the window, looking out, retreating into her home, only to repeat the process moments later.

After doing this several times, her head snapped up and her spine straightened, as though she had come to a decision. She again began to move toward the windows, but this time, instead of stopping there, she continued to the glass doors that led to her balcony and opened them. Stepping out onto the balcony, she waved her arms in wide arcs through the air.

He neither saw nor sensed any threat to her. Uncertainty kept him still, a sensation unknown to him before she entered his life.

After several moments of waving she brought her arms down and around herself, hugging her body against the cold. Her lips tightened, and she went back inside.

She could not wish his company, could she? She fought hard against any guards, so why would she seek him out?

But she kept looking out the window, her attention never leaving the balcony for more than a few minutes.

Standing, he snapped his wings in preparation, leaping in the air and gliding the short distance to her.

She heard his landing. Within moments she scrambled from her inner rooms toward the balcony door. Her eyes widened when she saw him. "It's you."

Did she not wish to see him again? They had parted on as pleasant of terms as possible considering the circumstances of their initial meeting. His shoulders went back as he braced himself. "Does this upset you?"

"Oh." She shook her head, the action appearing as a way to clear her mind than a motion of the negative. "I'm sorry, that sounded so rude. I didn't mean anything by that. I wasn't expecting you though."

"Why?"

She motioned at him. "You are the leader. I never expected you would be on guard duty."

Her words were intelligent, as under any other circumstances he would not be. Still, best she not know that. "A leader who views himself above any task is setting a poor example for his people."

The nod she gave was little more than humoring him, if the flattened twist of her mouth was honest in revealing her true thoughts. Still, she did not question him any further, and that was the outcome he desired. She asked instead, "Does this mean I'm going to see you often?"

*Yes*, but she did not need to know the truth at this time. "In the beginning only a handful of warriors will watch you as I search for information. I will be among them."

"Oh," she muttered, though he doubted she meant the word to be audible. She licked her lips, a nervous gesture. She looked around her apartment. "I'm sorry. I'm forgetting my manners. Would you like something to drink or eat? I mean, I don't know what gargoyles eat..."

The words trailed off and she was studying him again, her eyes stopping and lingering on the expanse of his chest, bare as his kind rarely wore shirts. The hint of a blush swept her cheeks, the color of springtime roses, which suited her pale hair and sky eyes.

"Water would be fine. As long as the glass is not delicate, I will be able to use it."

Relief washed over her features as her gaze met his again. "Not a problem. Please sit."

She motioned to the lone couch and walked into the adjoining kitchen area. Her apartment was small enough that the kitchen was readily visible from the living area, her graceful movements always in his view.

She brought the water, handing it to him. After drinking a sip, he put the cup down. "Your hospitality is gracious, so please forgive me when I ask if there was a reason you invited me in?"

Chagrin danced across her features before a smile crossed her lips. He easily saw her as a little girl, caught in her naughtiness by her father but trying to charm him from giving any deserved punishment. "I wanted to talk. I needed to ask some more questions."

"I am always willing to answer your questions, but I feel uneasy here. I am more effective as a guardian if I observe you from afar. I am more aware of the surrounding areas and can prevent anyone from getting near you."

Larissa took the seat across from him, drinking from her own water glass before answering. "And here I thought bodyguards always wanted to be closer to the people they were protecting."

He never had, not until her. "Gargoyles are not used to anyone wanting them near."

The wind howled past the glass, creating a haunting backdrop to their conversation. He missed the play of firelight over her skin. She was a creature of light. Sunlight or firelight, it did not matter. She should be bathed in radiance.

Her eyes were direct on his, proof that his memory was correct and he hadn't been imagining how bright and clear and true the blue was. "I still don't think I need a babysitter, but I'd prefer that whenever possible, you are close to me. It feels too weird to know someone is out there watching me when I can't see them." Her eyes flicked over his frame and before they shied from him they deepened in color to reflect a twilight sky. "But only you. No offense to anyone else."

Strange, his throat was tight. He swallowed before speaking. "If that is your wish, I will do so when possible."

She nodded, her fingers tangling together as she lost herself to her own thoughts. Then she let out a chuckle, the sound resigned humor. "Can my life get any stranger?"

No answer was needed, and she rose to pace the length of her living area again.

Movement seemed to calm her. Both at the keep and now here in her own home, her movements started frantic, mellowing as her body burned the negative emotion from her.

Once she reached calm, she turned her attention back to him. "A member of the Guild came to my school today. Well, I should say two of them. The redheaded woman I saw Friday night and an Asian woman."

"Yes," he said.

"My dad," she took a deep breath, uncertainty coating her words. "I don't think my dad knows about them."

"He may not. Or he might not know the extent of their influence. They would not bother him over the daily dealings of crime in this city. That is not their concern. Their concern is the battle with the necromancers."

"But my dad is chief of police. He's not some bumbling civilian – his whole life is dedicated to protecting this city. How could he not know that there are these people with all these powers waiting in the shadows?" Her voice rose and her fingers wound together, almost violent in how they twisted around themselves.

He stood, taking her hands in his. He eased them apart, massaging the soft digits. "What exactly upsets you so?"

She turned her head away, not meeting his gaze. "I've been thrust into some new dimension where up is down and everything I've given complete faith to is worthless. I've blindly trusted my dad and the system, and it's all a lie. Right now, whether I'm being targeted or not seems almost immaterial."

He stroked her forearm, willing her with his touch to relax. In small increments she did so, growing more pliant under his fingers. "Because your father does not know about the existence of a group who have long guarded their privacy is not a reason to start doubting him. Your father is a good man and a good protector. Your city could not be in better hands."

"I don't-" She backed away, but her movements had gentled, the tension gone. "I don't mean Dad. Not completely. But the wards are a lie. Zombies got past, you," she said, motioning at him as she paced, "Got past. My predictable life is turning into a minefield."

"And I am here to help you, little human. I do not wish you to carry this burden alone."

Her eyes locked onto his and he could not turn away from the hurt in them. "I believe that, but I also believe that is not the only reason. If you weren't also helping yourself somehow, I'm not sure you would be here right now."

She was withdrawing from him, even more than that first night, and being allowed to continue in her life was hanging on these next few moments. "And you are right, little human. Though I will admit to admiring your bravery, if I did not believe more forces were at play I would not be here."

"Bravery?" Shock colored her words, disbelief written over her face. "What have I done that's so brave? I froze. If you hadn't come, I would have stood there as those zombies tore me apart, doing nothing but screaming as I died. And after standing there like a log watching them attack you, I turned and ran."

"You did not know you could trust me not to hurt you."

She slashed her arm as though it were a sword, cutting through the air at her side. "Don't try to make excuses for me."

Terak stopped her pacing and brought her to stand with him. He cupped her face, that beautiful face that did not flinch as his clawed fingers came into contact. "I make no excuses. You are not a warrior. You are a scholar, one who cares for and nurtures younglings. That you did not act as a hardened soldier who has lived with death is not a reason to call yourself a coward. You feel shame because you ran, but I see that as only strength. You were strong enough to not let the horrific sights around you paralyze you until the battle was over. You broke away. Many can never do that."

She looked at him in wonderment. Fat, lazy tears started to roll down her cheek, burying themselves in the collar of her sweater.

His wings half closed around them as he used the pad of his thumb to wipe away her tears. "You confuse me, little human."

"How so?" she asked, her voice not much above a whisper. She closed her eyes and leaned into his palm, letting the weight of her head rest in his hands.

"Most beings I have known feel they are more important than reality dictates. You, though, you seem to not realize how special you truly are."

Her smile was small, quiet, but it suited this intimacy. "You seem to know a lot about me for having known me a weekend."

The warning from her words tested the mood, but did not shatter it. He must not misspeak. She could not know how long he had been part of her life. "My father once said that once you learn how to see people, it takes only a moment to truly know them. Everything after that moment is details and happy memories."

One of her hands covered his. "Your father sounds like a wise man."

"No son alive who loves his father would ever say otherwise."

Her eyes opened then. The tiny lines around them had eased and the sheen of tears was now absent. They were back to the bright sky color that had his heart beating a little faster as they stared into his. "And what would you say?"

He bowed his head, images of his father and mother from a time long ago dancing in his memory. A time before the Collision, when they had all been free of the burdens of this new reality, his father gathering his mother up and spinning her around, only to bring her in and kiss her, the sight embarrassing him, yet warming something in his chest as he beheld it. "My father was the wisest of gargoyles."

Terak moved his hands into her hair, pushing the blond strands off her face with gentle strokes. He continued, "My father would have enjoyed meeting your father. From what I have heard, they were very alike."

"You know about my father?" she asked, curiosity sparking her eyes and dampening the last of the pain that remained there.

"I am leader of my Clan. It is my job to know of all beings whose decisions could affect the balance of this world. Your father is one such man. He is well respected, and though he issues no decrees, his words are taken seriously by those who do."

Pride lit her features, her smile going wide and free. "Yeah, that's my dad."

The intimacy of their situation hit him then, his hands buried in her hair while his wings surrounded them, protected them in their own universe. Her own gaze held no discomfort yet, but it would in moments.

It was better to back away, remove himself from her space. He forced fingers that did not wish to unwind from the strands of hair. He backed away.

He shifted his gaze away and focused on her home, to give them both a moment to recover. The room was warm, blue walls and white furniture and a hint of everlasting summer. It suited her.

The title of the book on the table caught his eye and he reached down to grab it. From the corner of his eye he viewed Larissa as she made a lunge to grab the book from him before she stopped herself.

"*History of Gargoyles*," he intoned, reading the title. "I have never read this work. Is it any good?"

He turned his attention back to her to see her little chin raised. "I'm not going to apologize for trying to learn about you."

Of course she shouldn't. He would have not respected her as much if she took everything on faith. "I would not expect you to. A scholar always seeks more information."

Her eyes still held their earlier warmth, though a small shadow entered them. "There is not a lot of information out there, and what little there is, it's… mixed."

Here he needed to tread carefully. Her hesitation over the last word spoke volumes. He wanted to keep the level of camaraderie they had developed. "I do not know what the volume contains, but I can say with certainty that we are not as bad as many stories would have you believe."

Her fingers ran over the cover of the volume, which featured a gargoyle in battle mode. "If gargoyles don't deserve the bad press, why do you have so much of it?"

"Separation and isolation creates fear and mistrust, on both sides."

"Which is why you want to start living in the world?"

"Yes."

"But not all your people do, isn't that what you told me?" The shadow was growing larger.

He waved his hand over the cover, and need to make her understand struck him with the force of a warhammer. He didn't want her to look on him with fear. He didn't want to lose the closeness they were developing. He wanted to be able to touch her face again. "Stories like this tell only one side. They never speak to the many betrayals gargoyles suffered at the hands of other races. My people do need to move on, but many cannot forget the past, a past where they learned that they can only depend on other gargoyles, lessons learned with blood and fire. They have learned that other races would destroy us if they got the chance." He sat across from her, not wanting to force her to keep looking up at him. "But we must move forward now, not forgetting those lessons, but not letting them control us either. We no longer live in the Magic Realm, and I need your help to accomplish what I want."

The shadow was gone. Her eyes now held only curiosity, the question in them not on his trustworthiness but on the worthiness of his plan. "Spell it out for me. What exactly is it you want?"

"I want what every leader wants. I want to protect my Clan. My people have been in flux since the Great Collision. I want to bring calm and prosperity and peace to my people. I want us to be able to move in this world without fearing or bringing fear to others."

She motioned to the book with the gargoyle drawn to inspire fear. "And you believe helping me will help you achieve that goal? That it will change centuries of mistrust on both sides?"

"It is only a first step, but yes, it is a valuable first step, one that will set my people on that desired path. While the outcome is not guaranteed, I can only hope so."

She studied the book still in his hand. Reaching for it, her fingers brushed his as she took the book from his hand, soft and warm and gentle, the sensation sparking nerves and tendons in ways not even the fiercest of battles had ever caused. There was a split-second pause, a hesitation before she drew away and left him bereft. Without a word she went into her kitchen and tossed the book into the trash, the look she gave him almost defiant, as though she was waiting for him to comment.

When no words came from him she changed from defiant to bashful, pink once again dusting her skin while her hand reached up to rub the back of her neck. She cleared her throat. "Bringing the conversation back to my school crashers, Fallon said something rather interesting to me."

"I do not doubt that. What did she say?"

Larissa started giggling, sweet, nervous sounds that she covered by placing her hand over her mouth. She was as adorable as any youngling at that moment, her shining eyes still visible beneath half-closed lids and her cheekbones rounded in mirth. Something in him loosened at the sight, freeing space in him that let air travel easier and deeper, as though now was the first time he knew what it was to truly breathe unencumbered. "She is a very intimidating woman when you are up close and personal."

Perhaps a diplomatic meeting with the Guild was in order. He did not wish Larissa to fear in the place that should be her sanctuary. "Do not feel cowardly for thinking that. Most warriors would rather run than face Fallon in battle."

"Have you ever fought her?" she asked, stark interest in her tone.

"No, and while I would if I had no choice, I would never wish to. What did she say?"

"Well, like you," Larissa said, giving him a pointed look, "she didn't seem to believe me when I said I had no idea why I was attacked by zombies. I then asked her why she didn't know what was going on. Obviously, she had some information if she was there waiting. And she had the funniest look of annoyance come over her face. She said some meddling bitch sent her to my place that night and didn't have the courtesy to tell her why she was there. Would you have any idea who she meant?"

There was only one being who could possibly cause that reaction in a warrior of Fallon's caliber. "My guess would be the Oracle."

"The Oracle? *THE* Oracle?"

"As far as I know, there is only one."

Larissa's mouth hung open for a moment. "The Oracle," she repeated. "I've heard about her, but...wow."

*She is connected to the future of your Clan. Guard her well.*

"I don't understand," Larissa continued. "If the Oracle is involved, why didn't she just tell them who was behind this and what they want me for?"

"Yes, it would be nice if she were something other than inscrutable."

"Have you ever met her?"

No, he would not tell.

His protection of her was all that mattered. There was no reason to inform her of the Oracle's visit which started his interest in her, or the months he watched over her without her knowledge. He would not risk their fragile relationship over the truth.

There was no reason then for this gnawing sensation that crawled through his insides with sharp teeth, eager to tear into his flesh and let him bleed.

None.

"No, I have not."

A clock chimed in the background, bringing Larissa's head up. "It's later than I thought. I need to get to bed." She seemed to become unsure again, the same uncertainty that colored those first minutes. "Thank you for coming in and answering some questions. And thank you for..." here she colored again, her eyes softening at the memory that played behind them. "Thank you for everything you said to me tonight. I might not want what is happening, but I'm grateful to have you helping me."

His wings flickered, and for the first time in his life he had to hold them steady against him. "I would not have you afraid if I can prevent it."

Her hands were twisting together lightly, broadcasting her nervousness in the next question. "Is there some way I can contact you if I need to speak with you again?"

"I will be around often."

"Yes, but unless you want me jumping up and down on the balcony and hoping you are on guard duty to answer, I was thinking there had to be an easier method of communication."

With rare exception he was the only one who watched her. Her worry was for naught, but to not scare her he said, "You may ask any gargoyle any question. They have been given orders to keep you apprised."

"Thank you for thinking to order that, but," and here she licked her lips again, a pink and glistening temptation amidst silken hair and fathomless eyes. If he had not so much experience listening to those around him even as his concentration was directed elsewhere, he would have missed her next words. "I like talking to you."

Warmth lit up his chest, inappropriate and all-consuming. Clearing his throat, he gave a gruff nod and stepped back toward the balcony. "I will bring something the next time I guard you."

"Good. I guess I should see you out then." She stepped out with him onto the balcony. "Try to get some rest."

"I shall."

She looked down, pushing her long hair behind her ear in a nervous gesture. "Next time you come, you don't have to wait for an invitation. I wouldn't mind if I saw you knocking on the door." Without waiting to see his reaction to those words, she entered her home, turning off lights as she made her way to her bedroom.

Terak leaned against the wall. If he quieted his breathing he could hear her going about her nightly rituals, hear the splash of water and the soft music she used as a background noise to lull her to sleep.

Did he imagine it, or could he hear the graze of her shirt as it slipped from her shoulders and fell to her feet? The rasp of the pull of a zipper, and then those nimble little fingers tugging the coarse denim over the lushness of her hips, over the round swell of her backside, down those long legs.

His groan resounded through the otherwise quiet night.

# CHAPTER TEN

Running in the middle of the day sucked.

Early morning, great. Early evening, even better. In the middle of the day, she was a little too much white girl to enjoy the sun beating hard down at her.

It must not be an issue for gargoyles. It wasn't as though they were pasty like her, and the odds were good sunburn was an unknown to them.

That in a nutshell was why she had not been able to convince Terak to let her run at her usual times. He look mystified she would equate something as insignificant as turning as red as a lobster to the possible danger from attack, and since she would be safest from attacks in the middle of the day, that was when she would run. So sayeth from on high.

Damn stubborn gargoyle. The only thing she had to fear was heatstroke.

It was a gorgeous day, and in good news for her skin, there was a decent amount of cloud cover, though not enough to lose the cheer of the day. She was running on her favorite trail through the largest wooded park to be enjoyed while still within the city's limits. She might not have left the city, but darned if she didn't feel like she was in her own woodland habitat.

Two men came from behind and sped past her, both at a pace much faster than her own ten-minute mile time. One turned and ran backward for a couple of moments, smiling and winking at her before turning around and catching up with his friend.

Ha, ha! Still got it. Nice to know she could get a glance or two, being an old maid and all.

Up ahead a tall woman in a red running bra and matching spandex shorts came running toward them, jogging in the other direction. Both men slowed as they stared at her, eventually tripping over each other's feet.

Larissa half expected to see their tongues in that mass of body parts. The men righted themselves and took off at top speed to finish their run.

Her own oversize shirt and baggy shorts were a hell of a lot more comfortable than that red number. Who put lace edging on anything you were supposed to exercise in? That had to chafe.

Who cared what those guys thought anyway. Neither of them were built. Compared to Terak they were pubescent boys, and no doubt Terak could bench press both of them with his tail.

Terak...urgh.

The last two weeks were the most disturbing of her life, and yes, she was including the week when she first got her period. She had been attacked by zombies, kidnapped by a gargoyle, had both a brother and a best friend who were acting suspicious, and a father who was still upset at her for asking questions about the security of the city.

And she had a gargoyle protector she was starting to care about, maybe even like.

Out of all the above, that last one kicked her hardest in the solar plexus.

He had wings. And a tail. *A tail.*

How the hell did this happen? Stockholm syndrome? Some power dynamic because she was the helpless little woman and he was the big, powerful gargoyle?

No, it was because of his chest. No male should have a chest like that, and he never wore a shirt. Never, like they offended him or something. Maybe she should be grateful that at least he wore pants.

No, she shouldn't be.

Yes, she should.

*Well…*

Back to chests. Terak's was so broad it might take *hours* to explore every inch exposed. And that chest tapered to that stomach, which was not a six-pack but an eight-pack. What human had an eight-pack? How could a human guy compete?

Gargoyles were very unfair to humans. Maybe she wasn't right to help them become friendly with other races. All the other females of the various species would jump them on sight.

But if any of them jumped on Terak, she'd have to tear the female's hair out. To protect inter-races relationships.

Was inter-races a word? Well, it was now.

Sweat soaked hair fell into her eyes, and Larissa pushed the damp tendrils that clung to her forehead back into the mass of hair knotted on top of her head.

Heatstroke. Had to be heatstroke causing these freaking thoughts. No matter how much Terak complained, she was never running in the afternoon again.

Up ahead was the most delightful part of the run, a steep incline that always made her swear she would give up running every time she crested it. Turning up the volume, she forged ahead.

The scream rent the air, the sound of feminine terror stopping her cold. Instinct had her turning before her brain could warn her it was a bad idea.

A woman, the one in the skimpy running gear, six feet in the air and grabbed around the throat by...

Oh dear *gods...*

*Orcs.*

Why hadn't she fought her dad harder about the wards? But this... how was she to know this could happen? Orcs in the park, backlit by a hazy sun during an afternoon run where she should be safe.

Her hands hung there, cold, numb. Her mouth opened, she knew it was open, but no sound was coming out.

*Orcs.*

"Not her."

They spoke? Those monstrous creatures could *speak?*

And then one of them locked eyes with her. He threw his head back and roared, the guttural noise flaying her exposed nerves. The rest of the orcs turned their attention to him. He proceeded to point at her.

"Her!"

*By the gods,* me?

No.

No.

*Are you involved with the necromancers?*

But she wasn't. Never, she'd never had anything to do with them.

This couldn't be happening.

Orcs, larger even than Terak, their greenish skin oozing and oily, their heads misshapen, like someone used their skulls for batting practice.

A dozen orcs now chasing after her.

She was running, she was running even though she didn't remember turning from them, branches flicking over her skin as she crashed through the wooded area. The ground vibrated from the force of the running creatures, creating an uneven surface under her feet.

"*Terak!*" she screamed. She hadn't seen him during the run, but he had to be here. He had to be. He promised he'd protect her and Terak, Terak would always keep his promises.

She tore through the forest, bramble and brush scraping against her body with every step. Heavy footsteps were so close, the clang of metal and the rhythm of their stride gaining.

This couldn't be happening. She was a nobody, a nothing. This couldn't be happening.

A primal scream sounded from above and powerful relief surged through her body, stopping her in her tracks as she looked for him.

*Terak.*

He was here. She was safe.

Terak's arm emerged from the foliage up above. He grabbed the tallest orc and brought him into the air, wrenching his neck so hard to one side that Larissa heard the crack of bones.

The orc stopped moving, and Terak threw the body far away, then dropped to the ground and grabbed another orc, his clawed hands ripping into its chest through the metal casing.

The other orcs turned to Terak, all but one. One orc still had her in his sights. He shouldered through the others surrounding him, coming straight at her. Terak turned from the orc he was fighting to launch himself at that one, preventing it from getting any nearer to her.

That move left his back unguarded, and another orc took advantage, taking its sword and slicing through Terak's wing.

Terak made no sound or movement to indicate he had been struck with a sword. He never stopped fighting the orc in front of him, keeping it from getting near her.

She could get away. Now, while their attention was on Terak, she could run to her car on the other side of the wood and escape.

*An eye hanging from its socket.*

She had stood there, waiting for the zombies to grab her.

If Terak hadn't been there, she would be dead. Afterward he held her in his wings as she cried and he called her brave.

*I don't want to die.*

*I don't want to die and I don't know what to do.*

*But I never want to be that person in the alley again.*

There had to be something she could do beyond run away in her car.

Her car…

She didn't have a weapon but she had two thousand pounds of magic-fortified metal at her disposal. Could an orc survive being run over?

Only one way to find out.

Larissa ran to the vehicle. Her fingers shook as she turned the key in the ignition, but the car started readily. Snapping on her seat belt she jammed down on the gas pedal, then spinning the wheel so hard tires squealed.

Her massive SUV took the grass easily, the bumps and dips rocking her in her seat. The trees were spaced apart far enough that the car was able to drive through the openings.

The fight was in front of her. Several orc bodies littered the ground, but three orcs still fought Terak. Terak was holding his own, but his chest and arms were swathed in large splashes of red and one wing was useless, the torn skin flapping in the wind.

Larissa pressed hard on the gas pedal, aiming the car at the two orcs farthest from Terak.

The orcs responded a second too late to the sound of an approaching car, lifting their heads as the car rammed into them. She rolled over them, sickening thumps and crunches that had her stomach begging to lose its contents. She clenched her teeth against the urge to vomit.

One hand appeared from underneath and landed on her hood, and the face and shoulders of one orc came into view.

Ahead was a thick line of trees. Pressing down on the accelerator, her body went tight, bracing for the expected impact as she headed straight for them.

She closed her eyes before they hit.

The airbag deployed at impact, pressed into her face so she couldn't breathe, her nose flattened and her chest punched concave. The wait for it to deflate was eternity, but she pushed at it, speeding up the process the best she could.

She turned the key, and thank gods the car started again. She put the car in reverse and made her way back to Terak.

No more orcs were left alive. Terak had more wounds than before, blood streaming over a good portion of his body. He was erect but kept falling to his knees.

She parked and rushed to his side. His right side seemed the least injured, so she propped herself under that arm to help him toward the car. "Your wing," she said, though it wasn't as if he needed her to point out the obvious. There was no way he could fly.

What were they going to do? He wasn't allowed within city limits. If they were caught driving in the city the authorities would take him into custody. Her too, but what would happen to her wasn't the worry. If he was jailed the other gargoyles would attack to free him, stomping on the possibility of a peaceful coexistence.

It had *Disaster of Epic Proportions* stamped all over it.

Maybe it was time to call her father. He would be furious, but he would help Terak escape, considering the gargoyle had saved her life. Of course, she would have to tell him what was going on, and her father would lock her up before she finished telling him about that first night.

But she couldn't see an alternative. Terak needed medical attention and she couldn't risk a fight between human and gargoyles. She owed Terak that and much more.

"Terak, I'm going to call my father. I think he'll help us. At the very least we need to get you to a hospital."

"No hospital," said the gargoyle, sweat beading his forehead. "No father."

"I'm not a nurse. You're wounded and in no shape to fly or fight, and if a gargoyle is seen within city limits, they'll take you into custody."

"No father," he repeated, breathing rapid, his voice reedy. He was going to pass out soon. She could convince him after she had him in the car, and she needed to get him there before he passed out. There would be no way she could handle his weight by herself.

As she got him settled into the passenger seat there was a buzzing underneath her hand, a vibration so small she didn't bother to look as it was occurring, focusing instead on the belt buckle. She turned to Terak…

… And reared back, hitting her head on the inside of the car, the pain bringing tears to her eyes.

Larissa's eyes slid shut as her hands grasped the newly formed bump. Maybe she had seen wrong, but her eyes opened, and no, she hadn't been seeing things.

Instead of a gargoyle sitting in her passenger seat, now there was a human male – bare-chested and bloody, with black hair and stone-grey eyes.

"Say nothing," he said.

Then he fainted.

# CHAPTER ELEVEN

*Human.*
*Human.*
*Human.*

The words beat through her head with the same rhythm as her heart, which was currently doing double-time since she was carting two hundred and fifty pounds of a gargoyle-turned-human through her bedroom door.

The bed lay before her, smooth sheets and fluffed-up pillows, and it might as well have been a mile away. "Terak?" she asked, but a pained groan was his only response. He was fading out of consciousness fast, and there was no way she could pick him up if he crashed to the floor.

No way around it.

"I'm sorry, I'm sorry, I'm sorry," she muttered as she hefted his arm away from her and all but knocked him onto the bed.

He upgraded from a groan to a yelp as his battered body collided with the mattress. "I'm so sorry," she said again and again, the words on repeat as the maneuvering began to get him fully situated.

Finally he was settled and the growly sounds diminished to only a few every minute. Larissa pushed her hair back from her face with both hands. A rising tide of panic was coursing through her body, starting low in her stomach and rising up her chest.

No. That nonsense needed to stop. Panic was not allowed until after she got her gargoyle back.

*Breathe in through the nose, out through the mouth. Do it again. After this is over you better be prepared, Double Mocha Fudge Ripple, because you are going down.*

First she had to get Terak bandaged up. The first-aid kit was under the sink, so well-stocked a hospital could borrow it in an emergency. Only nurses appreciated a fully loaded first-aid kit more than a cop's kid.

Kit, check. She turned on the water and let it run for a few moments to warm up, then let a plastic basin fill while she grabbed a few washcloths.

Terak gave a loud groan. She scooped up everything she needed and hustled back into the bedroom. The items were placed around her on the floor as she took stock of Terak's injuries. Her goal was to bandage him up enough that when her next gargoyle protector came on duty, that gargoyle could then take Terak home, where his own people could heal him. Gods, please let him heal enough that a hospital visit wouldn't be necessary. He might look human now, but who knew if he was as human on the inside? He might have extra organs or something that would give him away. And that was assuming they could actually survive the trip out the building to the car.

Car! *Crap!*

Since her gargoyle-turned-human protector had been bleeding out over her seat on the drive here, it was understandable little things like orc parts possibly caught in the bumper or a front end that had held a strong resemblance to an accordion were overlooked.

No way could she leave Terak, and anyway taking the SUV to Cliff, the mechanic who usually worked on her car, was out. He'd be on the phone to her father in three seconds flat. Any body shop would, all of them by law were supposed to report anything suspicious.

Right now what was needed was a friend who'd dump it somewhere and could be trusted to not blab, and only one person fit that description.

On the second ring the woman on the other end of the phone answered, and before she could finish her "Hello?" Larissa started talking. "Olivia, I'm in trouble. Help me."

Olivia's tone was soothing. "Calm down, sweetie. Of course I'll help you. What is going on?"

Thank gods for Olivia. "I need you to take my car away and not ask any questions."

Confusion burned through Olivia's tone. "Take your car? To do what?"

And now came the hard part. "I was chased by orcs. I had to slam into one to escape and now my car is messed up. Please, Olivia, I need you to come get it and hide it somewhere."

There was a long silence on the other end. Before Larissa hung up to dial again, Olivia spoke. "I know someone. I'll get your car fixed for you. Don't worry, there won't be any questions."

Olivia's voice was calm and low and apprehension skittered the length of Larissa's spine at her friend's words. This was not what she expected when she picked up that phone. "You... *know* someone? Olivia, what are you talking about?"

"You said no questions, I'm going to say the same to you. We are going to have a nice long talk later, but right now, where is your car?"

"On the south side of the building."

"It's taken care of. Don't worry and I'll call you tomorrow." And Olivia hung up.

Were there any more surprises ready to drop down on her head? If so, a little advance notice would be welcome, because the nice people at the mental hospital might give her a discount rate after a certain number of shocks to the system.

Terak was still on the bed, his breathing not as labored as it had been. Picking up a washcloth, she ran it over his flesh, now a sun-kissed tone instead of stone grey. He slept through her ministrations.

The wounds across his abdomen looked the worst. Cleaning them would reveal whether she could wait with him here or she'd have to brave the hospital.

The washcloth cleared the blood away and a small giggle erupted from her throat.

Relief caused some weird reactions, but after everything that happened today, a little giggle was a nice surprise. The wounds weren't as bad as all that blood suggested. He still needed to be seen by a healer, but cleaning and wrapping the wounds would suffice for now. Her gargoyle was going to be fine.

He was going to be fine, and the relief flooding through her system left her light-headed in its wake. She closed her eyes tight for a moment to regain equilibrium before opening them to continue with the cleaning.

Through all wiping and bandaging he stayed asleep, even the groans becoming less frequent. And now, was that...*a snore?*

Some bodyguard.

His face was gentler now, softer. It wasn't the human features that caused the change, though that helped. Asleep, he lost the worry and the authority he always carried otherwise.

Not that the human features were bad to look at. The gargoyle made a damn fine-looking human. That had been obvious from the first moment he shifted, but it seemed impolite to ogle someone when they needed medical attention.

His chest was done, now his...pants.

Oh dear gods, she had to take off his pants.

Did gargoyles wear underwear?

Did they need to? Did gargoyle males have the same equipment...?

*No.* That was not what mature, adult women thought when taking care of an injured male. That response was more in line with pubescent males who hid the girlie mags they stole from their dads under their mattresses. She was above such thoughts.

She grabbed a towel and laid it across his pelvis. Eyes on his face, she reached under the towel to lay her hands at his waist, his skin as warm as a human as it was as a gargoyle. She inched fabric down, slow and gentle in deference to wounds both known and yet undiscovered.

The whole process to remove Terak's pants took less than a minute, and at the end of it she was breathing as heavily as she did after running a 5K.

She cleared her throat, embarrassment warring with the crazy, inappropriate thoughts that had somehow become embedded in her brain this last week. She was taking care of him, and that was why she was running her hands over his legs. There were a few scrapes and bruises, but his legs were fine. Well, not *fine* like that. No, wait, they were…

She rapped her forehead a few times. This was ridiculous when she was even a stuttering fool within her own brain.

A little more washing, a few more bandages, and a patched-up, human-looking gargoyle was now in her bed. "When you wake up, we are having a serious talk. Like about gargoyle emergency contacts, and this whole *turning human* thing."

If he was awake he wasn't admitting to it. His eyes stayed closed and his breathing stayed even.

Her warrior.

Without her bidding a smile curled in the corner of her mouth. Yeah, he was. He had been amazing, ferocious and unstoppable. He took on those orcs without hesitation, all to protect her.

She leaned back against the wall and slid down until her butt hit the floor. She could still see him from this angle, that human face displaying no signs of distress.

What did she have to do now? Car was taken care of, and the list of questions she was going to be asking Olivia tomorrow could be made later. Olivia *knew* people. When had she started *knowing* people, people who could fix a car filled with orc parts and not blink?

*Later.* Much, much later.

Blood. Maybe cleaning up any blood trail would be a good idea, yes?

Thirty minutes later, any signs she had hauled a bleeding guy around were taken care of, thankfully without any neighbors catching her in the middle of clean-up duty. The sheets and towels would need to be trashed, but other than that no worries.

Terak was still resting when she went to check on him. His breathing was easier and his color better than it had been when she left.

Pulling one of the bandages away from his chest she looked, then looked again, doing a double-take. "Oh holy *hell*."

He said no hospital and it wasn't him being a stubborn male. He was healing on his own. What had been a good-sized gash was now half the depth and width it had been when she had cleaned it.

It wasn't that she had misjudged the severity of his wounds at the park. It was that they had already begun to heal in the time that it took to get to the apartment.

Huh. So gargoyles could shift into human form, and they healed in no time flat. Handy gifts, those.

Larissa kneeled down beside him and smoothed his hair back from his forehead. The human hair was finer than the coarse gargoyle strands, but it was the same deep black. No fever, just warm, perfect skin. "Do you think next time you can share the important info that will keep me from worrying *before* you faint?" No answer, but his breaths were deep and regular without a hint of pain in them. She sighed. "You're lucky you saved my life today, or you'd be in for a serious talking to."

As she stood, splotches of red on her once blue T-shirt caught her eye. Oh, *ew*. Blood and sweat and dirt and who knew what else were all down the front of her clothing. And her hair was still damp with sweat. And her legs had stuff streaked on them that she didn't even want to identify.

Terak was still sleeping comfortably. A quick shower wouldn't hurt.

The hot water pounded her from above, working into sore muscles in a painfully pleasurable way. She had entered academia and not followed her dad and brothers into law enforcement for a reason. She was not cut out for all this physical stuff.

After tossing on some comfy pajamas and giving her hair a quick towel dry, she went back to the bedroom, where Terak had flipped over and was now on his stomach, his face at the edge of the bed and his arm hanging over the side of the mattress.

He had been so frightening and alien that first night, a monster who had grabbed her against her will. Now here he was, undeniably human, and there was such a strong physical resemblance between man and gargoyle that it seemed ridiculous she'd ever thought gargoyles were scary-looking.

Larissa smoothed the blankets over him since he was in danger of losing the towel with his maneuverings. Would he be embarrassed waking up without his pants? An embarrassed Terak – now that expression would be worth checking out.

She left the room and headed for the balcony. She never asked about the schedule on who watched over her when, so she didn't know when the next gargoyle would arrive. After five minutes of doing the arm-waving trick and no one showing up, she went back inside.

Someone would figure it out eventually, and it wasn't like Terak was in danger anymore.

She entered the living room, glancing at the clock. Dinnertime. Her stomach let out a low roar that would be highly embarrassing if anyone else would have been around to hear it.

Well, she was hungry, and everything that could be done was done. No sense starving while she waited.

The television caught her eye as she wandered to the kitchen. Sigh. It would be nice to have a television that worked, and she needed to make a note to call a repairman tomorrow.

What was being reported on? Was the city in panic? How was her dad going to respond to the news that the wards were broken?

Speaking of Dad, why wasn't her phone ringing off the hook? As soon as an orc invasion was reported, her father should have made a beeline to the apartment and proceeded to try to grab her up and bring her home.

Strange. Maybe not the strangest incident of the day, but strange.

She made a turkey on rye. It was nice to do something as normal as make food after the last few hours. Normal was severely underrated, and if her life ever went back to normal, she would never take it for granted again.

Normal was not a gargoyle who had the ability to shift into human form.

Human.

It had been so crazy today she hadn't considered how important this was, but this... this was big. How the zombies and orcs had gotten past the wards was still a question, but this ability was probably the way gargoyles were able to enter the city and pass the wards that guarded it – presuming the other gargoyles had this same ability. Only a human was supposed to be able to walk past them, and right now Terak was certainly human, at least on the outside.

Think of the implications. So many spells, especially protection spells, relied on that one designator. *Human.* An enemy who could bypass them at will, especially a race as powerful as the gargoyles – that would scare a whole lot of people.

Alone and unarmed, Terak had fought a band of orcs. He had been hurt, and yes, she helped, but none of that changed the fact he alone killed over a dozen of some of the most feared fighters in this world.

Gargoyles were not to be underestimated.

A hard knock sounded against the door.

# CHAPTER TWELVE

Surprise visitors had to be bad news. *Terak…*

Several loud thumps sounded in a row, as though the person on the other side were hitting the door with the side of their fist. "Ris, open up. Now."

Michael, using his patented *I'm the eldest and with Dad gone I'm in charge* voice.

Her brother the cop, who never came over without calling first.

As tempting as not opening that door was, that wasn't an option. Michael would kick it down in a heartbeat – any of the family would. And if she objected in any way, shape, or form or threatened parts of their anatomy, she would be met with a shrug and an insincere apology, and left with the full knowledge they would do it again if they felt it necessary.

With no other choice unless she wanted this to become a full-scale incident, she opened the door. "Michael, what are you doing here?"

He walked in before she had a chance to fully block the entrance or voice an excuse on why this was not a good time to visit, which translated meant he was not going to be leaving until whatever had brought him over was wrapped up to his satisfaction.

She shut the door with a quiet click. Michael wasn't yelling – not yet, at least – and it would be best to do everything possible to keep things quiet and prevent Terak from waking up during their little family chat.

Overprotective gargoyle versus overprotective big brother. That was a match-up she had no interest in seeing anytime soon.

Michael's eyes wandered her apartment, not in casual interest but in a hard sweep, searching out any hidden secret or concealed clue.

He was looking at her place with cop's eyes, and there went any hope that this was a friendly visit.

He'd never used the sweep on her before. He once joked this was the only place he could relax and not be a cop. Something had sent him here.

So what did he know, and how did he know it? If he knew she was at the park, where were the drawn weapons, and where were the other brothers and her father? And why wasn't he asking about the gargoyle sighted in the park? And if he was here only because there was an orc attack in the city, why wasn't he ushering her out of the apartment and straight to Dad's?

Nothing was adding up. This needed to be played casual, at least until she had a better idea of what her brother knew. "Michael, what are you doing here?"

"You went to the park today?" It was question and statement mixed together, a tactic used by cops where they were asking you a question, but in the words it was implied they already knew what was going on.

*Keep up the confusion act.* "Actually, I did. I went running this morning."

His voice was curt, not letting her sentence die before he asked the next question. "Did you see anything while there?"

"Yeah, lots of trees and two men ogling this one woman who was wearing red running lingerie."

"Anything else?"

In their usual conversations, now would be the time she would get annoyed with her big brother and start acting huffy. Crossing her arms and cocking her hip to one side, she added a touch of annoyance into her tone. "What's this about?"

Michael's eyes were cold and calculating. In that gaze, he was weighing whatever he knew in his head against what he had seen from her today.

Her brother was deciding if he could trust her. He was deciding if she was his baby sister, or if she was responsible for a wrong he needed to set right.

Damn, this hurt. And the worst of it was, he was right. He was right to question her and act as though she was some bum he grabbed from the street, because right now, right this minute, for the first time in her life, she was lying to him. Not a fib, not a stall for more time, but a lie.

A big lie. A lie over something that mattered.

*End this now.*

Maybe that would be best. This situation was spiraling out of control. If today proved anything, it was that the zombie incident was not a mistake. Something was hunting her for whatever reason.

What were the choices? Have a gargoyle sleeping under her bed all her life?

End this now. Confess everything and throw herself on Dad's mercy, then come up with a plan on where to go from here. He'd be mad as hell, no doubt about it, but that didn't change the fact they would do anything to protect her.

*And Terak?*

What would they do to Terak?

What would they do to the gargoyle who had been protecting her all this time, the being she had begun to call her friend? He fought and bled for her. He laughed with her. He snarked at her.

He called her brave and she knew, to the center of her soul she knew, he meant it.

Even if they didn't do anything to him, coming clean to Michael would mean the end of her relationship with Terak.

They would force her to let him go.

Michael's eyes were still indecisive.

Larissa raised her eyebrows at him. "Well, I'm waiting. What has you coming over here in such a snit? Couldn't you at least call me first and warn me you had attitude to spare?"

Michael relaxed, the signal that he had put his suspicions aside. He put his hand out to her, something between his fingers that he was giving her. It was her driver's license. "Did I leave this at Dad's?"

"It was found today at the park. There was an incident and I happened to notice it near the scene."

So that's what had started this. "What happened at the park?" *No, I'm not going to move back and live with Dad. No, I don't care if there was an orc attack...*

He shook his head. "Sorry, I can't give any details of an ongoing inves...Ris, you all right?"

It was a good thing she tripped and fell to the floor, otherwise Michael couldn't have missed the shock that had streaked through her body and had to be evident on her face, and he would have known she'd been lying earlier.

The zombies had disintegrated – at least, that's what she assumed was the reason the earlier attack was undetected. But the orcs? That was destruction on a large scale, and their bodies didn't disintegrate. They were in large heaps, bloody and broken bodies littering a little-used section of a public park. That couldn't be hidden.

Could it?

And if someone did have the ability to hide it? Who? And why would they?

What the hell was Michael part of?

She needed answers, but right now Michael needed to leave. There was still another large male she had to take care of. She picked herself off the floor and used her palms to dust off her legs. "One of these days I'll become graceful, you'll see," she said, picking the threads of a long-running family joke.

Michael fell into the rhythm. "The day that happens is the day I'll trust you with my computer."

"You'd be lucky if I broke that thing. There's old technology, and then there is technology that has seniors laughing at you for owning it." She walked into the kitchen and picked up her sandwich. "Well it was nice seeing you, and thanks for bringing back my ID. If that's all, I'm kind of busy. I'll see you this weekend."

He didn't take the hint, which was the usual for Michael. While he was no longer in full cop-mode, speculation was still clear on his face. "What are you busy with?"

Why couldn't her family be the type that avoided each other except the holidays? "Michael, quit treating me like a kid. I'm allowed to have a life and I don't have to run every decision by you."

"Who gave you that wrong information?" His eyes narrowed. "What are you hiding from me?"

A noise brought both of their gazes to the door of her bedroom.

Terak appeared in the doorway, the towel around his waist the only covering over his naked body.

# CHAPTER THIRTEEN

Warm honeysuckle drifted around him, tease and temptation. Just like her, sweet and comforting and sensual, she was able to ease his tension with a touch of her hand or have him hard and wanting with a glance of those eyes.

She had been delectable, her long legs bare and the sunlight exposing the multiple hues of blond in her hair.

A coppery tang worked its way past the honeysuckle. No, this should never touch her. It was his duty to protect her from necromancers, and from orcs…

Late afternoon sunlight filtered through his eyelids as he cracked them. Slow and steady, he forced his eyes open.

He was on a bed. Blue walls surrounded him, and on top of the furniture were feminine bottles and potions.

Larissa's bedroom.

Images were creeping back, the fuzziness of sleep giving way to the clarity of memory. Orcs were often allies of the necromancers but they were not slaves. If they were there on behalf of the same masters as the zombies, the necromancers must have agreed to a very high price.

Also, they were able to pass the wards, a situation that was very different from the zombies getting into the city. Zombies were once human. It would take powerful magic to confuse the wards enough to let the zombies through, but it was not outside the abilities of a master necromancer.

Orcs, though – orcs should have been impossible.

If the wards were completely useless, Larissa was in greater danger than ever, and a new plan for her protection needed to be drawn up.

But what? She would not agree to stay at the keep until the danger had passed. Indeed, he used that very suggestion to sway her away from the Guild.

And that was if she was still willing to let him guard her, now that she knew...

*She knew!*

He jerked from the bed, his half-healed injuries tearing anew at the sudden movement.

She knew. No.

*No.*

Had any of his Clan appeared? No, no one was to be here until the middle of the night. None would have come and seen him... human.

On unsteady legs he went to the bathroom. In the mirror was undeniable evidence, the face that of a human male. Larissa knew that he could shift into a human form.

From their earliest history, there only one absolute rule held by his race - if any outsider discovered that gargoyles could shift, the outsider was to be executed at once.

His clawless hands fisted against the white tile of the sink. He would be dead if she had not entered the battle. Instead of running for safety she had appeared to aid him in battle, as fierce as any goddess of war. She had taken him home, cared for him, nursed him. And he was to repay that with death?

No, no harm would ever come to his little human. She would never be hurt, even if he had to battle his own Clan for her life.

But the Clan's secrets must be protected. How could he ensure that?

Rubbing his hand over his face, he pushed back from the mirror.

There was nothing to be done now. It was time for more practical considerations, and later, he would reflect more upon how to contain the situation.

He took off the bandages and stepped into the shower, the hot water getting the last of the blood from this day's battle. There was very little that had been missed. Larissa had done well bathing him and tending to his wounds.

His hand stilled in washing his hair. He had been naked in that bed.

Larissa had stripped away his clothes. She had caressed his body with those soft little hands.

Did she like what she saw? What she *felt*?

His cock hardened, becoming as heavy and as stiff as the stone statues his kind resembled.

She would have been above him, leaning over him to tend to his wounds. She would have nibbled on her lower lip, as she often did when she concentrated, leaving it pink and swollen and glistening.

He palmed his cock, rubbing it with slow movements. Her little tongue would have come out to swipe over her lower lip after she had finished nibbling it, the way he wanted it to swipe over his body. He wanted her to peel the clothing from his body not because of injuries, but because she needed to know the taste and feel of him. She would get on her knees in front of him-

*Voices.*

His hand stopped. He tilted his head for clearer sound.

Larissa, and one other.

A *male* other.

The growl echoed through the shower stall. He grabbed a towel to cover his body and exited the room.

If the man threatened her, he was dead.

If the man was a rival for her, he would wish he was never born.

As he entered her living room, the two humans sensed his presence. Larissa's eyes widened while the male's narrowed, and the grinding of the man's teeth was sharp in Terak's ears.

The male was her brother, the only dark-haired one among the boys. She was not dealing with a male who desired her.

Larissa's mouth parted in surprise. Her hair was damp from a recent shower of her own, and she wore a shirt that hung off her shoulder, as if she had risen from the soft bed he had awoken in.

Her eyes locked with his, wide and blue and bright. The slope of her shoulder enticed him, invited him to nuzzle her, follow the curve of her skin wherever it led him.

She swallowed hard, her hand coming up to cover her bare shoulder, her thumb brushing the skin of her neck as he wanted to do.

The energy from her brother grew so dark Terak turned his gaze to the human male. He was murderous, his body tensed in preparation for a fight.

Larissa seemed to sense her brother's mood, for she broke from his gaze to turn to her brother. For a few long moments debate was clear on her features, a questioning on what to do next.

Then her chin came up, that little signal of defiance that often wrung a groan of frustration from him even as every cell filled with pride at the sight.

She walked over to stand in front of him. Sliding her hands up his chest, she stood on her toes to brush a kiss over his mouth, the pink lips softer than anything he had ever experienced before. "Baby, this is my brother, and we're having a sibling discussion. Why don't you wait in the other room and we'll be done in a moment."


Thank goodness Terak had done as she requested.

Of course, she still had a pissed older brother to deal with.

"Ris, who was that?"

Her hands went to her hips, an instinctive reaction when her brother used that tone on her. "You don't get to lecture me, Michael."

He stomped over to her, his eyes ablaze. "*I* don't get to say anything when my baby sister is obviously sleeping with some guy she never even introduced to the family?"

She poked him in the chest to get him to back up. "*Your* baby sister is twenty-six years old and lives on her own! Do I stomp over to your house to see what kind of hussy you are shacking up with?"

"We aren't talking about me!"

"Well, we aren't talking about me, either! My sex life is none of your concern."

He groaned, putting his hands up over her ears like he could block the words. "I don't want to hear my little sister use that word again."

"Grow up. You're the one trying to insinuate yourself into my life. Don't act like you can't handle it."

They eyed each other, both refusing to back down. Hands on hips, he said, "This isn't right."

Realization struck Larissa and she looked down to see her stance mirroring her brother's. They really were a lot alike.

Of course they were. They were family.

Larissa drew a deep breath, releasing the tension. She walked up to him and patted his chest, causing her brother to drop his hands to his sides. "I love all you guys. More than that, I like you all, and your approval means so much to me. But don't you feel it too? That sometimes it's too much, that you need a break from the family and their expectations, that you need your own life and freedom? Michael, you had to, you're the one who left us first."

Her brother's gaze slid across the floor, taking in her words. Her brother had been gone for eight years in the military, the only family member who left the neighborhood.

Her father had been so proud of his boy, talking to everyone about how his son had signed up, but Larissa saw it in him, the constant worry, the dread that gave him an ulcer and had him eating antacids like candy.

None of the rest of them ever left after that.

And Larissa would swear that the happiest she had ever seen her father was when Michael announced he was coming back and joining the police force.

"Larissa, is it serious with this guy?" Time to proceed with caution. If her brother thought Terak was trying to take advantage of her, he would go into the other room and dangle her guest off the balcony.

He wouldn't drop Terak though.

Probably.

"I'm not sure what we have together yet. I do know he's special to me. And I know, even if we separate, I will never regret him."

He sighed, rubbing the back of his neck, and Larissa knew she won. "Baby sister, you're killing me. Dad's going to scent I'm hiding something and he's going to make my life hell."

She gave him a hug. "Thank you."

He returned the hug, but then grabbed her by the shoulders and set her back from him, looking deep into her eyes. "You have a little time, but only a little. Figure out what you want, then either move on or the family has to meet him."

He sighed again, moving toward the door. "At least this will stop Dad from putting us all on Friday shift so he can introduce you to another guy."

The door closed. One male taken care of. Now the other to deal with.

# CHAPTER FOURTEEN

Terak was leaning against the wall, his arms crossed over his chest, waiting for her return.

At least he put his pants back on. As tattered as they were, it was still a lot easier on her respiratory system seeing him in those versus the white towel.

She put her hands up, a signal to please let her talk before any yelling started. "I didn't call him. He found my ID at the park when they were investigating the attack. I'm lucky it was him, otherwise there would have been a whole squadron of cops at my door."

His features were a shade different, softened into human lines, but the intensity of his eyes and set of his mouth was pure Terak. She'd recognize both no matter what else changed. "I know this. I am curious why you did not tell him about me?"

"Why would I? The whole reason I agreed to your people guarding me was so that I didn't get my family involved in this mess. Running to them would kind of defeat the purpose."

He started shaking his head, his arms coming to his sides as he propelled himself away from the wall. "Why did you not tell your brother about my abilities, that the human male in front of him is in reality a gargoyle?"

There was a strange tension in Terak, his usual intensity magnified. He was waiting for her answer, his now-clawless hands clenching and unclenching at his sides. The question of whether she should be scared popped into her head, but she pushed it away. Nothing about him scared her. What he was...was...hopeful. "Why would you even ask that? This is your secret. I would never tell anyone about this."

Terak challenged her, that deep voice still the same in this form. "He is a protector of the human world. Information on your enemies is what any protector would wish."

Before she could stop herself, her hands went to her hips. "There is nothing I want less than to get into another fight with a stubborn male who is trying to drive me crazy. Now, I don't know what's going on in that human-looking gargoyle head of yours, but quit it. You saved me multiple times. We've fought together. More than that, I consider you a friend, and I trust you. I would never betray a secret I discovered from my friend."

Terak reeled back as if someone hit him. "You would call me a friend?"

He looked so adorable and bewildered, and while the smile curling her lips couldn't be stopped, there was a pang in her chest over what this male's life was like that the thought of someone calling him friend elicited a reaction like this. "Shocking, huh? Kind of surprised me to. Maybe that kind of stuff only becomes apparent when you're watching someone bleed and praying he doesn't die."

His face held wonderment. It was if he received a rare gift, something he always wanted but never thought he would get for himself. His gaze roamed over her face, like he was committing everything in this moment to memory.

"So," Larissa said, wanting to stop the awkwardness creeping through her skin, "how does this work? You look pretty healed up, I'd say. Does this mean you are healed as a gargoyle? Your wing was torn pretty bad."

He shifted. Strange, this big, bad secret, but it bordered on anti-climactic seeing it in action. He went out of focus – only for a second – and then became the other form. If Larissa took a long blink she would have missed it.

She walked behind him to check his wing, stroking her hand over the membrane. It felt like leather, but that soft, luxurious leather, the kind where a jacket would cost most people's yearly salary.

Her hand traveled to the frame. Even this was warm, his body heat coming through. The muscles bunched under her hand as she took in the area where the frame met his back. This body was that of a warrior. He was hard, perfectly formed. This body was her salvation, her sword and shield in a world that made no sense.

Tiny tremors rippled under her fingertips as she stroked down his muscles. Which shook, her hand or his back?

Her thumb brushed over the tiny hollow in his back that separated his wings. She leaned closer, breathing in his smell as she did that night where he held her in his arms. She'd been so scared that the sensation of flying was a blur. She couldn't remember if she enjoyed it, even on a subconscious level. Would he take her flying again if she asked?

Adding more pressure, she ran her thumb down the strong curve of his spine

Would he let her follow it with her tongue?

Larissa pushed back even as her mouth parted to make the thought a reality.

Sleep, that was the ticket. She needed a break from this day in the worst way. Sleep would be good. Sleep would get her emotions back in line. Clearing her throat, she said, "You look completely healed. I'm not a nurse though, so you should have one of your people look at it."


His muscles still trembled where she had caressed him. His lips still carried the warmth of hers. Her scent filled his nostrils.

This woman was consuming him, bit by bit. She was becoming the reason and the reward of his existence, and if he did not shield himself, everything he did not have to give would belong to her.

He turned and brought her back into his sight. She was so appealing standing there, the over-large shirt hanging from her frame, her hair still damp and laying along her back.

Her hands were twisting together in a nervous fashion, her pupils dilated, darkening her eyes to the color of the stormy sea.

Once he had boasted to a group of young warriors that he could withstand any torture. The woman before him made him realize the fool he had been.

She forced her hands apart, a deliberate relaxation. She was trying to bring normalcy back to their interactions. "So, gargoyles can shift, huh?"

He hung onto the safety line she provided, willing to walk away from whatever edge they had been traveling. "We have hidden it for a very long time. In the distant past other races knew. In return for our trust, we received death."

Her eyes widened. "Your allies turned on you? How did they succeed?" She paused, then in a mutter meant for her own ears more than his, said, "I've seen you guys in battle. I'm not sure anyone could win against you."

Pride swept through him at her assessment of his skills. "We are more vulnerable in our human form. We are stronger than humans, but nowhere near the power of our gargoyle forms. We foolishly let others know of this weakness."

His thoughts drifted off into memories until he was a boy at a fire, listening to the weathered elder tell the darkest moment of their race, the only story that ever brought him to his knees.

Soft skin cradled his face, breaking the memory. Larissa was before him, her warm eyes pleading for him to confide in her, promising him she would be strong enough for them both. "What happened?"

"There was a great celebration. Gargoyles were invited, including the children and the elderly. We were asked to come in our human guises. We did."

His eyes closed and his head bowed. He did not want to finish the story. Not because he did not want to relive the elder's words as she warned them all on that firelit night to never trust an outsider again, but because he wished Larissa to never be exposed to the depths of depravity some were capable of.

Those soft hands slid around his neck, pulling him down into her arms. She buried her face into his neck. He leaned into the silk of her hair, pulling in breath after breath of her beloved scent.

"I'll never tell," she said, low tones that still displayed the steel of her will. "I swear to you, I'll never tell."

He wrapped his arms around the little human and into her hands, he placed the fate of his people.

They stayed still for long moments before Larissa broke the contact. "I'm sorry you are in this position. I realize now how hard this is for you, making the decision between staying separate and entering this new world."

"I wish," he paused, the words stopping on his tongue. Uncertainty was not something he shared with others. The leader must be invulnerable. Still, she was not a member of the Clan. His doubts would not be held against him. "I hope that those who do not agree with my decision to help you will understand when this is over. They are so intent on never being vulnerable again that they lose all the possibility that this world can offer. But then I remember what has come before when we opened ourselves up, and I wonder if I am the naïve fool many call me behind my back."

"Terak, you are not a fool. You are a great leader, one who cares for his people more than he cares for himself. Your instincts will not steer you wrong."

"There are many of my Clan who do not possess your surety." He backed away from her, the weakness that demanded he take her in his arms becoming stronger the longer he was near her. "I owe you a debt. You protected me."

She snorted, the tiny sound adorable to his ears. "Well, you protected me. I say that makes us even. Or if you argue it, I'm probably still in your debt with your two life-saving rescues against my one. Besides, it's a moot point. The way I see us, we are now allies trying to figure out what is going on."

"You now accept that you are in danger?"

She sighed. "Guess I have no choice, do I? When a bunch of zombies and orcs come after you, it's kind of hard to argue that it is one giant mistake."

The teasing words came to him, another impulse he rarely experienced before entering her world. But though his first inclination was to swallow them, instead he freed them, directing them toward her. "I do not know, little human. You seem to have a great gift for arguing any situation."

Her eyes widened. Were his words not received as they were meant? Perhaps...

And a huge smile broke out on her face, the effect that of the sun escaping from a dark grey sky. "Is that so, oh Great Leader? I'm honored that you noticed my wondrous skills in that area."

He pushed back, gentle, not wanting to end their ease with each other. "I am sure the most silver-tongued of all elves could not argue more effectively than you."

"That's because no elf grew up with my family."

He had nothing to add, so he stayed silent, letting the playfulness rest peacefully between them.

She spoke again. "How do we discover why they are after me? I acknowledge that they are after me, but it doesn't change the fact that I don't know why I have been singled out." She ran her hands over her arms, the playfulness fading from her features to be replaced with a fearful uncertainty. "I'm scared."

He did not dare touch her again, but he projected every ounce of his strength into his voice. "No matter who your enemy is, I will protect you."

# CHAPTER FIFTEEN

"Why don't they call this place '*Goths R Us*' and be done with it? And seriously? Red velvet? Even I wouldn't go there."

Fallon didn't waste the movement it would have taken to look down at the mouthy mage. Goth overload was an apt description of the vampire club. Black and red was the color scheme of everyone and everything, the haze of smoke beneath the dim lights could have been from the multitude of clove cigarettes or a few more nefarious drugs of choice, and with the attire on display, there was a good chance a leather-and-lace factory nearby had been robbed.

"And considering all the places you have gone, Laire, that is a statement." She scanned the contours and corners from where they stood at the entrance. Invitation or not, this place was dangerous. Life-ending dangerous. Soul-stealing dangerous. Invitation or not, there was no letting down her guard. "Besides, do you really expect us to defer to your color judgment? Bubblegum pink? Why?"

A vision in leg warmers and a miniskirt, Laire pushed back her feathered, pink-tipped hair. "Just because you can't understand color, don't try to bring me down. Black should be an accent, not your whole color palette. I'd almost say you fit right in here among the groupies."

"Bite your tongue."

"No thanks, I don't want a horde of suckers descending on me if I drew blood. And you," Laire said, turning to the man who rounded out their spectacularly *not*-happy-to-be-here trio. "You need to up your act as well."

"Hey, I do blue." His dark blond hair was a shaggy mess that hung over his forehead, almost covering yellow eyes but not hiding the scar that ran down the right side of his face into his well-trimmed beard.

"Wulver, blue jeans every day are as bad as Fallon's forever black. I do not give you a pass."

"But jeans do good things for my tushie." He turned his back to Laire, raising the lumberjack overshirt with one hand while pointing at his derriere with the other. "See? Proof right there. Why mess with perfection?"

Laire ogled him a touch longer than necessary before giving her nod. "You win. That is a great butt, truly a class by itself."

"Thank you."

"Before Laire comes up with a reason why we should start removing clothes to prove some theory, I got a question." Fallon said. "Can we teleport out of here if this turns ugly?"

"Nope, our only hope will be for you to swing your sword, Wulver to fang out, and me to set everything on fire...*Ooh!* Liquor," And Laire turned away to scamper to the bar.

"Laire, get back here! You do *not* drink before we meet with our mortal enemy." Not even a stutter-step to indicate she heard. Fallon's head fell forward, the annoyance-and-more-annoyance mixture swirling through her synapses so familiar when dealing with Laire. She turned to Wulver. "Can't you control her?"

Wulver snorted. "Can you?"

"You are the boss."

"Like that's ever worked."

They went over to Laire who was pounding on the bar. "Hey! Walking blood bank, I need some service."

The bartender, a woman was in her mid-twenties, was beautiful, of course, because vampires would surround themselves with nothing else. She kept to the red-and-black theme in her tight corset and red lips. Her expression was a mixture of disdain and horror – but to be fair that was how most people looked at Laire's outfits. "I don't think you belong here."

Laire plopped down on the barstool. "And I'm supposed to care about the opinion of someone who drools over corpses? Your implants have more sense than you do. Get me a boilermaker."

The woman's nostrils flared, which probably hurt when you took into account all those piercings. Still, she started to fill the order. Laire called after her, "And hurry. Who knows when we're going to be interrupted, and I want my drink."

"What are you, an alkie?" Fallon stood to the left of the mage while Wulver sat on the right.

"You are the one who said I needed to be pleasant to a suckhead and not start a war. Don't harsh my means of achieving it."

The music was low, played more to enhance the dark, sensual mood than as a main attraction. The majority of beings here were human, though a few elves and a couple of nymphs were visible in the crowd. All of them beautiful and most of them women.

So where was their host?

Fallon extended her senses for the magical signatures. There by the far wall, a pulse of necromantic magic. And another in the middle of the dance floor. Neither were strong, acolytes monitoring the outer club or other low-level duties.

She extended further, discarding the signatures of the weaklings. They would pose no threat if she needed to kill them to escape. Stronger here and there, but not yet, not quite…

Tendrils vibrating with a heavy thrum of magic wrapped around her senses, caressing down the length until it reached her body. Without her shields it would have engulfed her and demanded she kneel in its wake, shudder with despair, degradation…desire.

*Reign.*

A big tankard was placed in front of Laire, leaving the mage clasping her hands in childish display and with a gleeful, "Sweet! I was afraid all they would have was absinthe or shit like that."

Wulver was on the stool next to Laire, leaning back so his thick forearms rested behind him on the bar, the movement stretching his blue T-shirt tight across his chest. "I know we're on time. How long do you think before they notice us?"

Fallon catalogued all eyes on them from both living and dead. "Oh, they've noticed us. But Reign wouldn't be Reign if he didn't exert his authority."

Wulver nodded. He tried to appear nonchalant, unconcerned, but he failed so spectacularly the passersby were giving him looks of pity. Not unexpected, since there were few things bossman hated more than being surrounded by suckheads.

Then he tensed, his gaze fixed on the far end of the bar. "What's this?"

Laire turned to look. She straightened in her seat, her hand going to fix her hair. "Oh, he's cute!"

"Sure is. Too bad he's up for sale to the highest bidder," Fallon said, taking in the V-shaped torso and long legs of the man at the end of the bar.

"For sale?" parroted Laire, and damned if she didn't reach for her purse.

"Give me that." Fallon grabbed the purse and threw it to Wulver, who threw it behind him. "Please tell me you recognize the most in-demand mercenary in the business."

"Why, did we have a drunken one-night stand you forgot to tell me about?"

The jeans and T-shirt combo marked the man as much an outsider as they were. Anyone without training would buy the good-ole-boy obliviousness he projected – if good-ole-boys had thick black tribal tattoos running over large chunks of exposed skin and long black hair with dyed-red streaks in it – but the defined lines of his body were a little too tense, his stance too close to battle-ready for those used to war to mistake this man as a non-threat.

Motioning toward the end of the bar, Fallon said, "Since we're waiting for Reign anyway, I'm heading over and saying hi, maybe ask him about a certain rumor we've heard."

Wulver nodded, while Laire asked, "Can I come too and get his number?"

"I'm going to say no."

When she was only a step away he called out, "Fancy meeting you here, Dragon Slayer. Hanging with vampires...seems I should have given the stories I heard a little more consideration."

Leaning against the bar so her sword hand was free, Fallon said, "I was wondering why I'm seeing you here as well, Merc. I never took you for a guy who was interested in the lace and tights crowd. Searching for a new personal style?"

"No, not me. Only male elves can pull that off."

"So why are you here?"

His shrug was perfect nonchalance, the movement hiking the shirt from his waistband and giving a quick glance of muscled torso. "Blood banks are legal under the treaty between the Seven Houses. No reason why I shouldn't be here."

"No, no reason. Meeting anyone special?"

He smiled at her, a deep dimple appearing with the movement. "Why? You looking for a date? While I'm flattered, I tend to like the ladies a little darker-haired and darker-skinned. However, I might know the perfect guy for you."

"You are sweet to be so concerned over my love life, but I've decided only to date guys who have bigger swords than me."

"I can see how that limits your dating pool."

Reign would send for them any minute, and Merc wouldn't meet with his client, not now that he'd seen them. So when he reached again for his drink, Fallon placed her hand over the glass.

His fingers folded into a strike form, but there were no further signs of aggression as he took her in and awaited her next move. Fallon said, "I'm not interested in a fight. I want to give a friendly warning. You've always been under our watch, but you've never done anything stupid enough to warrant being placed on our shit list. I advise you not to change that habit now."

His smile held the same level of friendliness as a shark's. "Whatever could you mean?"

"I've heard things about a spellbook and an auction run by a certain facilitator. Ring any bells?"

"Not a one. But if I hear anything, I'm coming straight to you."

He was good – impossible to read and giving nothing away. Such a waste he hadn't joined them when he was invited. "Appreciate that. Think about what I said. I'd hate for us to end up on opposite sides."

Merc grabbed his shot glass from the table. After saluting her, he brought it to his lips and drank the contents down, the strong column of his throat advertising the liquid's path. "I find I'm a little tired. If you'll excuse me." With that, he left.

Wulver's eyes were on her as Fallon made her way back. He gave a small shake of his head, indicating he didn't want to talk about it yet. Yeah, probably best not to discuss their business around here.

Moments after Merc walked out of the club, a vampire walked through the crowd and toward their little group. While his necromantic energy was unmistakable, his eyes were not red. So not a true vampire, merely one of the serving boys.

One who had overestimated his power, the poor deluded bastard, because instead of stopping some distance away he came to stand right before the three of them. Holding out his hand, he said, "I need your sword."

Laire snorted into her drink while Wulver's chuckles sounded on Fallon's other side. Smartasses. Fallon really didn't want to deal with baby vamp right now. Going to see Reign was never an activity that put her in a happy mood, and if Reign was tempting her into a fight by sending some fool into her path, it was a ploy that had a good chance of working. "Everyone needs my sword sweet-cheeks, but I'm the only one who's going to be holding it. Now run along, because I'm not supposed to fight anyone tonight."

The vampire's eyes narrowed. His lip curled, flashing a hint of fang. "You will give me your sword, or I will beat your insolence out of you."

Laire laughed so hard she proceeded to fall off the chair. Through the slightly-screechy, slightly-snorty display, she managed to eke out, "He's killing me here. Tell him to stop."

The vampire was young and wanted to start a fight. Fallon was feeling charitable enough to give it to him, but if she started one, Kyo would scold Laire, and Laire would mope for a week, and all in all, it wasn't worth it. Besides, she could turn this around and work it to her advantage, maybe get out of this damned meeting. "Tenro goes where I go. I'm either admitted to Reign with my sword, or I leave."

Wulver's low, "Don't even think it, Fallon," squashed that plan. Damn.

"Master Reign, human. Do not take such liberties with his name."

Laire had calmed down from her laughing fit enough she could stand by her chair again. At the vamp's words she piped up. "Trust us, junior. Reign wants nothing more than for her to take liberties with him."

Before Fallon could smack Laire, a bald, dark-skinned man appeared behind the young vampire. Sleek and elegant, he was all smooth lines, from his expensive suit complete with tie and cufflinks to the well-trimmed mustache and goatee. He bowed. "Lady Fallon, please forgive your treatment. I am here to escort you to Master Reign."

The young vampire voiced his displeasure. "But the human has a sword."

The man's gaze beat into the young vampire, and the vamp shrank from it. The man spoke. "Listen well. Whenever Lady Fallon appears, you are to immediately bring her to our Master. Do you understand?"

The vampire bowed and scurried away, escaping the anger emanating from the suited man. The man's almost-black eyes focused on Fallon, deliberate in his exclusion of Laire and Wulver. "My apologies, Lady Fallon. If you and your guests will come this way."

Wulver looked at her with a *told you* expression. Letting loose her sigh only in her own mind, Fallon took the lead and followed the man.

Laire spoke low at her side. "Who is that?"

"Zemar. He's Reign's personal bodyguard."

"But he's human?"

"I have no idea what he is."

Zemar led them to the back of the club, where a well-hidden door awaited them and opened to a hellish wonderland. The outer club Outside was decadent, but in here, in this room, it was the first level of Dante's Hell. Everywhere was flesh and pain and degradation and underneath it all, the copper tang of blood, oppressive and inescapable.

Wulver's energy flared and Fallon turned back to see his eyes brighten and turn translucent in the dim light. She put her hand on his arm, his skin shuddering under her palm.

It was unfair that Kyo sent Wulver instead of coming himself. None of them liked being here, but a place like this was special torture for Wulver. But he was here, and none of them could be weak in front of an enemy. Fallon's fingertips bit harder into Wulver's forearm in wordless demand, and he blinked, his eyes back to their normal yellow the next time they met hers.

They followed Zemar, passing scenes of damaged carnality on all sides. One woman was flat on a table, her legs spread wide as a man pounded into her with inhuman strength. Two vampires hovered over her chest, biting her breasts as she screamed out her pleasure. Another corner held a woman being whipped. With each stroke, vampires would come to lick the trickling blood off her back.

The back of the room had a wide set of stairs that led to the second floor, an open space that overlooked the cavernous club area. Here the gothic scheme morphed into chrome-and-glass and clean minimal lines.

A large, luxurious white couch spanned one end of the back wall to the other. A dozen beings sat on the couch – all but one a woman, all of them otherworldly beautiful, all laughing as though they weren't part of a nightmare. Blood and alcohol lined the table in front of them, as well as other stimulants that guaranteed they wouldn't have to live with their conscience for yet another night.

In the middle was the lone male. Physically, he appeared to be a human man in his mid-twenties. Impeccable grooming and stylish dark good looks, and an old-world manner evident even though he was doing nothing save sitting on the couch. Ungodly beautiful, with a square jaw and thick brows over deep-set blood-red eyes, nicely formed mouth and a straight Roman nose.

He had a woman on each side, both of them stroking and nuzzling him. He paid them no mind.

His eyes sought and stayed fast on Fallon, roaming the contours of her face, her body, the marking so intense it was almost physical. "Fallon."

Fallon swallowed, caught in that gaze. Inside her was a shifting, a growl, a warning to leave that she ignored. She inclined her head in acknowledgment. "Reign."

Reign murmured, "It's been a long time."

Wulver stepped in front of her, protecting her and partially blocking her from Reign's gaze. "Vampire Reign, thank you for seeing us."

"Wulver." Not bothering with any courtesy, Reign turned his attention toward the male of the group. Reign's voice was deep, cultured, giving even ugly words an elegance they did not otherwise deserve. "Make no mistake, I granted this meeting as it was a personal request from Fallon."

"We appreciate it no matter the circumstances. We can only hold the peace as long as all stay within the boundaries that were agreed on after the Great Collision. This protects both your interests and ours."

"Not that you have any boundaries, huh?" Laire piped in, gesturing to the many scenes behind her.

Reign's attention turned to Laire for the first time of the evening. "Everything done here is consensual, as was agreed upon in those long-ago talks and sealed by each leader of the Seven Houses, *including* Kyo. Blood is life, and we agreed not to seek it out from unwilling sources as long as willing sources were not stopped from seeking us."

Laire looked like she wanted to say something else, but Wulver raised his hand in signal to stop. Wulver's voice rang out, no diplomacy left in his tone. "There was a zombie attack in the protected zone two nights ago. Do you know anything about that?"

"No."

Wulver waited a beat, but when Reign said nothing else, Wulver continued. "This attack was done by a master. The zombies were not created by someone new to the craft."

Reign shrugged, the movement more eloquent then it deserved to be. "No master under my control had anything to do with the attack. My people know the rules. I'm sure you have studied them for magical brands – use those."

"The zombies disintegrated once they were no longer functional. As I said, they were not created by a novice."

Reign made a dismissive gesture. "My magical kin are not exactly unionized. I control those under me. I do not ask what others do."

Wulver's back was a mass of knotted muscle, but his voice was even as he continued. "There was also an orc attack in the city. Would you know anything about that? Orcs would never be able to get in the city on their own, and they would have no reason to do this without someone bargaining with them."

"I'm afraid I do not. Is there anything else before you go?"

Laire made a great display of looking over her nails, saying in an offhand manner, "No surprise you suckheads are so weak you can't keep tabs on one another."

"Would you like to see how weak I am, Battle Mage? Do you truly believe I fear your little fireballs?"

Reign began to rise and Wulver began to growl. This was going FUBAR fast.

Fallon sidestepped Wulver, only the inches of the table separating her from Reign. She kept her hands down, away from her sword. "The only one here you should fear is me. I told you long ago, *I'm* the one to separate your soul from your body."

Reign's full attention was on her, those blood eyes as light as she'd ever seen. He reached toward her, the smooth skin of his fingertips grazing over her forehead while his thumb made sure, short strokes over her cheekbone, the strokes coming ever nearer her mouth.

She didn't object. Her gaze stayed locked with his and her hands stayed at her side. With a slow, deliberate movement, he pushed his hand into the fall of her hair, wrapping a thick strand around his fingers and wrist. His voice dropped, deepening as he spoke words meant for her. "I love your hair. The color of blood at its most fragrant and powerful."

The light tug on the strands didn't hurt. Instead it sensitized her. The swirl of color in his eyes was myriad shades of red reflected and magnified. "You should let go now," she said, low even tones that matched his own.

The corner of that edible mouth lifted, baring a fang. "Never." He pulled her closer, keeping to that edge of discomfort that never crossed into pain. "Stay by my side."

She ghosted her mouth across the air over his, one inch all the space that separated them, that he could feel the warm, moist puff of her breath a certainty. Her voice held a low, breathy undertone she had never heard come from her lips. "Never."

He gazed down at her through heavy-lidded eyes, the pull on her hair now a welcome pain that did nothing to break her away from him.

Wulver's voice came from behind her, tones that spoke of barely leashed violence. "Is there anything you wish to tell us about the zombie attack? If not, my people and I will take our leave."

Reign's lips thinned, the muscle in the corner of his jaw betraying itself with a small tic. His hand clenched in her hair, his greedy gaze roamed her face once more, lingering over each square inch of her skin.

Then he pulled back into himself, cloaking himself with decorum. He unwound her hair from his hand, sitting down on the couch. In moments the two women were back at his side. "I know nothing about the zombies. Good luck in finding their maker."

Fallon turned to step down from the platform, Reign's voice following her. "You are welcome anytime, Fallon, but please do not invite your friends again." Without stopping she walked toward the exit, the shift in air currents preceding Wulver and Laire as they followed her.

Once they were in the car, Laire spoke. "That was productive."

"To be expected," Fallon said. "We knew talking with him was a longshot at best."

Laire pursed her lips, studying Fallon with an intensity rare outside of a shoe sale. "Vampire boy is a little too touchy-feely with you, and you aren't afraid of getting in his space. You sure you two never dated?"

Leave it to Laire to start awkward conversations at completely the wrong time. "Are you serious?"

Laire shrugged. "He may be the scourge of all the realms, but there is no denying undead boy is damn, *damn* fine."

"So you think ultimate evil necromancer is my type?"

"I'd be really thrilled to find out you had a type. It's not like I see you dating right now. Or ever."

"Why is everyone suddenly worried about my dating habits?"

Thank the gods Wulver had the sense to interrupt this line of questioning. He directed a question to Fallon. "What information on the teacher?"

"Tec hasn't found any info that would suggest why she's targeted. The only interesting pieces of trivia we found are she was born the day of the Great Collision, and big brother isn't as finished with the military as his family thinks he is."

"What about fangwhipped?" Laire asked, bringing her hand in front of her mouth and using the first two fingers to mimic fangs.

"Who are you, vampire bunny? And no. There is no sign of it."

"Laire," interrupted Wulver. "What about her birth? If she was born around the time of the Collision, could that have affected her?"

"I would normally say yes. There were large amounts of wild magic, and a new life would be very susceptible to any effects. But by twenty-six she would have manifested any magical abilities."

"I want you to keep researching that angle. It's a long shot, but that's a hell of a coincidence." Wulver turned back to Fallon. "And Terak? Why is he so interested in her, and are we any closer to discovering how he and all the other races have gotten into the city?"

"No and no. We have all of our own people going over each ward individually, so hopefully we'll know about that soon. But as for Terak," Fallon's hand did a quick triple-beat against her leg, an outward sign of frustration. "I don't know why he was there, and I don't like it, especially since I don't have much more faith in gargoyles than I do necromancers. Right now sucks, because all we're doing is sitting on our hands waiting for something to break."

Wulver smirked at her. As glad as Fallon was to see him relaxed again after getting out of the blood bank, it wasn't pleasant to have all the relieved energy directed at her, peeving her off when she was already in a sour mood. "Then be glad you have Merc to take care of in the meantime until something pans out. Any word on the Dream Crafter?"

"None yet, but she can't hide forever."

"And Rhaum?"

"He's being his usual inscrutable self and making a crazy request as payment. I agreed to it. We need her. Merc is too good and has too many defenses against any of our other means to get to him. I wouldn't want to go against him unless I had no other choice."

"But has he committed to guarding the spellbook? He's never done a job for anyone evil."

"No, but he's going to." Fallon looked out the window, the occasional streetlight only deepening the gloom of the road in front of them. "And we both know why."

# CHAPTER SIXTEEN

Knocks on the door tended not to mean good news these days, but Larissa rose to answer anyway.

Olivia stood there, carrying take-out bags with the name of a nearby Thai restaurant and emitted an amazing smell that started Larissa's stomach growling. "I come bearing gifts to make up for not calling ahead."

Larissa jerked her head. "You're in. I'll grab some plates."

After food had been dished out and wine had been poured, the women retired to the couch to start their feast. "So," Olivia began, "your car will be ready in two days. My friend was impressed by the damage you did."

Larissa swallowed a spring roll. "Thanks. I was rather impressed to have caused it."

"You know there was never any mention of an orc attack in the news, right?" Olivia waited until Larissa nodded to continue. "What is going on?"

Taking a swig of wine – fake courage at its finest – Larissa said, "Does this mean you are going to tell me how you know someone who'll fix a car full of orc splatter?"

Without answering, Olivia stood up and walked toward the kitchen. "Olivia?"

Opening the refrigerator door, she held up a couple more bottles of wine. "With all the stories we are going to be telling tonight, I think we're going to need these."

Larissa lifted her glass. "Top me up."

After wine was poured and they were once again settled, Larissa started. "I have no idea what's going on. None. Zilch. I'm as in the dark as I was after I was attacked by zombies. The only difference is I know now that it wasn't an accident. I am the target of all this."

Olivia tilted her head, disbelief written all over her face. "How can you not have a clue? These people... this isn't tiny, this isn't a scrap of information you might have stumbled across in a book or the wrong person crossing your path."

That was the same question on endless loop since she accepted the attacks were meant for her. Frustration beat a strong rhythm through her head and had her digging her toes into the carpet. "Believe me, if I had ever done anything that might be causing this, I'd be confessing it in the town square, in front of Dad and whoever else might be watching. I don't want any of this."

"Speaking of dad," and Olivia ran her hand through her brunette curls, the aftereffect a tousled look most women paid salons big bucks for. "Could this have something to do with him or one of your brothers? Have you talked to them at all about this?"

"No."

"Why?"

Larissa ran her hand through her own hair. Through long experience she knew the look was nowhere near as flattering as Olivia had achieved with the same motion. "Because Dad can't help me, and if I bring him into this, I'm going to get him killed. You know how he is, how my brothers are."

Narrowed-eyed disbelief met that statement. "Maybe – *maybe* – you can justify not telling the family when you thought it was a mistake or a one-off. But now, it's wrong to keep them out of this."

Larissa quelled the urge to squirm like a seven-year-old under the Olivia's look. "If I go to Dad, he's going to lock me down. I won't be allowed out of the house."

"Yeah, that's horrible, having a family love you that much. What was I thinking?"

The urge to squirm morphed into an urge to hang her head in shame under the harsh tone. It wasn't something they talked about, but Olivia had been abandoned when she was little and had been on her own most of her life. Though she never voiced the thought aloud, Larissa was sure one of the reasons Olivia hung out with her was to be able to experience a tight-knit family.

"You're right. I am a lucky woman to have these people back me up. They would put their own lives on the line to protect me." Larissa kneaded the back of her neck, her fingernails scraping the sensitive skin there. How to make Olivia understand? "Would you give up your freedom for prison? A wonderful prison, one with amazing people and great food and lots of love within its walls, but still a prison."

Olivia wasn't about to be placated. "You have no clue what a prison is like, or being on your own."

"No, but I do know what it's like to suffocate because no one around will let you breathe. No matter how loud you yell, or what you say, it's always a pat on the head and they send you down the path they want you to take, no matter what your wishes are." Larissa placed her hand on Olivia's forearm, forcing the brunette to look at her. "I was a good daughter, and I did what was expected of me, and you know what? I'm happy I did. I don't have any regrets, because I love my family and I love my life. But if I go to Dad now, I will never have another moment in my life where I am not under his thumb, and he'll justify every second by saying he's protecting me. And I love him enough that I'll let him do it, because the only other option is to lose him, and I can't abide that thought."

Olivia covered Larissa's hand with her own. "So you're saying family is a little overrated?"

Larissa smiled, though she couldn't quite manage the laugh Olivia was angling for. "I'm saying my family has to stay in the dark, at least for a short while. I'm not yet at the point where I have no other choice except to inform them and take the consequences."

Olivia squeezed Larissa's hand before letting go, and Larissa removed her hand from Olivia's forearm. "How are you going to protect yourself? You are the only one of the Miller clan who doesn't know at least three martial arts and can shoot a gnat from a mile away."

If only she could blame her father clinging to outdated gender roles for that fact. Reality was

Larissa never had any interest in learning any of those things, no matter how much Dad tried to get her involved. She preferred spending her time in the library, always had. It was still her favorite hangout. "I have someone looking out for me."

Not good. Olivia's eyes widened a fraction, then took on a gleam of devious speculation. "Oh you do? Who would this paragon be, and why have you never mentioned him to me before?"

How to explain Terak in terms that would not have Olivia salivating and asking ever more uncomfortable questions? "He saved me from the zombies, and said he wanted to protect me."

"Did he have a hand in getting you away from the orcs?"

"Yes."

"And you've never mentioned him before because...?"

"He's... shy."

Olivia leaned closer, practically climbing on top of her. "Who is he?"

"I can't tell you."

"Why not?"

"Olivia!" Olivia took that as her cue to back away, though still within pouncing distance. "It's a secret."

"I thought we weren't having any more secrets."

"That's right," confirmed Larissa. "No more hiding my secrets. That doesn't mean I can tell secrets entrusted to me."

"He's trustworthy, you're sure?"

*You would call me a friend?* "Yeah, I'm sure."

Olivia nodded. "You're covered in the bodyguard department, good news. Now, how are you going to figure out the whys and wherefores of what's happening on your own?"

Larissa reached over and grabbed Olivia's hand. "I'm not on my own. I've got you."

"Fat chance. We get chased by orcs, I'm tripping you and running the other direction." But Olivia twined her fingers with Larissa's, giving a reassuring squeeze.

And now came the part of the evening where Olivia had to answer a few questions. "Since you know people, do you think you know anyone who can help me figure this out?"

Olivia's gaze became distant as she considered. "I think I do. But he's a hard one to get hold of, and he isn't a certainty. He's got his own demons chasing after him."

"Figuratively or literally?" Larissa asked. Olivia rolled her eyes but didn't answer the question. "I'd be grateful if you can try to get him, even if he isn't a certainty."

"I will. I'll put in a call when I get home."

"Thank you." Eyeing her wineglass, Larissa refilled it and took a long drink. She'd probably need it for this portion of the evening. "Just how do you know people?"

To her credit, Olivia didn't pretend ignorance. "You know me. I talk to everyone."

Olivia certainly did that. It was talent and gift rolled together, the way she was able to bond with anyone no matter their background. Within minutes, she went from stranger to beloved family friend. "Why didn't you tell me?"

"Why would I have?" Olivia's face held a hint of censure. "Before this happened to you, you were content to live far away from any of the New Realms. It wasn't a part of my life that I thought you would enjoy. Maybe I didn't think you'd approve of it."

"I wouldn't have approved or disapproved, I just wouldn't have been interested in it. That sort of dovetails back to our previous discussion about being surrounded by a loving family who think they know best for you, being in a prison that isn't really a prison."

An *o* of surprise formed across Olivia's mouth. A shading of understanding crossed her face as she closed her mouth, bowing her head slightly. "Sorry."

"Yeah." The wine was more than half gone by this point, but despite being a lightweight when it came to alcohol, Larissa wasn't affected by the hazy happiness that usually accompanied consumption. "Don't worry about it. Honestly, I didn't realize I was in a prison of my own making until recently."

"And now?"

Larissa drained the last of the wine in her glass. "Jailbreak."

# CHAPTER SEVENTEEN

Larissa leaned on her balcony railing, looking toward the sky. Olivia had left twenty minutes before following a lot of food and a lot of conversation that didn't revolve around the crazy turn her life had taken recently.

It had been a great reminder of normalcy, but now she wanted to speak with Terak.

She hadn't seen him since the day of the orc battle. He said he would be gone for a few days to fulfill his responsibilities at home, then had flown away.

Should she call out, maybe wave her arms like she had done the first day?

Her reverie was interrupted by Terak dropping beside her.

"Terak!" she cried, her hand going over her heart. "You scared me!" That was what one called an understatement. These days a stray leaf was enough to get her jumping.

"My apologies," he replied, but that deep voice didn't quite convey that sentiment. He sounded far away, his mind and thoughts in another place and another conversation.

Leader of a Clan. She watched over one hundred students on a regular basis and sometimes she wanted to explode at the end of the day. To know a whole race depended on your every decision? She added a note of teasing to her voice, to let him know no harm done. "If my life keeps up at this pace, I'm going to have a heart attack by the time I'm thirty." She took a deep breath, trying to settle her racing pulse, when a thought struck. "Do gargoyles age like humans?"

He turned his attention to her, finally shaking off whatever shackles he arrived with. "Yes, our lifespans are quite similar."

She motioned to his wings. "But you guys have that cool healing power."

His brow bone arched above his right eye. No fair, even without eyebrows he could do the eyebrow arch. Why could she never manage that? "Cool?" And she might be wrong, but there sounded like a hint of tease underlining his words, the same tone he used after he had been healed.

She crossed her arms over her chest. "Are you asking me what it means, or are you questioning my choice of outdated slang?"

He mirrored her body language, though watching those massive arms stretch over his impressive chest made her heart pound in a way that had nothing to do with fright. "You are a teacher. Do you not know the new slang by listening to them?"

"No, kids only speak new slang when they don't want you to know what they're talking about. They use the classics around us old people." She motioned to his wing again before returning to her arms crossed position. "Healing factor?"

Instead of his usual almost smile she got the real thing, small and quick and unexpected and it wasn't until her lungs told her to bring in some oxygen that she remembered – breathing, it was a good thing. "I am glad you approve of it, though I do not think of it as cool, more as necessity. You need every advantage in battle."

She nodded. "Understood. I'm still going with cool."

"You do that." Damn, she really liked that teasing note in his voice. It was rusty, hesitant, and she held close the thought that it might be because he used it with no one else but her. He continued, "I have a gift for you."

"A gift?" Her inner seven-year-old was jumping up and down with excitement. "What did you get me? It wasn't necessary."

"This gift is practical, not celebratory, but as you requested it, I wished you to get it as soon as it was ready."

Into her hand he placed a small silver ball with an unknown script etched into the casing. "What's this?"

"A way to contact me. Hold it in your hands and think my name, and I will answer you."

"We'll be able to talk telepathically?" Wow, this was... this was... Yes, everything ran on magic these days – from cars to telephones – but in the city, people tried to minimize that as much as possible. They used magic only for the necessities, and they never used it in such a way that it was obvious magic was responsible for what was going on.

This was something she'd never had before. Pure magic, and a being who encouraged her to use it.

"Yes. No matter where I am in this world, I will hear your call, and I will answer."

Her fingers curled around the silver ball, so tight the mysterious script might have imprinted itself into her skin. "Thank you so much."

"Do not thank me. It is a selfish gift."

"Selfish?"

His midnight gaze locked with hers. "Now I will always be able to talk with you."

Didn't gargoyle men know you couldn't say that to a human woman? Not if you didn't want her to lose her ability to think and definitely not if you wanted to keep any kind of emotional distance.

Human men needed to explain the basics to him. A *How to Deal with Women* summit. Nothing would bond the races faster.

But this gift also meant another obligation on him, on top of the thousands of obligations he was answerable to every day of his life. And as amazing as this feeling was, she didn't want to experience it if all he received on his side was the look of burden he had arrived with tonight. Pulling herself away from his gaze, she motioned to the empty expanse of horizon before them. "It's a gorgeous night. Don't you get tired of watching over me? There must be other things you could be doing."

"Would you wish another to watch over you?"

Maybe it was her wishful thinking, but she could swear she heard the barest trace of hurt underlining the words. She put her hand over his forearm, an echo of what had happened with Olivia earlier tonight. "No, I'm glad it's you, I really am. I worry that if you keep up watching me, your people will suffer."

He didn't cover her hand with his, but he did lean close enough to her that they could share a breath. "I am gratified that you worry over my people, but they are able to function without my presence for this period of time."

"But not for long, not if you are a good leader. And I know you are a good leader."

He stepped even closer, and his wings half-closed around her, blocking her peripheral vision. "You do?"

"You have this way about you. I've seen it before." She bit her tongue to stop any more words from flowing out with what else she thought – that he was good and honorable and walked the edge of humorlessness in his determination to make every right decision. "Anyway, all I meant is that I know you make your people proud. You can't waste all your time watching over me."

"It is not a waste, little human. It could never be a waste. We have shed blood together, have shared secrets and held them honorably. You are my comrade in arms, and my friend. I would not have anything harm you."

Yes, she should request that summit immediately, because this night was turning her into a puddle of emotional goo.

His wings flared, and she held onto that to pull herself out of this emotional morass she was falling into. "Do you like flying?"

It took him a moment to orient himself to the new thread of conversation. "Like it? How do you mean?"

"Well, I guess flying for you is like running for humans, right?" After his nod, she continued. "Some humans hate running and will never do it. Some force themselves to do it, but there is no joy in the act. And some humans love to run. Which is it with you and flying?"

"I have never thought on it." His eyelids lowered, bringing his eyelashes into relief against his skin. No eyebrows, but yes to eyelashes. Hair on his head but none on his chest or arms. In this form, did he still have hair in his private regions?

The split second after that thought crossed her brain – *Damn you, Id!* – the most intense heat in the history of the blush raced over her skin, from her cheeks to her forehead and down her neck to the top of her chest.

His eyelids raised and his brows furrowed the moment he saw her face. "Are you well? You appear overheated."

"I'm fine, really hot all of a sudden." One hand pulled her hair away from her face while the other fanned away. "No worries. You were saying about flying?"

He glanced around to see if he could ascertain the cause of her reaction. Thank gods there was no way that could happen. Not finding anything, he turned back to her, answering her question. "There is a freedom in flying that I can find nowhere else. I am away from my obligations and only answerable to the elements."

"Sounds like you fall into the *love* category, then."

He considered some more before giving a final, decisive nod. "That is a fair way to put it. I cannot disagree."

She was going to ask. Worst that could happen, he would say no.

Best that could happen, he would say yes and she would be cradled against the large expanse of chest, breathing in the smell of newly cracked stone as she saw the world as he experienced it every day, his deep voice low, intimate breaths against her ear as he kept her close so his words weren't lost on the wind.

On second thought, maybe that was the worst that could happen.

She was going to ask anyway.


"Terak?"

It would take mere moments to reach over and cradle her heated cheek in his palm. His claws curled, eager to experience the feel of her warm flesh. A deeper blush than he had ever seen on her, apparent even in the dark of the moonlit night.

So appealing, his little human. She spoke words of duty to him, her certainty of his leadership flinging open passageways to deep caverns, shining light on hidden doubts and tenacious worries.

And after the comfort brought by her declaration, she immediately caused discomfort to throb through his body by the lift of her hair and the curve of her neck.

*To follow that blush as far down as it goes, and then to go further...*

Her eyes were luminous in the moonlight, a warmth even in the midst of the coldest night.

"Yes?"

"I-" She broke off, letting her arms down so her hair fell around her face. She licked her full lips, a nervous gesture he was growing familiar with, coming to loathe as he could not follow where that pink little tongue led. "Remember that first night?"

The first night? "Impossible to forget."

"True." Her smile held for long moments, not a product of nervousness but of fondness. While he thought on it with a certain amount of pleasure as well, he never dared hope she shared the sentiment. "That was the first time I ever flew."

"Not even in one of the human machines?" He could see no pleasure in flying if it was in one of those contraptions. Where was the pleasure without the wind on a face or the force of wings slicing through air? No, it would only be good as a means of transportation.

She shook her head. "No. My only family lives here, and my father said there was no reason to go elsewhere."

He had never thought to ask her, afterwards. Understandable. While at the end of that first night a cautious truce had been declared, she had been a far way from trusting him and he wished to make no mistakes that would change that. "Did you enjoy it?"

"That's the thing. There was so much going on, and I couldn't see beyond my own fear and then later my exhaustion. But I think I might under other circumstances." She reached out to touch his wing but caught herself, bringing her arm back with a jerk. "Would it be possible for us to go flying another time?"

To have her in his arms. To cuddle her generous body against his and have her arms wrapped around his neck, her warm breath rhythmic against his neck. "I would enjoy that very much."

"You would?" She let out a small, audible breath, and it was only now when she let it go he saw the nervousness interwoven throughout this entire conversation. "So would I."

*So appealing...* "Why not now?"

"Really?" She looked around, though what she thought she would see he did not know. "Are you sure it would be okay?"

He held out his hand. "Come, little human. Let me show you your city from above."

She stared at it for long moments, and as she looked, he began to see the appendage as it looked from her point of view. Did the sharp claws frighten her? Did the grey skin bring her distress?

She laid her small, soft hand in his and her gaze showed no distress when it met his, only excitement at this new adventure.

He came to stand in front of her, taking in those miraculous blue eyes. He bent to accommodate her smaller frame. "Wrap your arms around my neck," and the words were a rumble, coming out from part of him he dare not explore.

She was hesitant, her fingers first resting on his collarbone before moving over the planes of his shoulders to twine around the curve of his neck.

His arms snaked around her, one over the long curve of her torso to rest at the small of her back, the other curling under her lush thighs.

With a sharp exhale that had nothing to do with physical exertion, he brought her fully against him.

The movement brought their faces within a beat of space. Larissa's gaze darted to his mouth.

Terak flung himself from the building. He heard Larissa's sharp inhale as they plummeted and then her small, relieved gasp as the wind caught under his wings ringing in his ears.

He went as low as he dared over the city, but after a few moments she shook her head. "I have no desire to see the city, so don't tempt fate over being caught. I want to fly."

As though to emphasize her words she nestled her head into the valley between his neck and shoulder, a placement that would give her limited visibility but allowed him the full experience of her body against his.

He took her outside of the city. He flew high, the chill in the air biting into even his skin. He went low, where there was the chance of feeling the scrape of foliage.

She egged him on with her sounds and her sighs. She laughed and she screeched, and at one point she stretched her neck out and tilted her head, her hair a banner behind them.

"I can see why you love this. I do, too."

The pleasure from those words was out of proportion to their importance.

She leaned up, her eyes on the sky. "Gods, look at that sky. It's amazing. You can't see a sky like that in the city."

"Why have you never traveled outside?"

She was quiet, her exhale forceful. Finally, she said, "Dad never had much use for the New Realms, but I could never blame him for that. My mom died in the Great Collision."

"I am sorry."

"I..." she exhaled, and from her weighted pause he knew this was the part that was hardest for her to share. "She died giving birth to me. There were complications during the birth, and in the chaos after the collision the hospital was overwhelmed. Probably any other day she would have survived, but I chose to make my appearance in the world right then."

She looked up at the sky again, and her eyes held a sheen that told of tears. The burden she carried was palpable, the blame she accepted immutable and undeserved. There would be future days to tell her this guilt was misplaced, but now was the time to be quiet and listen to her story.

"Dad never blamed me," she said, looking up at him with the defense of her father. "He never spoke about it much, except to say how much Mom loved me, and he knew she was happy, because she finally got her little girl. When I turned twelve I tried to combine my birthday with a memorial for her. Dad wouldn't have it. He said there were other days and other ways to show we loved and honored Mom. My birthday was a celebration that I'd been brought into this world."

"Your father is a good man."

"My dad's the best." Her eyes shone with pride. "My whole family is. I couldn't have had better if I had been able to order them to my specifications. Well, except for the over-protectiveness."

"Overprotective? Your father makes my Clan look permissive by comparison."

She laughed. "You got that right. It's probably one of the reasons I came to enjoy history so much – I got to investigate actions and ask questions and actually have them answered." She took another deep breath, her mouth turning inward. "I can't blame my dad too much, though. He was a cop during the Great Collision. Now that I'm older and realize how horrible the first few months were, and then the uncertainty the following couple years... I can't blame him. He did his best to care for and protect us while the world was going crazy and had taken his wife away from him."

"That is all any of us can do, they best we can under the circumstances we are given."

She nodded. Her fingers were curling themselves in his hair. The unconscious stroking soothed him, the intimacy of the act yet another chain binding him to her. "What about your parents? What were they like?"

The air shifted around him, its currents disturbed. He tightened his grip on her, pulling her close, so close her face smashed into his neck. "Terak, what's wrong?"

From the left it whizzed by them, clipping his wing enough to throw him to the side until he righted himself.

"Terak?" and all pleasure was gone from her tone.

It came down from above several yards in front of him, far enough away that he could pull himself short and hover there, his wings flapping to keep them steady in the air.

A small human woman, with Asian features and hair such a blinding color of blue it hurt his eyes. "Boo."

# CHAPTER EIGHTEEN

"Like I said, romantic. Can I call them or what?"

They landed some twenty feet away from the waiting group in a cleared section of woodland, far outside the city limits. It was Fallon who had called out to them, that giant sword strapped to her back, with the same combo of black leather-ish clothes, though this time she wore a coat that fell to the ground. Laire was standing to the right of the swordswoman, her outfit tonight a neon-blue ode-to-naughty Alice in Wonderland ensemble, full of lace and Victorian trappings, but if she bent over, Larissa was sure any underwear would be exposed to the world.

If she wore underwear.

Shaking off *that* thought, Larissa turned her attention to the third and final member of the gang. Her breath hitched as she beheld the newest woman, the same wonderment she experienced moments ago as she flew in Terak's arms spreading through her now.

This woman's height was average, but nothing else about her could be described that way. Her pale blue eyes glowed against the light tan of her skin and her long silky hair was so black it had a blue sheen in the moonlight. Her face had an appealing pixie-ish quality, but Larissa could tell nothing about her body, which was hidden underneath a long brown cloak.

A gust of wind ruffled her hair, giving a glimpse of a long neck, delicate jaw, and pointed ears.

*Pointed ears.* "You're an elf, aren't you?"

The woman inclined her head. "I am Aislynn." Her voice held the clear luster of ringing bells.

Being in front of an elf must not have had the same sense of awe for Terak, if his clenched jaw and the tight lines of his body were anything to go by. He said, "What is it you wish, Dragon Slayer?"

*Dragon Slayer.* In reaction to his words Fallon held herself even straighter. Why would he call her Dragon Slayer?

Fallon said, "I make no move against you or yours, Clan Leader of the Gargoyles, but I wish to talk to this woman. She is a human who lives in the city, and thus is under my protection."

"I saved her. Therefore, she is mine." Terak's voice pitched low while his clawed hands flexed, and while it held warning for the women in front of them, for Larissa it sparked a heat that spiraled through her torso and down the length of her body.

"Is that so? Shall we take it before the Seven Houses to hear their verdict?"

Terak held himself still, but his anger was palpable. "Beware casting your fate in that direction. Do not think my Clan powerless."

Enough of this. Whether this was jockeying for some kind of position or they really thought they could argue about her as if she was a lost pet, it was over now. "Don't talk about me as if I'm not even here," Larissa said, meeting the eyes of each of the women before turning a quick glance toward Terak. "I'll decide who I'm going to talk with and when, and flying out of nowhere and then hitting us with these intimidation tactics isn't going to endear you to me."

Aislynn came forward, bowing slightly. "Forgive Fallon. She is so single-minded she forgets to show any manners."

"Hey!"

Aislynn continued, not sparing the swordswoman as much as a glance. "We have not detained you for any fight-"

"Speak for yourself, Ais."

Aislynn rolled her eyes heavenward but showed no other sign that she heard Fallon behind her. "-But we must ask you questions. The appearance of the orcs signals an escalation. We must discover the reason behind this."

How had they connected her? Was this a shot in the dark? "I don't know what you're talking about."

Fallon started looking around her, quick movements of her head in all directions. Laire was watching her teammate with a puzzled expression on her face. "What are you doing?"

"Looking for a brick wall to hit my head against. I'm sure I'd have more luck with it than with her. You know, Teach, you might want to stop and think for a moment. Do you really believe Terak is the only one watching you now? How do you think we were able to plan this little get together?"

Oh gods, why hadn't she thought about that before? These people knew everything about her.

Why wouldn't they also be watching her? She had been so focused on Terak...

A warm, calloused palm met hers, and Terak's large hand squeezed, snapping her out of her daze. She raised her face to his. His dark eyes reassured her.

She squeezed back, and was rewarded with that almost smile.

Aislynn took another step forward and spoke not to Larissa, but to Terak. "Clan Leader of the Gargoyles, while we may not be allies, we are not enemies. Our goal is a common one, to protect this woman. Everything we have done has been with that purpose."

"And how would you do this?" Terak inquired of the elf, his voice stilted but no longer furious. "You have not protected her thus far."

"We have tried. We would have protected her had you not that first night." Terak tilted his head as if acknowledging the elf's words, but didn't speak himself. Aislynn continued, "We ask to be brought into your confidence. We may have information that you do not, as you may also have information unknown to us. We wish to protect this woman. We wish to protect the Realms. We wish to defeat the necromancers. Surely these commonalities outweigh our differences."

A play of emotions crossed Terak's face as he kept his gaze steady on Aislynn. Larissa wasn't sure what she thought about what was being proposed, but there was no doubt in her mind that the elf had been brought here as the peacemaker and dealmaker. The other two women deferred to her, keeping silent as she talked to Terak. Larissa would place money that wasn't a common occurrence.

Decision sharpened Terak's expression, and he looked not at the elf, but at Fallon. "And which of these goals is your priority?"

Fallon's head tilted, assessing Terak. "Why do you ask? Isn't it enough they are goals we share?"

"No." Terak's baritone was laced with finality. "Only when there is no conflict can there be truce. We are not the same, Dragon Slayer. Even if you could bring yourself to lie and tell me otherwise, we both know the truth."

What was he talking about? But even before the echo of the words faded Laire's expression turned serious in a way Larissa never would have believed possible. She reached out her arms in front of her, fingers splayed wide, and with a quick movement flung her arms out to the side.

Around them dozens of floating spheres appeared, bright white with a core of black through the middle. Laire clenched her hands into quick fists, and the spheres exploded in balls of flame. "We need to leave," Laire said, but before she could be made, she jerked and fell forward as if someone punched her in the stomach, though no one was near.

Fallon was at her side in two quick steps, grabbing the mage's arm and helping her straighten. "What's happening?"

A howl sounded, far away, and then a legion of answering howls, growls and almost-human screams of such menace that Larissa's blood turned to sludge and flowed through her veins, weighing down her limbs and making fleeing impossible.

Terak wrapped his arms around her, bending to speak into her ear. "Calm, little human. I will protect you. Have I failed you yet?"

*No.* No, never.

*My sword and my shield.*

She wrapped her arms around him, returning the embrace. "Sorry about the momentary freak out. I'm good now."

From behind her Fallon's voice ground out, "Laire, what's going on?"

With a final squeeze, Larissa let go of Terak and turned back to the group of women. They were standing in a close circle. Laire looked recovered from whatever had attacked her. "Someone was watching her," she said, nodding toward Larissa. "When I destroyed their little spies, they must have decided to send something after us."

"Let's get out of here."

Laire shook her head, looking up to the sky. "Magic barrier, which means they have a mage and there is no flying out of here."

Fallon turned to the elf. "Ais-"

Before Fallon could finish, Aislynn ran past them toward a large outcropping of rocks, jumping onto the largest of them with a grace and an athleticism no human could ever match. She peered into the dark, the full moon only giving a little help in illuminating their surroundings. Within seconds she called down, "Direwolves, ridden by goblins. We have a battalion of them coming fast. I see bows, so expect to become target practice."

"Ais, a volley as soon as they're in range." Aislynn must have been expecting this order, because even before Fallon stopped talking she threw her cloak off, revealing a bow and a quiver of arrows. She grabbed the bow and an arrow, putting them together and getting into a firing position, all with such speed that Larissa couldn't tell what was happening as it occurred, only filling in the blanks once Aislynn was still and prepared for battle.

Fallon turned to Laire. "Why didn't they arrive closer to us? Why that far away?"

Laire twirled a finger around a curl of blue hair. "Don't know. It would be impossible to teleport that many with pinpoint accuracy, but they should have gotten closer than what they are."

"Maybe there is something wrong with their mage, or maybe they only have a wizard. Any feel on what we're dealing with?"

Laire's eyes…*swirled*. There was no other word to explain it. Her eyes lost color and iris and became a violent mass of movement. "Defensive magic specialist. And yes, only a wizard. Male. And young. Each of them has a personal shield spell, so Ais's arrows won't do jack and damage will be minimal until it's dispelled." Her lips tightened, hard anger on her face. "Who do they think I am, sending a pansy-ass like that against me?"

Fallon patted Laire's shoulder, a *there-there* motion. "I don't think they knew we'd be waiting when they prepared this trap. But for you, we'll send his head back to them with a note to not insult you again. Does that make you feel better?"

Laire gave a long, theatrical sigh. "I don't know, maybe."

"Think on it." Fallon turned, the full weight of her gaze back on Larissa. "We have a battalion of direwolves – and a wizard – running around the exact area you are in. Care to reassess that whole *I don't know what you're talking about* line of crap?"

They deserved something. She wasn't sure of their exact motives and didn't fully trust them, but they were about to fight to save her life. "I don't know why they are after me. If I ever find out I will tell you, but right now I do not know."

Fallon's one eyebrow arched, the swift look of surprise crossing her face before it morphed into a speculative cast. She turned to Laire, who shrugged and said, "I believe her."

"Hell of it is, I believe her too." Fallon drew a deep breath. "We found the ward that allowed the orcs and zombies to get in. It was set by a powerful wizard who has since disappeared. He was thought to be above reproach, so the standard triple-check wasn't done. Of course, that doesn't explain how *you've* gotten into the city," Fallon finished, giving Terak a pointed glare.

"No, it doesn't," he agreed, and said nothing more.

Fallon unsheathed her massive sword, a faint glow coming from under her coat, no doubt that same scrolling that Larissa beheld that first night. "Well Gargoyle, do we fight each other, or do we fight what is coming to meet us?"

"This night I will fight at your side." Terak turned to Larissa. "Stay near the mage. She will protect you."

He was a great warrior. She had seen it herself. That didn't change this hollow ache inside her. It was unnecessary, but she had to say it. She had to know she said it, a charm that would protect him. It had to. "Terak, be careful."

"I will be." He gently pushed her toward Laire, holding the mage's attention with a hard glare. "If she dies, Battle Mage, until my last breath, I will dedicate every moment of my life to the destruction of your world."

For once, Laire was not the smartass Larissa expected. Giving a perfect bow, she answered, "I will protect her, Clan Leader of the Gargoyles."

Fallon broke in. "Now that we got the mushy stuff out of the way, let's go meet us some goblins." She turned to Laire. "Shield Larissa. Don't worry about the rest of us. Break the wizard so we can cut through the army."

"Understood," said Laire. She grabbed Larissa's hand, bringing her over to a nearby wall. "Sit on that stone wall. I'm putting a barrier around you."

"A barrier?"

"A magic shield. It will keep the bad guys out."

Larissa sat. The Asian woman made a motion as if she were clutching a ball in her hands, then pushed out toward Larissa.

Nothing happened. Larissa looked around her, but nothing was different. "Is it working?"

Laire yelled out, "Aislynn, help me here."

The elf turned and shot an arrow right at Larissa, the point heading straight for her forehead. It came closer and closer and-

And it stopped dead, falling to the ground several feet away, as if it had bumped into something solid.

"There's your proof," Laire said. "So don't do anything stupid like try to run out. It wouldn't work anyway, you'd only hit the barrier, but those things hurt like hell if you run into them full speed."

"I won't."

"They're in range!" Aislynn started firing arrows again, this time at the upcoming army. They were still far enough away that they looked like little more than black dots in the distance, but the elf called out, "Laire was right about the shield spell, the arrows are bouncing. Laire, you need to do something."

"Working on it," called out Laire. What it looked like she was doing was working on her statue-mimicry skills. She stood stock still, her hand held out toward the open field with her thumb perpendicular to the ground and her first and middle finger curled above it, the other two fingers pressed against her palm.

Her body might have been still, but sweat was beading on the skin of her forehead and neck, the same way it would for most people who were in the middle of intense physical exertion.

"How long?" Fallon asked.

"Don't know. He's good."

Fallon smirked. "Are you saying some pansy-ass is getting the best of our mage?"

"Instead of flirting with me, why don't you swing your little sword and hit a couple of them? Just because they have a shield over them doesn't mean they would like it if they were batted around like a baseball."

"Good idea." Fallon turned to Terak. "You might not be able to fly up high, Gargoyle. Doesn't mean you can't fly at all, and a shield won't prevent them from being picked up and thrown from their mounts."

Terak looked back at Larissa. She smiled at him, with what she hoped was a reassuring smile. "You saw the arrow bounce. Out of everyone here, I'm the safest. If you think meeting them is the best way to end this, you need to leave me here."

He nodded. "I will make this as quick as possible."

"I know."

Terak's wings snapped out to their full wingspan. He ran a few steps then took off into the air, his battle cry quieting the wolves coming toward them and even Fallon looked a little in awe as she said, "That's impressive."

They were arriving fast, what only moments before looked like black dots were now fully formed silhouettes of small creatures riding atop vicious-looking canines.

Terak reached the army. Some must have seen him coming, because she heard the ping of fired arrows at him. He didn't react as if he had been hit, but in the past no matter how beaten up he was he never stopped fighting. He swooped down, grabbing some of the creatures and lifting them into the air. He flew high and dropped them down. Once they hit the ground, they didn't get back up.

Fallon was right. Whatever shielding was on them wasn't helping against Terak.

Arrows were flying at them now. Aislynn hid in cracks in the stone outcropping, while Fallon stepped in front of Laire and drove her sword into the ground. "Tenro, *shield*," whispered the swordswoman, and the sword glowed. The volley of arrows that should have hit her and the mage instead disappeared into the light emitted by the sword.

Laire never moved a muscle throughout any of this.

Terak was swooping in and out of the army, grabbing as he did. The goblins waved their swords at him, but he never stopped.

The direwolves were closing in fast, close enough now that the moonlight glinted off rows of teeth a shark would be jealous of. Fallon pulled her sword out of the ground and started toward the incoming army, her movements fast but deliberate, her sword out straight at her side.

Laire yelled out, "Aislynn, fifty degrees, eye level, four-hundred feet. On my mark!"

Aislynn got into firing stance, holding still despite the arrows falling around her.

"Now!"

Aislynn fired, the arrow disappearing within the army.

"You got him!" Laire yelled, glee in her voice. "Rock on!"

Aislynn began to fire into the throng. Wolves howled in pain and fell to the side, knocking over those closest to them and causing chain reactions of wolves and goblins falling atop each other.

The voices of the goblins rose, words indistinct but confusion and panic clear in the sound. Laire brought her hands together and flung them out, and a ball of fire fifteen feet in diameter hurled through the air and smashed into the advancing creatures.

Screams rent the air, burnt flesh and ash swirling in the currents and reaching Larissa even through the barrier.

"Laire, how much spell power do you have left?" Aislynn asked, still firing arrows into the fray.

"Not much. I wanted to make sure the wizard was out of the equation for good."

"Then keep it in reserve. We'll be okay without it."

*How much.* That's right, wizards and mages could only do so much magic a day, the strength of the caster being the deciding factor on how much they cast and how strong those spells would be. Larissa looked over towards the Asian woman. So Laire either wasn't very strong or this was the end of a very busy day for her.

Fallon had arrived in front of the advancing direwolves. The animals snarled and hurled themselves at her, as if they were delighted they finally had an enemy in front of them to tear into.

She swung her sword and cut through a half dozen of them, their blood flying through the sky in splatters as thick as paint. She whirled, the battle becoming a dance, the wolves and the goblins her partners in a death waltz.

The three warriors were swift and sure, their movements as choreographed as any on stage. They weaved and they jumped, making graceful arcs with their bodies and their weapons.

The bodies of the dead were piling up, lying across the once-empty landscape. Thank gods it was dark enough that the small details were not visible, like the pools of blood and the strewn body parts such a display must leave behind.

Finally, few enough of the army remained that Terak landed, battling now with claws and wings. A direwolf lunged for him, but Terak tore through the creature's throat, slicing through it with his claws. The goblin riding on it tried to stab Terak, but he grabbed the sword with his other hand, impaling the goblin on its own blade.

The mad rush was now over and those remaining were more precise, taking their time and studying Terak and Fallon.

Terak's wings flared, his clawed hands coming up before him, blood dripping from the ends. "You think you can come here and take what is *mine*? Go now, go and tell your masters that the woman is under my protection. Tell them that no one will ever touch her, and anyone who comes. Against. Me. Will. *Die!*"

He was a god of vengeance, a demon arising from the night to destroy everything in his path. The direwolves bent before his final roar, their heads dropping and their ears flattening against their heads. The goblins cowered as well. A handful turned away at that point, racing back into the night.

"Cowards. Like the necromancers aren't going to kill them for failing." Aislynn's approach was silent and Larissa jumped when she heard the voice. "Laire, drop the shield. It's over."

The mage did as requested, and the elf came to sit on the wall beside Larissa.

Laire came back as well, sitting on Larissa's other side. "Aren't you two going to help finish this?" Larissa asked.

"What, and mess up my hair?" Laire's hand went to plump up her ringlets. "Heck no. Besides, Fallon loves this shit."

Larissa's attention went to Terak first, but he had finished with the creatures near him. She turned to

Fallon to see the woman bring her sword on an upstroke and slice both a direwolf and the goblin riding it in two.

There was something amazing watching Fallon wield her sword, the arc of metal and the sureness of movement the woman displayed, slicing through her enemies without pause. A brutal, bloody beauty. As if she read Larissa's mind – and who knew, maybe she did – Laire sighed in admiration. "Watching that woman, it's like *damn*."

Aislynn nodded in agreement.

One final move, one final death of an enemy at her hands, and Fallon landed on the ground before them, her hand and one knee resting on soil, her sword held high in the air, surrounded by the dead. She rose, slow and sure, a goddess of war demanding her beaten, ravaged due, leaving no space untouched with her eyes as she circled and surveyed the battlefield.

Satisfied with what she saw, Fallon turned to the three of them sitting on the wall. "And that is how you do it! You may bow before me now, peons."

To Aislynn and Larissa, Laire said, "And then she opens her mouth, and all wonderment vanishes."

Aislynn nodded in agreement.

# CHAPTER NINETEEN

"Are you ashamed that you're with me?"

They were in her home now, and these were the first words Larissa had spoken since the end of battle. After their enemy was defeated, Terak had gathered her close and flew away, not giving the Guild members time to respond. She said nothing and cuddled close, burying herself in his arms.

"What?" Why would she ever think that?

She shrugged, the movement jerky, her shoulder half-hunched inward. "I'm useless. I sit on a wall surrounded by a magic barrier while Aislynn fires an arrow a second and Fallon slices through an army."

He despised the beaten note that threaded her voice. "I would never be ashamed to be at your side. And you must stop comparing yourself to them. The world needs its warriors and it needs its peacemakers. You have experienced too much war these last weeks. It has you questioning your worth." Why did the one woman he wished to keep far away from the brutal reality of this world find herself always buried in yet another battle?

Larissa unfurled her body and looked at him. Instead of fear or loathing clouding her gaze, he saw warmth.

Thankfulness.

*Admiration.*

"I know you're right. No one can be all things." She shrugged, her mouth flattening. "I never cared about fighting or... any of that. When I was a kid, I never wanted to play cops and robbers, though it was the only game my brothers *would* play. Too violent and I didn't like all the fighting. I just wanted to read."

"So you didn't play with your siblings?" That didn't seem to fit with the closeness he had witnessed between the siblings.

"Oh no, they forced me to play. They always made me the robber and would cuff me, though Dad said never to play with his handcuffs. Joke was on them, though." She lifted her arm until her hand was in his line of vision and rotated her wrists. "Double-jointed. No matter how tight they made the cuffs, I could get out. Made them so mad."

Her fondness for her siblings banished the last lingering traces of any self-doubt. Her eyes brightened with memory and glee before she banked both, her gaze now holding a question. "Back to tonight. You called Fallon *Dragon Slayer*. What did you mean by that?"

"Her sword, Tenro, is a sacred weapon and known as the Slayer of Dragons."

"But I thought dragons didn't exist – never existed – even in the Magic Realm." His face must have betrayed his feelings because Larissa's own eyebrows drew together and she asked in a hesitant voice, "Did they?"

"I have never seen any true record of their existence," he conceded, letting the full weight of his misgivings play into his tone.

Her face still held the same hesitance. "But…?"

"But I cannot forget something my father once said. He said with all the terrible creatures we have that are real, why would anyone create the myth of the dragon? And if dragons are even half as powerful as they are portrayed, would it be any true test for them to disappear without a trace if they so wished?" Though he could only hope his father was wrong, and that dragons never existed, or if they did, they would stay far gone.

"What are the Seven Houses?"

It took a beat of time to follow the change in topic. "Where did you hear that?"

"When Fallon started threatening you. She asked if she should let the Seven Houses sort it out."

"Ah." Now he remembered. "They are connected to the New Realms."

Larissa's gaze went unfocused. "I remember when I was little and first heard the term *New Realms*. I thought that to get to those places, you needed to go through some magical door. For a long time, I opened every closet door in every house I entered." Her gaze sharpened again as she came back to the present. "I was so disappointed when I found out it was just a term for the governments and lands of the different races. What's the importance of the Seven Houses? I'm positive I've never heard that name before."

"They are a shadow council which wields much power in the New Realms. They deal with matters outside the purview of any single race."

"Any humans on this council?"

"Yes, one, though I do not know her name or status within the human world. The leader of the Guild is another member."

"The Guild have their hands in lots of places, don't they?" Larissa asked, though her tone made clear the question was rhetorical. She continued with barely a pause. "Why have this council? I thought the various races all kept their own ways of government, just as the human governments remained as they were from before the Great Collision."

"The Seven Houses have always existed. When you have a threat such as the necromancers, you must have a governing body that can answer that threat."

"And the gods? The Oracle? Where do they fit into this?"

"They are all powerful beings outside of all. They have their own agendas, would that we knew them. Never doubt that there are always deeper powers and deeper secrets at play."

She wrinkled her nose, and he stifled the urge to lean down and nuzzle it with his own. "Have I ever mentioned I hate cloak-and-dagger stuff? I don't even watch spy movies on TV."

"I am sorry this has been brought into your life."

She looked at him again, and to his surprise a brilliant smile dominated her face. "Have I ever told you that our dates have been some of the most exciting and eventful of my life?"

"Dates?" he asked. While not a custom gargoyles engaged in, he did know the meaning of the word. What she meant by that phrase interested him.

When hearing the word repeated to her, Larissa's cheeks went scarlet. Ducking her head, she said, "I was kidding, being humorous. Trying to lighten things up."

She was curled against him in her attempt to not be seen, her soft warmth a balm after the fierce battle. He could offer her nothing less and met her attempts at normalcy with his own. "I was thinking on how our next date could go. Maybe we should fight a cave troll."

She looked up at him. Her face was still red, but her eyes shone with laughter. "Only a cave troll? I demand that we go to the top and meet a necromancer."

Terak shook his head. "I am afraid that is too advanced for you. I'm willing to show you a wraith, but no more than that."

She was smiling, and... Terak stopped.

He was smiling.

He was smiling and laughing and teasing the woman in his arms.

What's more, he hadn't put her down. They had been in her apartment for fully five minutes, and never had he the desire to let her go.

"Terak, what's wrong?"

What could he say?

*I would give everything to you if you always look at me with those eyes.*

A *thwup* sounded on the balcony, and Terak turned to face their intruder. Valry stood there, her gaze held by how he cradled Larissa against him.

Anger surged through him, anger at the interruption, and anger at the reminder of his responsibilities. "Valry, what is the meaning of this?"

She strolled in, undaunted and unstoppable. "We were alerted to the battle tonight. When I heard of it, I had to make sure you were unhurt."

"You were told never to come here."

"My need to know my Intended was safe overrode all other concerns."

"*Intended?*" Larissa's voice cut through the words Terak was about to speak. He looked down at her, still cradled in his arms. Her eyebrows drew close together, and there was a shadowing, a hesitance in her eyes that he had not seen since the first night they had met. "What does that mean, *Intended*?"

Valry's voice was quick, malicious. "I believe you humans call it an engagement. Lord Terak and I are to be mated."

Larissa's eyes were wide and round and hurt. "You're going to marry her?"

Terak began to shake his head, and it took force of will to stop the movement.

Larissa started to look around. "I feel much better now. You can let me down."

In reaction to her words his fingers gripped harder, disobeying the command from his brain to follow her order. He forced himself to let her go.

She continued, not meeting his eyes. "Once again I seem to owe you my life. Thank you for saving me. But I'm very tired right now. Would you please excuse me?" She turned and walked into her bedroom, closing the door behind her without a backwards glance.

Terak left, leaving Valry to follow him. He did not wish to bring her to the perch he had spent so many nights watching over Larissa, so instead he brought her to another, further away but still with a view of his little human's abode.

He wasted no time after they had landed. "Why did you say such a thing?"

"Why would I not? She asked a question and I answered it honest. Why are you upset she knows you are promised to another?"

"Part of protection is having her comfortable with me. I do not wish her to feel uncomfortable."

Valry studied him, a hard look in her eyes. "Why would she care about our customs?"

He would not let himself be baited. "It matters not. You have defied my wishes, the wishes of your *Mennak*."

Her claws ripped through the air in fury, her mouth in a snarl. "I am talking as your future mate! Why is she allowed more liberty with you than the female who will bear your young?"

"I am your lord first, your mate second, always."

"And would you say the same to your human, Terak?" Her tone was disgusted, filled with her contempt of anything that was not gargoyle.

*...which of these goals is your priority?*

*My priority will forever be her.*

A human whom his Clan would never accept.

He must bring the Clan together. They were too fractured now, stresses from both within and without crushing them.

To be a leader meant sacrifice. His sacrifice was staring at him with hard eyes.

No, his sacrifice lay on soft blue sheets within blue walls with a halo of gold always surrounding her.

The anger left him. Weariness, bone-deep and aging, settled in. He looked at Valry, and whatever she saw had her reeling back. "We will be mated, Valry. You will bear my young and stand by my side. But never forget this – I mate you only out of duty. You knew this from the first as I never hid my motives, and you accepted them. So do not now or ever pretend to be an injured party, and never ask again which has the most importance to me. The answer will always be the Clan. Now, do you wish to be released from our Intention?"

She shook her head, mute before him.

"Return to the keep. Never come here again."

She left without a word, and once she was out of sight Terak flew to his usual spot. As he watched over his little human he allowed himself one brief moment never to be repeated, a moment to imagine a life without sacrifice.


Why was she so shocked that Terak was engaged?

Larissa rolled over onto her side. Though only moments before she willed her eyes not to look at the time, the little buggers betrayed her. *2:43.*

Terak was going to be married.

Larissa flung the covers aside and sat up. Screw this. If she was going to be up, she was going to watch a movie and eat some ice cream.

She strode into the living room and picked up the remote.

*Click.*

And then she remembered her television was on the fritz.

The remote fell from her hand and she collapsed back in the couch with a heavy sigh. With all the commotion of the last few weeks, getting a wizard out here to recalibrate it had been nowhere on her list of priorities.

Now she had no television and no ice cream. Sure, she could go to the refrigerator and eat the ice cream, but then she wouldn't be a woman who was eating ice cream because she wanted a snack with her late time viewing.

No, she would then be a woman who was eating ice cream after hearing a guy she knew had a girlfriend.

No, make that an Intended.

Larissa rubbed the back of her neck, trying to ease the tense muscles she found there.

Why the hell would she be upset over this?

She took a deep breath, a slow and forceful inhalation to expand her lungs and clear out the cobwebs.

Okay, she had gotten used to having Terak around and had some proprietary feelings where he was concerned. He'd saved her several times over, so it was understandable and natural. Anybody would react the same.

And tonight, he had stood between her and an army, a warrior whom demons bowed before, and said *mine*.

The shiver raced up her spine at the memory. It was said on a harsh growl, claws and blood entwined in his promise. Only death awaited anyone who challenged him.

*Mine.*

She owed him her life. She owed him so much.

*Mine.*

That was it. It was gratitude mixed with shock and the closeness you can only feel with someone when you have faced death with them.

There was nothing else to this insomnia.

She'd feel better tomorrow.

And she'd call the repairman.

# CHAPTER TWENTY

The ringing phone awoke Larissa. Even as she reached for the phone she looked at the time. *4:59.* If someone wasn't dead, they were going to be. "Hello?"

"Sweetie." Olivia's voice was soft on the other end. "You have to wake up."

"Says who? What's going on, Olivia?"

"The person who I said might help? He wants to see you, and he wants to do it now. I'll pick you up in twenty minutes."

Olivia's words wound through Larissa's mind three times before she realized the implication. "I'll be ready – wait, Olivia," she said before the other woman could hang up.

"What?"

"People are watching me."

"My friend already assumed that. I've got it covered. Just be waiting in the lobby."

"I'll be there," said Larissa, hanging up the phone even as she went to her bureau for shirt and pants.

Gods, it would be so good to get some answers. If she knew the why, maybe Terak...

Terak.

His name brought her up short. What should she do? Who knew if he was guarding her? Maybe he left with his *In-ten-ded*.

She winced. Who knew her subconscious could be so bitchy?

Larissa sat down on the bed, wasting time she didn't have but needing a minute. If she had gotten two hours of sleep she was lucky, and even that short time was filled with unremembered but unsettling dreams, the type that sour your mood the next day even when you can't remember a single detail about them.

This needed to be put to rest inside her, fast. She didn't have the luxury of acting all junior high school, pouting because the boy she liked didn't like her back and taking it out on the world.

She liked Terak.

There. She admitted it. Damned junior high.

Maybe more than like, or within easy distance of that thought. But even if he didn't have an Intended – not like that was a small issue – they still could never be together. He was a leader who was dragging his Clan into this new world and dealing with the consequences of those actions. And she was a human who once this was finished would go back to teaching kids and pretending everything outside the city gates didn't exist.

Right?

*No.*

No. It was loud and clear and certain. No, she wouldn't be going back to that life.

She could picture clear as day the look on her dad's face as he worried over Michael, the only child who had ever left the nest.

Larissa loved her father, but for the first time, the thought of that look wasn't enough to have her backing down.

No, when this was over, it was time to explore this world, to learn all the things she wanted to learn but denied herself out of the fear of hurting her father. It was time to make her place. It was time to cut the strings and leave the nest. She fooled herself in thinking moving out of the house was the only step she needed to take to make that happen, but she wouldn't make that mistake again.

A lightness hollowed out her chest, and she couldn't breathe deep enough to fill it. Tears and laughter were threatening in equal measure, and it would be really nice if her mind would choose a more appropriate time to make known these little revelations. She had ten minutes before she had to leave to meet someone who might know what's going on.

Which brought her back to Terak.

And any more revelations would be for later. Right now, she would leave it at she needed him near and by her side. He was the only one she could trust.

Dressed, teeth and hair brushed, shoes on with five minutes to spare, she went out to the balcony, waving her arms and jumping up and down. If he wasn't near the silver ball was stashed in her pocket and she'd call him on the road.

Within moments Terak landed in front of her. Relief and a whole slew of emotions she threw into her mental lockbox ran through her. "You're here."

"Where else would I be?"

"I have some news. My friend Olivia knows someone she thinks might be able to help us. She called me and is on her way here to pick me up."

Terak stilled, his claws flexing at this unexpected piece of news. Damn, she should have told him about this possibility earlier, but so much had happened and she forgot all about it. "Who is she taking you to see?"

Larissa shook her head. "I have no clue. Olivia wouldn't say, but from what I gather he is a difficult man to talk to. He's in hiding from something, I don't know what."

Terak was already shaking his head. "I do not like this. I do not want you going to an unknown."

She wasn't thrilled about the thought either. She was still shaky from earlier – both of the night's surprises. There was nothing to be done though. "In this case, I don't think we have a choice. The chance to learn something supersedes the fact we're flying blind."

Terak snarled, but Larissa paid it no mind. It was aimed at the situation, not her. "This Olivia, you are sure she is trustworthy?"

Talk about echoes in conversation. Larissa could only answer the same way she had earlier. "Yes, I'm sure. Of course, I don't know him so I'm not trusting him. That's why I want you to come with me."

Surprise crossed his features. "You are not going to fight me on this?"

"Remember when I told you I'm not stupid and won't go into situations alone I have no business in to try to prove something? This is what we call a case in point. But you can't come as a gargoyle. You are going to need to switch into human form." Terak's mouth tightened and his tail twitched. Time for some charm. "You can protect me, I know you can, no matter what form you wear. And you can switch if it becomes necessary. But like you said, we're walking into an unknown, and they don't need to know I have a gargoyle watching over me. The less information we give them the better. So please, trust me?"

In his human form, Terak rode in the backseat of the car as it traveled outside of the city limits. Larissa was at his side and her friend Olivia drove the vehicle. Olivia kept glancing at him via the rearview mirror, but didn't say anything about the man who had unexpectedly joined them.

He wore a shirt that belonged to one of Larissa's brothers. It was small, but not so much that he could not move in it. He wished that one of her brothers had left their human weapons at her home. He flexed his hand, despising the flimsy fingernails where claws should be. Yes, he could change, but what if those moments were the ones that decided Larissa's fate?

They stopped in front of a large building, no decoration on the outside and no other buildings around it. It was a unique location, giving the impression of being completely insular, but in reality only minutes away from the bustle of the outer metropolis.

Upon entering, Larissa exclaimed, "I was not expecting this from the outside."

He believed humans called this a "bar", a gathering place for celebrations. But even without personal experience, he could see this was a place the very powerful and important would inhabit. Everything gleamed in rich tones and sumptuous fabrics, and one could almost feel the wealth that had gone into creating it.

"Right on time."

Terak zeroed in on the voice that came from a door on the side. It was a human adult male, but he stood no taller than a youngling who had not yet reached majority. His brown hair hung in a careless fashion around his face, but his green eyes did not project carelessness – they were lit with intelligence and an edge that Terak ground his teeth against, and he fought his instinct to step closer to Larissa. He would give away nothing to this man.

Olivia motioned between everyone. "Rhaum, this is my friend Larissa and her friend, Terak."

Rhaum's eyes flickered between them. "Pleasure to meet you both."

"Where is Simon?"

Rhaum answered Olivia's question with a movement of his head, motioning to stairs across from them.

"Thanks," said Olivia. Turning to them, she said, "Let's go."

Terak's impression of wealth only intensified as they walked up the stairs and toward a hidden room in the corner. This was an important place, and that man – Rhaum – was not one to be disregarded.

Olivia reached the door first, opening it and going inside. When Larissa made to follow, Terak held her back, placing her behind him. Her mouth tightened but she did not gainsay him.

He edged in by only scant inches, enough to take in the room and the lone male inhabitant.

*"What trickery is this?"* Olivia had betrayed them. He would tear her limb from limb to inflict the same hurt upon her she had visited upon Larissa.

"No! No, I promise, it's not what you think!" Olivia's wails were entwined with Larissa's scared, confused words behind him. "Terak? Terak! What's happening, *please*."

"So you know what I am, do you?"

The male's steady, even voice cut through the confusion. He didn't look up. Instead, his concentration was on the vials and beakers before him, all filled with a multitude of bubbling and colorful concoctions.

Terak felt Larissa's chin graze his arm as she looked around him into the room. She gasped, and he knew then she saw the man as well. His skin was sallow with a flaky appearance. His hair was thinning, dandruff thick on his scalp. He was thin but bloated.

He looked up from a purple concoction, zeroing in on Larissa. "Hello, young lady. Do you understand your protector's worry now?"

Terak knew she nodded by the scrape of her chin against his arm. "You're a zombie, aren't you?"

"Manner of speaking," Simon said. "Most zombies don't have their original thoughts left and were created to mindlessly follow the orders of their master. That was not the case for me, which is why I'm not aligned with bad guys and am hanging here."

Larissa was pushing against Terak, without words telling him to let her in the room. Olivia was standing on the side, her eyes begging him to believe this was not a trap.

He had thought he had prepared for every possible situation, but this…this was beyond his comprehension. Before him was an abomination, the culmination of a necromancer's lust for death and destruction. He spoke to the creature. "Why would they create one such as you? I have never heard of any like you before."

Simon had already turned back to his bubbling tubes. He was studying one of them, making notes. "They turned me because I am a being of exceptional brilliance."

Larissa gave a small laugh behind him. "Not exactly modest."

"I'm a man of science. I deal in truth, not obfuscation." Simon finished his notes, then after lowering the heat on the tube, turned his attention back to them. "That truth was why they made me undead in the first place. Cancer would have killed me within six months and they didn't want to lose me."

"Who is your master?" Terak asked.

"Don't have one."

"Do not lie to me, creature. All of your kind has a master."

Simon shook his head as a teacher would at an unruly student. "I don't lie. A necromancer created me, yes, but he is not my master. No one controls me."

"I have never heard of such a thing."

"Yes, well, weren't you the one who said you never heard of anything like me before?" The zombie motioned toward Larissa. "Can the young woman come in now? I understand she has questions for me."

There was a poke in his ribs, no doubt from Larissa's finger. She did indeed want to enter. With ill will he let her enter, but when she made a move to stand in front of him he held his arm to the side, not letting her any further than his side. Again she gave that small huff, but she stayed put.

He might be willing to accept this was not a trap, but he would not let her nearer. No matter what the creature believed, a necromancer created him and a necromancer would always be master to him. "Why would a necromancer create one that had free will? It is counter to their interests."

The zombie shrugged. "I'm a man of science and I don't know the intricacies of necromantic magic. My understanding is if they had imprinted me, I would have lost my genius and been useless to them."

"Then why are you not with your creator now?"

"As my free will and my genius remained, so did my morality. I may be a zombie, but I am in all other ways still the human male who existed before the Great Collision." He motioned to himself with a sweep of his arm down the front of his body, and for the first time Terak detected emotion, a flicker of disgust at what was beheld. "Do you think I want others to become this? The necromancers to win? No, not at all. I want them defeated."

"If they are defeated, you will cease to exist." Cruel words, but truth. How would the zombie react?

The creature took the news as calmly as one would a situation that peace had been made with long ago. "I should have died seven years ago. Even if I expire this moment, I've gotten more than my share."

Larissa's hand touched Terak's shoulder, giving his arm a small caress. "Do you know anything that can help me?"

Simon shook his head. "I don't know any specifics about you. I've been away from them too long. But I do know what their ultimate goal is, and with what Olivia has told me, I have to assume somehow you are mixed up in that."

"Ultimate goal? You mean beyond the usual of bringing death and mayhem wherever they go?"

Simon's face showed no response to Larissa's attempt at levity. "They want to rip the Human Realm and the Magic Realm apart."

"Impossible," Terak breathed, unable to stop his head from shaking, unable to stop his body from backing away even as the gasps from both Olivia and Larissa sounded in his ears. "You speak of the impossible. The realms are forever entwined. All the great mages have proclaimed it."

Simon's eyes bore into his. "The realms can't be separated in a way that won't involve carnage and destruction on a scale unparalleled in the history of either realm. When has that ever been a deterrent to a necromancer?"

Terak thought back to the First Council after the Great Collision, where various leaders came together to understand how to proceed. His father had journeyed forth against the advice of many in the Clan, bringing him and his mother. He remembered how one – an elf? – asked if it was possible the realms could ever be separated.

The mage hesitated, then replied, "No spell is impossible, only the conditions that surround it."

It was double-speak at the time, a way to say no without appearing less powerful, and he and his father, as well as the cadre of leaders, paid no mind to those words. But if this creature was correct? He asked, "This separation of the realms? What would happen exactly?"

Simon shook his head. "I don't know any specifics. I know we are entering a short period of time where it will be possible to rip the realms apart – planets in alignment and other mystical happenings. If they are able to make this happen, the Human Realm will be destroyed while the Magic Realm will revert to the way it was before."

Larissa's hand went to her throat. "The Human Realm will be destroyed?"

Simon nodded. "Since the Human Realm is dominant, it would take the brunt of the destructive force and become the Realm sacrifice required. Anyone who was originally from the Human Realm would die with it. Those who have been born since the Great Collision it's less clear. With as complex a spell as we are talking about, I doubt any magic user truly understands the full impact."

"And me? You think them coming after me is somehow related to this?" Larissa's tone held the fear and uncertainty of a child who had lost sight of her family and was now alone amid a large, uncaring throng of adults. Anyone observing be damned. Terak took the step needed to be situated behind her and wrapped her in his arms, bringing her close to his body. She leaned back into him, her arms circling his own.

If Simon took any special notice of the display he didn't let on. Instead his attention turned back to his beakers, one of which looked to be on the verge of bubbling over. He went to it, saying over his shoulder, "I don't see how you could be connected. There is nothing I've heard about you that makes me understand why they would pick you as a target. At the same time, this is what they have been planning for since the Realms first collided, and considering the effort and the risks they are taking to collect you, I see no other possibility that explains their interest."

In the thickness of the ensuing silence, only the zombie appeared to not be troubled by dark and heavy thoughts. Olivia shook off her own worries first, and she smiled at the zombie, small and trembling, but warmth still evident in it. "Thank you for seeing us, Simon."

"Anything for you." It was the first spark of human feeling the zombie had exhibited, this response to the dark-haired woman. She was important to him, though in what way Terak could not fathom. Simon then turned to Larissa. "Young lady, I can't press this upon you enough. If you are somehow connected to this, they will stop at nothing to get to you. This is all they exist for. They want their world the way it once was. They hate this new reality. They still have power, but not the complete domination and utter subservience they enjoyed in the other realm. They want it back, and will do anything to get it."

# CHAPTER TWENTY-ONE

Back in the car, Terak watched as Larissa continued to absorb the information. She was pale, almost as pale as the abomination, and her arms were wrapped around her stomach as though it were the only way to keep herself from flying apart.

Olivia looked into the rear view mirror. "Larissa? You okay, sweetie?"

She was anything but okay, but the question brought some strength back to her. She straightened in the seat. "You know a zombie, Olivia. A sentient *zombie*."

Olivia's eyes went back to the road. "I never planned for that. I kept getting introduced to more and more people, and the more people I talked to, the deeper I got sucked into the politics and the backstage goings-on. Believe me, right now I really wish I didn't know so much. This shit with the necromancers…I could happily have lived in ignorance."

"Yeah," Larissa said. She absently started to pick at her fingernails as she looked out the window.

"Are we still friends?"

Larissa's head jerked at that statement. "Of course we are. You've stood behind me since all this started. Why would I leave you after you've put yourself in danger helping me?"

Olivia's shoulders relaxed at the sincerity in Larissa's tone. "What are you going to tell your family?"

Larissa shook her head. "I'm not quite sure where to go with this yet."

Olivia laughed, a harsh sound. "I got you. Right now I'm so messed up I can't remember how to diagram a sentence. My kids are going to eat me up and spit me out."

"Jason Evans will be king for the day. I hope the school is still standing tomorrow." Both women laughed, a call to move beyond fear and back to normalcy.

After the laughter died down, Larissa breathed deep. "Thank you again for setting up this meeting. So please don't think me ungrateful when I say I wish he had been a little more helpful. I'm still no closer to knowing why they are targeting *me*, and that's what I was hoping to find out."

Olivia smiled, and Terak saw mischief in her features. "Well, if you weren't here with a fine-looking man who happened to be in your bedroom at five in the morning, I would have said it was because you were a virgin."

"Olivia!"

Larissa's scandalized tone was barely heard over the sudden pounding in Terak's ears.

She was untouched?

"I'm just saying..." Olivia didn't even try to hide her smirk.

"Well, don't!"

Yes, her father was protective, but from what he knew of humans, they did not reserve sexual intimacy solely for their mates. She was old enough that not having a lover would be unusual.

Larissa refused to look at him, her face scarlet and muttering under her breath on how she would take revenge on Olivia.

It was still early morning when they arrived back at her apartment, but late enough that she would have awoken already to get ready for her day. Larissa motioned toward the balcony. "Thank you for coming with me, but I need to get started-"

"Is what Olivia said true?" he broke in, no finesse in his words. He needed to know, now.

Her face flamed immediately, but Larissa pretended ignorance. "What are you talking about?"

"Are you untouched?"

Larissa turned to walk into her room. "My...sexual life...has nothing to do with what is occurring."

He came before her, not letting her escape into her bedroom. "You say that you can think of no reason why the necromancers are targeting you. There is no overt reason, but there is some reason. They have gone to extraordinary lengths to apprehend you. No possibility can be overlooked."

Larissa would not look him in the eye, instead tried to step around him. When she failed in her quest, she went still, looking down at the floor. Finally, she said, "Yes."

*Yes.* How could one small word have such power over him, delivering a punch greater than any enemy who ever came before him? He worked saliva into his now-dry mouth to speak, feigning a calmness his heartbeats would easily belie. "Why does this embarrass you?"

She shrugged, still looking at the floor. "People usually don't discuss their sexual history, or their complete lack thereof. And most people my age don't have a complete lack thereof."

The defensiveness in her tone hurt something in him. He did not like her feeling she was inadequate in any way. "I do not know the ways of humans, but while virginity is not held sacred, most of my Clan do not engage in sexual acts with anyone before they take a mate."

That brought Larissa's head up, her interest in the subject easily read on her face. "Really? Why is that?"

"Vulnerability."

Larissa's eyebrows creased. "I don't understand."

"A gargoyle is vulnerable during intimacy. There would be no better time for an enemy to strike."

Her lips twisted, a smile that couldn't quite form. "If that wasn't so sad, there is a pithy comment in that statement."

He reached out and smoothed back her hair. "What statement?"

"Your people have trust issues."

"I have never denied this."

She laughed a little, but her eyes widened, her lush mouth opening in surprise. "Wait. So does this mean you are...?"

She let the question hang, but what she was asking was clear. "I have never had a lover. I am as you are."

"Oh." She cleared her throat, her head once again hanging down, her gaze on the ground. Then without lifting her head, her eyes came back to his. "Valry?"

"No."

Now her head lifted. "But you two are engag – I mean, Intended."

"Yes. It is my duty to mate with her. As the strongest female, she will protect the Clan well, and any young we have will have the strength to protect the Clan in the future."

Her eyebrows furrowed. "Wait, you don't love Valry, but you're going to marry her?"

"I must do what is best for my Clan, and my Clan will prosper with Valry as my mate."

Larissa shook her head, though she seemed not aware of the movement. "You can't be serious. Life isn't worth living if you're not with the one you love."

"Humans can live with such fanciful notions. As leader, I am allowed no such luxury."

"That's bull!" The exclamation was a surprise, as was the finger that poked him in the chest. "I understand you are under pressures I can't comprehend, but there is nothing strong or noble about picking a female you don't love as your wife. It's a cowardly way out."

"Cowardly?" He had never been described that way in his life. He was the leader of the greatest warriors of this realm, and this little human would call him a coward? "Watch your words."

"Oh, I am!" Her eyes were blazing, and in her anger she seemed to grow in size. "Only a coward would marry someone he doesn't love. You know why? Because love is the ultimate vulnerability. It can put you on your knees and destroy parts of you that will never function again when it's gone. A coward couldn't handle that, so they would instead marry someone that could never happen with."

"What would you have me do? Would you have me defy tradition and the will of my people?"

"Yes! Isn't that the point of being here with me, to bring your people away from what they know to something better? Be with someone you love." Her eyes were bright, shining with the ferocity of her belief while she spoke of love and cowardice.

"You do not understand."

"Then make me understand. Make me understand why you would be with a female you don't love when there is a female in front of you who…"

She faltered, her hand going over her mouth and stopping any more words from coming forth.

A female in front of him. A female who was warm and loving and brave and so damn desirable his teeth ached in want of her. "Make you understand, little human? How can I make you understand something that becomes less clear to me every time I am near you?"

He picked her up by her waist, bringing her to eye level. Before the question in her eyes could translate to words, he leaned down, pressing his mouth to hers.

Her lips were soft, as soft as he'd imagined those rare moments he was away from her. Even then, she was as much a part of him as when she was in his sight. There was never a moment he was free of her.

She didn't respond as he moved his lips over hers. Maybe this was not correct. It was perfect to him, but...

Thought left as her mouth opened under his, pressing against him to push closer. Her tongue slipped past his lips, a tentative touch against his own.

Her tongue was becoming bolder, tangling with his in long strokes. He raised one hand to grasp her hair, slanting her head so he could dive deeper into that warmth.

Her arms wound around his shoulders, her own fingers digging into hair as her body writhed against him. Gods, that body, that soft, sensual body was draining the strength from his. He leaned her against the wall, bodies now tight together. Her chest was against his, her nipples such hard points he felt them through the cloth that separated their bodies.

She moved against him with that sinuous grace he had seen so many nights from a distance, the movements slow and sensuous and reducing him to a mindless beast.

He wanted her skin. He wanted her naked. He wanted his mouth on every inch of her – her breasts, her stomach, that valley between her thighs.

Especially there. He wanted to live there. He wanted to wring every ounce of pleasure from her body, and once he did, he wanted to do it again. And again. And again.

She pulled her mouth from his, her eyes wide and shocked as she looked down at him. She opened her mouth, closed it. Opened her mouth again, licked her lips, closed her mouth.

He looked at her mouth and a vibration rolled through his chest. That mouth was far sweeter and softer than any dream had promised.

"I..." She had gotten her voice back, though shock colored her tone. "School. My kids. I need to go."

He let her go and backed away before he convinced himself of the wisdom of taking her back into his arms. With a bow, he returned to his gargoyle form and leapt from the window.

# CHAPTER TWENTY-TWO

"Miss Miller? You're about a million miles away today,"

"Huh?" Larissa looked up to see half of her first-period students staring at her. "What?"

Jason Evans sighed. "You might consider making all your classes study periods today. You keep zoning in and out."

*Damn it! Stupid gargoyle.* No, no fair blaming Terak for her inability to do her job. The fault lay squarely with her and her hormones. "Thank you, Jason. I'll take that under advisement. Any other questions before class ends?"

Jason spoke. "You never answered my question. If the necromancers are such bad guys, why didn't everyone band together to destroy them?"

Every day Jason somehow brought up either necromancers or vampires. Older teachers told her there was one kid every year who fixated on them, but Jason didn't fit the mold. He was the golden boy, an athletic genius who was adored around the school, not some emo kid who had no other way of expressing dissatisfaction with their lot in life than by thumbing their nose at society's conventions and openly embracing something everyone else feared. "Necromancers are very powerful, so it's not that easy to fight them. Plus there is due process to consider."

Jason shrugged. "Or maybe everyone makes them out to be the bad guys to keep all the attention on them and away from the other races."

The intensity in Jason's eyes, the set of his shoulders and the line of his mouth, had warning bells clanging in uncomfortable cacophony. When had this unhealthy fascination begun again? "Jason, while I am not one who swallows the party line completely, trying to make necromancers in any way good is a bit of a stretch."

"And I think we're only being given one side of the story," Jason argued back, his arms crossed over his chest with typical teenage mulishness.

The minute bell rang, saving Larissa from this conversation. "Okay, everybody, no homework tonight, but review the last few chapters. Big hint here – expect a pop quiz."

Disgruntled voices followed that announcement as the kids grabbed their items and left. Jason went against the tide and came over to her desk. Before he could say anything she took the initiative. "Jason, you're entitled to your opinion, but you're not going to convince me otherwise."

He smiled, the earlier intensity gone. "No, I understand, Miss Miller. I was actually going to ask you something else. Would you be my sponsor for the upcoming fall carnival? I want to do a dunking booth. "

"An oldie but goodie – I approve. Who would be the one dunked?"

"You, of course."

Of course. When *don't* the students want to dunk the teacher? "Ah. Silly me for asking."

"Maybe we can meet up after school today so I can show you my designs and go over a few ideas I had. How about we meet in the gym?"

The gym, which was a separate building from the school and would be very empty after classes were done for the day. Goosebumps rose across the back of her neck. "I'm busy after school. Seventh-period study hall, why don't you meet me in the teacher's lounge?

"C'mon, Miss Miller, it will only take fifteen minutes, and I need you in the gym so you can see what I've done so far. We've been keeping all the supplies in the back." The wheedling tone was in direct contrast to that intense look that had once again entered his eyes.

"Sorry, I can't. Let's plan it for next Tuesday, I'll meet you then." *Like hell I will.*

His lips thinned for a long moment and his eyes grew stormy. But he came back to himself and all traces of anger at her pronouncement disappeared. "Sure, next Tuesday. But let me know if you have an opening before then. I'm really eager to get on this design." He turned and left the classroom as other students came filing in.

Jason Evans, all-star quarterback and the golden boy of the school, who was unnaturally fixated on necromancers and was doing his best to get her someplace alone.

This needed to end, because either she was starting to jump at shadows or those evil creatures were coming at her through her kids, and like hell she'd let them near her kids.

For the first time since she finished the student side of high school and began the educator side, the final bell ringing brought sweet, sweet relief and thankfulness that the day was done. She was out of the building before most of her students, her little yellow loaner car tearing up the asphalt to get her home. Once home, she closed the curtains tight, hoping that would discourage any knocks from her gargoyle guardian.

She was being a coward. Fully admitted it, would sign a note to that effect. But what else could she do after that kiss...

That kiss.

*Gods.*

Never had anything like that happened in her life, that flint-to-wood inferno that exploded the moment his lips touched hers. If that was what happened when you called a male a coward, it was something that needed to happen a lot more often.

Every millimeter of his skin branded hers and demanded she press closer, and she wanted to do nothing except obey. There had never been anyone else who had ever caused that reaction, that desperation to have him trapped in the most intimate embrace she could hold him in.

It would have been the most perfect moment of her life, except he was the member of another race, she'd just called him a coward, and he was engaged.

She didn't mess up often, but when she did, she went big.

The memory brought the 20/20 cringe. Somehow at the time it made sense, she was saving him from a stupid mistake – never mind it was self-serving bunk.

Gargoyles were hardly alone in their philosophy of strength, and not everyone was meant to have the fairy tale that her parents did. Even her parents hadn't had the fairy tale. Reality needed to be acknowledged.

But he was the one who kissed her. He cradled her in his arms and held her tight and made her feel so cherished. If he didn't return her feelings, if he was at peace with his people's traditions, then none of that would have happened. Right?

A knock sounded on the door. No, not a knock. Several heavy thumps and a loud, "Damn it, Ris, open this gods damned door now!"

Couldn't she have one day alone to mope and obsess? After checking the peephole and seeing it was indeed family, Larissa pulled the door open, fixing in place a scowl that would signal her extreme displeasure. "What do you want, Michael?"

He pushed past her, kicking the door closed with his foot. "Don't you dare lie to me. What are you involved in?"

Oh, he did not. It didn't matter if he had eight inches and a hundred pounds on her, like hell she was letting him get away with this bullying. "You might want to stop with the attitude right now and back off. I don't know what you mean."

Michael was pacing, his hands running in his hair as he talked, the way all the males of her family acted when they were upset. "You aren't going to throw me off that easily. I'm fucking mad as hell I let myself become so wrapped up in seeing that guy in your apartment that I forgot myself the first time and let you talk me out of what my gut was saying."

"Nothing was left unfinished the last time."

"Red running lingerie."

The out-of-the-blue statement jarred her. "What are you talking about?" she asked, the volume lower than before.

"The woman in red running lingerie, that's what you said you saw at the park. Except how could you have seen the woman who had barely started her run when she was grabbed by the orcs if you weren't there at the same time? And where is your car? Shall I tell you what lot it's in and what the current shape is, because I made a point to find it when I realized it *disappeared* the same day as the attack!"

He tried to tower over her but she wasn't having it, stepping forward to make him break away. "What orc attack, Michael? The orc attack that was never reported on the news and there is no police record of? You might be on the force, but being the chief of police's daughter has its own set of advantages. Don't think I can't find things out."

"Why the hell did you go behind my back?"

"*That's* all you have to say to me? You come here full of righteous indignation while you are hiding all sorts of crap from me, and when called on it you get huffy because I was a little underhanded in finding things out? I'm not playing that. You either come clean or you can get out."

He raked his hand through his hair, creating chaos in the formerly smooth strands. "This isn't about me."

Really? He thought he could play that with her? "It sure as hell *is* about you! It's about the fact that I don't know what's what in this world anymore, and even those closest to me have secrets I would never have imagined. So you tell me, Michael – does Dad know? Whatever you're involved in, does he know about it?"

Muscles ticked in his jaw as he contemplated her, anger still within easy reach but banked at the moment. "Are we coming clean with each other?"

She sat on the couch in front of him, crossing her arms. "You tell me."

The drumming of his fingers made a staccato against his jean-clad leg. He lowered his head as if in defeat. When he brought it up all heat was gone from his gaze. "I wasn't in the military, not like you think."

The world shifted beneath her feet, a roller-coaster sensation she didn't expect and didn't want. "That isn't funny."

"Not meant to be." He shook his head, coming to sit beside her on the couch. "In basic training, I was recruited for a Special Forces-type team."

"You mean like the SEALS?"

"I mean…" He trailed off. The late afternoon sun came through the window, casting half of him in shadow and making his features a little starker, a little harsher. "There are a lot of dangers in this world. Humans can't completely place our protection under the control of members of other races. We need to keep a hand in things ourselves."

"The Seven Houses," she muttered, and was rewarded with his surprised jump.

"You really do know a lot of things." He picked at his pants leg. "We're not enemies and this isn't about trying to start trouble, but yeah, we can't leave things entirely to the Seven Houses or the other races' governments. We need to remain strong on our own, and I was part of a group whose job is to protect us."

"Why are you telling this to me now?"

He took a deep breath, his face filling with sorrow. "I've never left it. I'm still part of that Special Forces team."

She jumped up, away from him. If he slapped her it would have shocked her less. "You're a cop, Michael. You're a cop with Dad and the bros."

"I came back because it was part of my cover." He looked up at her, his eyes tired, haunted. "I'm not a cop, I'm undercover. I'm sorry, Ris."

Her father... "Does Daddy know?"

Michael shook his head, his eyes breaking away from hers.

"This would kill him." She rubbed her hand against her upper arm, trying to warm herself against this sudden cold. "He'd never recover from this."

"I know." Flat, blunt, taking full responsibility for the damage.

"Then why?"

He stood then, his posture not showing any further apology. "Same reason you're keeping secrets now. To protect him. To protect all of us. All I ever wanted is my family to be safe. Dad buries his head in the sand. I don't blame him, and I never want to force him to do otherwise, but I knew I had to do things differently."

When put like that, she couldn't argue. Everything he said was true, and wasn't that why she had gone against what she knew her father would have wanted? Having your own thoughts spoken aloud by someone else made it really hard to remain mad at them.

"Your turn. What are you involved with?"

Tiredness hit her like a sledgehammer. These last twenty-four hours had been hell, and she wasn't out of the woods yet. She wanted to sleep and process, but Michael wouldn't let this go, not until he knew everything. "How did you know, and don't tell me lingerie girl – you pieced that together after the fact."

His eyes narrowed and became cop's eyes, questioning and searching out the truth. "A woman named Fallon came to visit me. She said you would recognize her name."

If she lived a thousand years, Larissa was pretty sure she'd never forget Fallon. "What did she have to say?"

"She didn't give me any details. She said she had more information about the attacks for you and your guardian, and gave me directions of where to bring you tonight if you wanted to meet." The pacing started again. "Who does she mean, *guardian*? The man in your apartment?"

"Yes, he's been protecting me."

"And what have you needed protection from?"

She didn't want to say it. She didn't want Michael to become part of this nightmare. But he had told his secrets, and that was the deal. "Necromancers."

Michael's knees buckled before he righted himself. "Fuck no, fuck no...*Necromancers*, Ris? You don't know what they can do, the horrors I've seen..." He grabbed her hand, pulling her closer. "You're sure?"

His terror was bringing her own back, batting down walls she'd been using to keep it contained. She had to get away or she would be curled up on the floor. She pulled her hand from his, wiping it over her face as she nodded, the only answer he was going to receive.

He stayed still for several moments, looking lost, his hands clenching at his sides. A word floated through the air. "Why?"

She would give anything to fully know the answer to that question. "They're going to use me to somehow rip the Human Realm and the Magic Realm apart and return the Magic Realm back to how it was before."

If Michael was unhappily stunned at the prior mention of necromancers, he was poleaxed at this latest revelation. "Impossible," he whispered, the slice of sound low and haunted.

She said nothing and let him come to terms with this newest revelation in his own time. When he came out of his stupor, his eyes were a laser focus on her. "This Fallon, she's from the Guild, isn't she? Fuck, I should have known."

He didn't sound happy about this new bit of knowledge. "You know of the Guild?"

"Not because I want to. I've been very happy that I haven't had any run-ins with them this far in life, though I guess that's changing now."

"What did you think of her?"

He didn't hesitate. "That she's scary as hell and you'd be ten shades of stupid to mess with her." He took a few moments then, and she saw protective older brother fade to be replaced by cool cop logic. "That doesn't mean you shouldn't meet up with her and see if you can learn something, as long as you have your back-up guardian – who, by the way, you haven't fully explained yet."

"I can't explain him."

Michael narrowed his eyes at her. "Larissa…"

She held up a finger in warning. "Don't take that tone with me. I can tell you my secrets, but I won't betray those who have been protecting me all this time. I would be dead several times over if it wasn't for the man you saw. He's been by my side throughout all of this."

Michael's hands slipped into the back pockets of his jeans. "I'm sorry you didn't feel like you could have come to me, to the family."

"It's not that I couldn't, it's that I wouldn't. Protection, right? If something had happened to any of you because of me…it was easier to risk myself alone."

He came over and enveloped her in a giant hug, squeezing her so hard she was lifted a few inches off the ground. "Never again. No matter what, you come to us."

"No." She pushed away from him. "I still don't want Dad to know, and I have others to protect me, people more qualified than Dad or the other bros."

She could see the war behind his eyes at that statement, but after long moments he nodded. "Yeah. I hear you."

"Thanks."

He looked around the room, taking in the family photographs that lined her walls. "So what now, Miss Hear-Me-Roar?"

She smacked his arm, a giggle escaping. Gods, it felt good to laugh again, even such a small sound. "I need to see Fallon. It's time we all laid our cards face up, because cloak-and-dagger is not my thing, and if the Guild can help, I want to meet with them." Jason's face flashed before her, the weird intense look in his eyes as disturbing in memory as it was in person. "This might be affecting people close to me. It needs to end, no matter how unsure I am about my possible allies."

"I agree. I'll talk to my superiors and see if I can bring my people into it." He took a strand of her hair, curling it around his finger and pulling slightly, like he did when she was little. "We'll figure this out. I'll pick you up tonight and we'll see what this Fallon has to say."

"You'll pick up me and Terak."

"Terak? That's the guy's name?" Michael's mouth thinned and turned down. "You sure you still want him if I'm with you?"

*I can't do this without Terak.* The response almost leapt from her throat before she tamped it down. Probably best not to go into that minefield with her brother. It was an area she wasn't sure how to handle yet, so discussion with her brothers – all of whom had less than enthusiastic responses to any male who had ever gotten close to her – was strictly a no-go. "It would feel weird if I didn't bring him with me, like a betrayal. He's been through every step with me."

"When I see this guy again, I'm going to shake his hand and thank him for taking care of you."

"Aw, Michael, that's so sweet-"

"And then I'm beating the crap out of him for being naked in your apartment."

Men were stupid. It was all she could come up with most days. Change of subject. "What time are you going to pick us up?"

"Seven."

"We'll be ready."

He leaned down and kissed the top of her head. "Love you, baby sister. No matter what else, you have to remember that."

"I always know that."

When Michael was gone she went to the balcony and did her patented wave and dance, which had always worked in the past to get Terak's attention.

No Terak. Not then and not for the next several minutes.

The image of that little silver ball popped up. Yes, thank gods Terak had the foresight to get it. Going into the bedroom and opening the top drawer of her nightstand, the silver ball was where she left it, safely stored in a velvet bag in the corner.

All right, hold it tight and start speaking in your head. *Terak. Terak, I need you. Can you hear me? Fallon wants to meet with us tonight, and I need you here.*

Thirty minutes later she had a pounding headache and not heard a word from her erstwhile gargoyle.

The next two hours were spent between going to the balcony and trying to use the silver ball, but Terak never arrived at her side.

This couldn't be about the kiss, could it?

Did he hate himself?

Did he hate her?

Maybe he felt guilt. It didn't matter if he wasn't in love with his fiancée. The fact was he was engaged to marry one woman while he kissed another. She wouldn't like him if he was the type of male who thought so little of his promises and responsibilities.

Whatever the reason, he wasn't here, and Michael was arriving in five minutes for their meeting with the Guild.

This meeting had to happen. Working with the Guild was her best bet of finding out the information needed. She wasn't going to let necromancers use her to destroy this world, and she needed to protect her kids and anyone else close to her the necromancers might use to get to her.

Terak would hate that she left without him, but there was no choice.

It was time for her to step up.

Michael arrived at seven sharp. A smile plastered on her face and her hands stuffed into the pockets of her slacks to hide the shaking, she said with all the false confidence she could muster, "Let's go meet with the Guild."

# CHAPTER TWENTY-THREE

Michael drove to the town hall, parking in the back. There were no other cars around, and all the lights had somehow stopped functioning, making the parking lot pitch-black. Nice touch.

"This way," Michael said, guiding her toward the emergency exit. No alarms went off as they opened the door. He led her to the elevators, and they went up to the fourth floor where the meeting rooms were. They walked three doors down into the only lighted office.

Fallon and Laire were waiting, tonight's outfit of choice for the mage a lime-green catsuit. Maybe she was colorblind. Or someone who really hated her bought all her outfits.

Fallon nodded. "Thank you for coming. Did your bodyguard decide to take the night off?"

Larissa might want a truce with the Guild, but that didn't mean she was going to become best buds and tell them everything. "Terak has other duties, as you well know. Besides, considering how *tense* conversations can become, I thought it might be best to leave him out of it."

Fallon nodded again. "I hear you. That's fine by me. In fact, it makes my life lots easier."

Warning bells went off at Fallon's words and the smug way she held herself. *This was a mistake.* Larissa shouldn't have come here without Terak. "Tell me what you wanted to tell me, and then I need to go."

"Sorry, not going to happen."

"What the-" Michael's voice cut-off and Larissa turned. The shadow man from that first night was emerging from the wall, at least his torso was, the rest of his body still hidden. He wrapped his arms around Michael and pulled, taking Michael...

...through the wall.

"Michael!"

She ran to the wall and beat on it, but it was unyielding. "Michael!"

"He's safe, I promise," and Fallon was there in front of her. Larissa shrank back, but the wall was solid behind her, not allowing any more movement. "Sorry, Teach. You need to come with us now. The time of pussy-footing around is over."

Laire's voice popped up. "Is that what pussy-footing means? Why was I thinking it was something sexual?"

"Just read from the scroll." Fallon sounded like an annoyed instructor during last period instead of someone in the midst of a kidnapping.

Laire huffed, but brought out a parchment sheet. Larissa recognized it from pictures in her lecture books. It was a magic scroll, which gave a magic user the ability to cast spells they normally couldn't. There were several conditions to be able to use one, not the least of which was the magic user had to be a powerful caster – the book said only ten percent of casters were powerful enough to make any use of scrolls.

"What are you going to do to me?" Larissa hated that she couldn't keep the tremor entirely out of her voice.

"You are going unconscious. This is the easiest way," and even as Fallon explained, Larissa could hear Laire chanting in some strange language, a mixture of smooth vowels and guttural consonants.

Laire finished.

Nothing happened.

"Laire," and Fallon's annoyed voice was now ratcheted up several notches.

Laire was looking at the scroll with confusion plain on her heavily made-up face. "I have never had a scroll not work before. It's a beginner spell – there should be no way they could mess it up."

Larissa made a break for it, sprinting past the women, but as she stepped out the door someone picked her up, giving her body a hard squeeze. Even as she struggled a blindfold was placed over her eyes and ropes wrapped around her body.

"Hard way it is."

It was an interrogation room – big and white, with a long table and two chairs in the middle, a couple spare bulbs hanging overhead, and one wall consisting of what was undoubtedly a two-way mirror.

Larissa sat on one of those chairs, looking toward the mirror. She wasn't going to throw anything, not until she had a living, breathing target. Those mirrors were notoriously hard to break.

Fallon and Laire walked into the room. Well, more accurately, Fallon glided in, her balance centered on the balls of her feet. In contrast, Laire was wearing six-inch stilettos and was doing a hurried shuffle to keep up.

They stopped in front of the mirror. Fallon never so much as glanced at her reflection and leaned back against it. Laire was the opposite, leaning close to the mirror fix her make-up and slick on a very shiny gloss on her lips.

"My brother?" Larissa asked. Keep it cool. She could do that.

"He's perfectly fine," Fallon answered. "He's back at his home right now without so much as a hair out of place, though *very* pissed over what happened. He's calling his commanding officers even now."

Several moments of silence followed. "*Why?*" So much for playing it cool. The word exploded out of Larissa. "Why am I here? Why did you kidnap me? You said we were meeting to talk, and I *trusted* you."

"Told you we should have waited for Aislynn," said the tiny mage to Fallon, still looking at herself in the mirror.

Fallon's jaw tightened. She probably wasn't the one often engaged in diplomacy, and the peeved look on her face told Larissa everything she needed to know about how Fallon felt being put in that position. Fallon said, "This was necessary. You are in a lot of danger and we had no other way to keep you safe."

"Don't try to sell me that crap. You're mad that I didn't play your game, and you decided to change the rules."

"It was necessary," Fallon repeated. Her sword kept peeking out from behind her head, a deadly reminder of what she could do. Well, she might be counting on that to help her out, but fat chance. This woman's intimidation tactics weren't working today.

Larissa put as much scorn in her voice as she could. "Keep telling yourself that if it helps you sleep at night, though I can't imagine anything could."

Laire, in the process of adding more eye shadow, spoke to Fallon then. "You aren't helping the situation."

Fallon turned, narrowing her eyes. "I notice you aren't speaking to her."

"I'm smart enough to recognize my weaknesses. I don't do that empathy shit. That's Ais's department."

As if in answer to their words, the elf came through the door, followed by a man Larissa had not seen before. Overlong dark blond hair and deep-set yellow eyes, and a scar that ran from the bridge of his nose below his cheekbone to end somewhere under a close cropped beard. He wore blue jeans and an open flannel shirt over a T-shirt.

He came to sit in front of her. "I'm Wulver," he said, smart enough not to offer his hand when his advance caused an involuntary flinch on Larissa's part. "I'm leader here."

Fallon was still standing with her back to the mirror, not reacting to those words at all. Larissa pointed to her. "I thought that was her, the way she acts."

He smiled but refused to be drawn in by her words. It was a nice smile, his teeth white and sharp.

Maybe a little too sharp.

No, no she was not going to ask. There was enough on her plate right now without wondering if the guy in front of her was a human or not.

Guess the human. That might make a neat game.

Well, he said he was boss. It gave her someone else to yell at. "Since you are in charge and not her, I'm assuming it was your order that brought me here?"

He nodded. His eyes did hold some compassion, but something in the set of his shoulders, the way he carried himself, all told that while he might be sorry she was so upset, he felt no remorse in grabbing her and bringing her here against her will. "I'm sorry it was done this way, but with that last attack, we decided it was too dangerous for you to be free any longer."

That was an interesting way to put it. "Who's this *we* if you are the leader?"

Once again, he didn't answer her question, the compassion in his eyes morphing into something harder. He said instead, "We want your stay to be enjoyable. Is there anything we can bring you?"

"A nail file."

"Sure. Any nail polish? May I suggest red? It's a personal thing, but I prefer when women stick with the classics." He smiled again, and in that grin she saw the easy charm he possessed and could project when he wanted to. That might be the secret why he ran things, because in moments she was half under his spell, imprisonment be darned.

Enough of that. Charm wasn't going to get her home. "How long are you going to keep me here?"

His grin faded, and her stomach sank to the soles of her feet. "You must understand how much danger you're in-"

"How long?" she repeated.

He leaned back in the chair, trying to project nonchalance but failing. "Until you're safe."

She crossed her arms and directed at him her hardest stare, the one that kept even her most unruly student in line. It didn't do anything to free her, but she got some satisfaction in using it. "Meaning you're keeping me here indefinitely, unless you know why I've been targeted and are only holding me here until you get your man – well, necromancer. Is that the case?"

"There are things going on-"

Screw this. She was here against her will, but she was here, and she was going to get some gods damned answers right *now*. "How are they going to use me to rip the realms apart?"

Wulver jerked, and she'd bet money he rarely looked as surprised as he did right now. He looked at Fallon. Her brows were lifted slightly, the lines of her face softened from their usual intensity. She shook her head.

He turned back to her. "You've learned a lot in a relatively short period of time."

"Did you think I was sitting on my butt waiting for the zombies to eat my brains?"

Laire turned away from the mirror. "It's not really true that zombies eat brains, it's an urban legend...*mrph*."

The impromptu lesson was finished when Fallon clapped her hand over Laire's mouth. Wanting to move the conversation forward before any possible explosion between the two could take place, Larissa said, "So why me?"

Wulver settled in the chair, the smile and charm fading as weariness settled over his features. He half-opened his mouth before closing it, his gaze shifting away for a bare moment. His confusion was tangible. "We've searched and dug and researched and watched, but there is nothing about you that tells us what is going on."

That was not telling her anything she didn't already know. She pressed on. "Do you know how the spell works that the necromancers would use?"

"It isn't one spell. There is a final spell that would need to be cast at the end – the one that rips the realms asunder. That one doesn't change, but before that spell can be cast, certain requirements must be met. The problem we have is there are a lot of ways and a lot of roads to get things ready for that spell." Wulver's jaw tightened, and certainty once again infused his demeanor. "Bottom line is you are in danger. We still don't know why you've been targeted, and all the paths we've traveled thus far have led to dead ends. With you here, maybe together we can figure this out. Isn't that why you were going to meet us tonight, to get some answers?"

"Yes, by talking and working together, *not* to be treated like a criminal. I came to you in good faith, to answer questions and open up my life to you so we could get answers together. But now I'm in jail and while you can take your sweet time figuring out what's going on, my life will be in shambles. Isn't that special?"

"I promise I'll get you home as soon as possible."

"Forgive me for saying that your promises don't mean squat."

He drew in a deep breath, his eyes searching hers, as though he was trying to figure out how she worked, at least enough to say something that would have her agreeing to stay by her own free will.

The door creaked and opened and a man entered. He had curly ginger hair with sideburns and was wearing jeans and scuffed up tennis shoes, with a grey T-shirt under a battered dark brown leather jacket. He walked over to Wulver, leaning close and whispering into the leader's ear.

Wulver's eyebrows furrowed and he stared at ginger boy. Ginger's mouth turned down and he nodded, then left the room.

Laire, Fallon, and Aislynn looked on with curiosity. Not a sliver of sound reached Larissa, but from the way Wulver's mouth tightened and his eyes narrowed, she knew he didn't like what he heard.

His eyes settled back on her. "For having the cleanest record I've ever seen, a whole lot of people want to meet you. What is your secret?"

"Wulver," Fallon called. "What's going on?"

*Yes please, what the hell is happening now?*

Wulver sighed. He closed his eyes and scrunched up his face, the way people do when they're expecting an explosion. "The Oracle has summoned her."

"*Ah, hell no!*" Fallon said, and Larissa flinched. Wulver really could have warned her about the volume Fallon could achieve, at least given her some ear plugs. "What do you mean *summon*? We only just got her to the safety of the compound."

Wulver stood, facing the swordswoman. "The Oracle commands that Larissa be brought to her at moonrise."

"The Oracle can also feel the backside of my boot."

Anyone who irritated Fallon that much couldn't be all bad. This might be fun. And hey, she was an Oracle – hence the name. Maybe answers would finally be forthcoming.

Larissa stood, looking to Wulver. "Can she tell me why all this has been happening to me? Is that why she wants to see me?"

Wulver didn't look like he believed that was a possibility, but after a moment he plastered on a smile and said, "I don't know why you've been called, but yes, the Oracle may give you some answers."

"Wouldn't count on it," Fallon muttered.

Wulver pinned his gaze on Fallon, command and authority in his bearing. Yes, this man was leader here. "She is to go to the Oracle." *Do you understand?* was unsaid, but Larissa felt it.

Fallon crossed her arms, slouching back against the mirror. "Yeah, got it."

Wulver left the room. The second the door closed after him Laire started jumping, a huge smile on her face and her body shaking in repressed excitement. "I'll go, I'll go, I'll go! You don't even like the Oracle. Let me."

Before the first words were out of Laire's mouth, Fallon started to shake her head, and as soon as the green-haired woman took a breath, Fallon used it as her opportunity to say, "No way."

"Please please *please*."

"Let me rephrase. No way in the four hells."

Laire stopped jumping, a small pout coming to her lips. How she had been able to prevent an ankle fracture on those spikes, Larissa didn't know. "Why not?"

"Because if they have an orgy going on, you'll want to join. And if they don't have an orgy going on, you'll want to start one. I'll take Aislynn with me." Fallon looked over at Larissa. "Congratulations. You are about to do something many mortals dream about but few get to experience. You're about to meet the Oracle."

# CHAPTER TWENTY-FOUR

The acolyte was a young elf male, no more than hundred years old. His hair was shorn in the way of all those newly pledged to their necromancer master while the scar pattern on his chest denoted who his master was to those that knew the code. His eyes gleamed with a feral and fierce devotion, one the gargoyles had yet to crack.

Terak stood before him as he had the last several hours. "I ask again, why are you here trespassing on our lands? Your master knows my kind is resistant to your magic, so it is not in his best interest to court the wrath of gargoyles."

The high-pitched giggle teetered on the edge of sanity. "Perhaps my Master knows he has nothing to fear from a gargoyle obsessed with a worthless human woman. Tell me, Gargoyle, is what's between her legs so unique that you let it take you away from your Clan?"

There was nothing Terak wanted more than to feel flesh shred beneath his claws, but long training kept him still. This was the most the acolyte had offered all day. There would be time for vengeance later. Now there were only answers to be found.

"Not so worthless. You have been unstoppable in your quest for her. Why should only necromancers possess that type of power?"

For the first time, a gleam of intelligent cunning peeked out from behind the madness. "You don't even know her secret."

"I know you want her so badly you go against the Guild to collect her. What else do I need to know to realize her worth?" Only when the words were spoken did Terak realize their truth. He had been so focused on the necromancers and the new knowledge of their ultimate plan he never considered all the other avenues where danger now lurked. She was a prize of great worth. His stomach wrenched hard at all the ways she could be now used to further various interests.

"Our source never indicated you felt this way."

*Source?*

Betrayal.

A gargoyle was in league with this evil, feeding them information. Who? In exchange for what? He pushed the bitter burn away to think on later. To the acolyte he said, "I am *Mennak*. I am answerable to no one, and your master is pitiable if he does not know even that about my kind."

The acolyte made no reaction to the offense. Instead, his mad smile gleamed brighter. "Only time will tell us if your words are true, gargoyle. We should like to see you prove them."

And a gut-deep realization spread through Terak that he would get no more from the acolyte, no matter the methods he used.

Malek waited outside the thick cell doors. "Does anyone else know he is here?" Terak asked once he cleared the prison. Malek had been the one to find the acolyte, and had come straight to Terak.

"No, just as you ordered."

"You heard what the creature insinuated?" Terak wanted his second-in-command to gainsay him, to tell him he was wrong in thinking one of their kind turned on them.

Instead, Malek nodded. "I wish I did not believe it, but it makes sense."

Terak placed a hand on his shoulder. "At this moment, I trust only you. Keep watch on the grounds. With the capture of the acolyte, the necromancer may try to force a meeting with the betrayer."

Terak headed for his chambers, but was waylaid by Krikus. "There is an issue with the human woman," the old councilor said without preamble.

Cold, sick fear spread through his stomach. "Is she hurt?" and even he could hear the terror the tone held.

"She was captured by the Guild. We do not know where they hold her."

A powerful relief hit so hard he was dizzy, and he almost embarrassed himself with the need to lean against the wall. Instead, he forced his legs to stiffen and hold his weight upright.

His first instinct was to pursue her, to gather warriors and fight. But even if he knew where she was held, he could not leave. His Clan was in danger, and he needed to find the threat within. With the Guild she was safe.

Later, the Guild would pay for taking her. Now, they were the best option to keep her protected.

To Krikus, Terak said, "Send out our scouts to be on the lookout for her. As soon as she is found, they are to send word. We will take her back…

…by battle if necessary."

"You would betray me, Valry?"

She had arrived to her meeting with the accursed vampire with her shoulders squared and her head high, but now, as she saw Terak step from behind several rocks and Malek at his side, her body hunched over, losing her usual arrogance.

She reached out, beseeching. "This is not betrayal. I would never betray you. Everything I have done was so our people can become great again." She motioned to the vampire who was still several feet away. "He is here to offer a bargain."

"Which means you do not believe us great now, under my leadership and the leadership of my father. If that is the case, I wonder then why you would *not* betray me."

"You are a great leader, but you are blinded by a utopian vision of living in this world as equals among the other races, but they will never accept us. We must always live separate, and they must know our strength so they will never come against us!"

It should hurt more, the female with whom he had once meant to mate aligning herself with a man with the blood-red eyes, a mark of a true vampire and necromancer. It should tear at his chest, drive him to howl at the moon and claw the dirt around him.

And he did feel that, but for another female. Larissa was apart from him and the ache in his chest would not abate. He could not lean over and pull her toward him. He could not see her little chin lifting as she fought him or those blue eyes laughing and inviting him to share in her joy. All he could not do was tearing at him, pulling him apart at the seams.

He would get her back, and if the Guild fought him, he'd destroy them all.

The only emotion he could spare for Valry was anger, anger that she was keeping him from finding Larissa.

Betrayal or not, perhaps some good could come of this night if he could discover why it was Larissa these beings were obsessed with. Terak turned to the vampire. "What is your name?"

The vampire cocked his head in surprise. "You would speak to me, Terak, Clan Leader of the Gargoyles?"

"I would be a fool to not listen to your words now that you are here before me. Valry spoke of a bargain. Tell me what it is."

"I am Garof."

"And who is your master?"

"That does not concern you, Clan Leader. That knowledge will not affect the words I speak. I hope my lack of answer will not stop you from listening to my other words."

Terak inclined his head. Vampires never gave the name of their Master; it had been a desperate attempt, nothing more. "I will listen to your words. What actions I will take based upon them is not guaranteed."

"My people want the woman. She is needed for a spell."

"She is needed to rip the Realms apart, this I know." Terak watched the vampire closely, but to the vampire's credit, the only sign this might have been a surprise was an extra-long blink. "How would she accomplish such a task? Why her?"

Garof shook his head. "You do not need to know the specifics. What I am willing to divulge is that we need her and her alone. To possess her we would be willing to pay a very high price."

What did the vampire think to offer? "How high?"

"Since you know the ultimate purpose the woman would serve, you will understand when I say this. Once we return the Magic Realm to its former state, we will have gargoyles rule over all, second only to the necromancers."

They would never quit hunting her.

As Valry gasped and even Malek let out a grunt of surprise, this knowledge pounded through Terak. She would never be safe again. There was nothing he could do to blunt their interest. With his words and his covetous gaze, the vampire showed how much they desired her.

For him to stay with her was to put his Clan in the direct path of the necromancers. They would go from neutral parties to fierce enemies.

But to walk away from her was as good as handing her over to them.

She was sunshine. She was light and laughter and the key to a part of him that had sat, unused and rusty, since his mother had died. She was gentleness that surrounded a will of steel, and a fierce protectiveness to her family and her students and whoever else she considered her Clan.

She kept the secrets of a gargoyle and had fought to save him. She told him her secrets and let him wipe away her tears.

Calm descended, thick and complete.

She was his heart, his life, and he would forever protect her. Whatever he needed to do, whatever he needed to give up, he would keep her at his side and ally with whomever he must, as long as she was safe.

The vampire was watching him with careful eyes. This channel had to remain open, for the hope of future information. "What if the spell does not work? What will you give that will serve my people here, in this realm?"

The vampire looked surprised. "The Magic Realm will once again exist, Clan Leader."

"Do not talk to me of certainties. Yes, the Magic Realm may once again exist, but I will not make my people an enemy of several powerful Houses on that hope. I want to know what I will receive should this not come to pass."

"I would need to talk to my Master and ask him what he would wish to give." Garof nodded at Valry. "I will contact the female in our usual manner when I have a response for you."

"You speak of this one?" Terak grabbed Valry's wing and flung her toward Malek who caught and bound her.

"Terak, *no*. How can you do this, when you yourself are talking to the vampire?" She struggled against Malek's hold. "Let me go."

"This one," said Terak, ignoring Valry's pleas, "has betrayed her *Mennak* and kept secrets that might have placed my Clan in danger. Look at this female tonight and remember her face, Vampire, for you will never see it in the flesh again."

Garof smiled. "I have high expectations for our future conversation, Gargoyle. I will be in contact with you."

The vampire disappeared, teleporting away in less than a blink of time.

Valry cried as they flew back to the keep, struggling against the ropes that bound her. They landed among several warriors. Terak ignored the questioning gazes on him and told Malek, "Lock her away." Malek nodded and led her to the dungeons.

Before anyone could voice their questions, a cry of "*Mennak*!" sounded through the crowd. A warrior broke through and stood before Terak.

"What is it?" Terak asked.

"The warrior Fallon has been seen in the Wilderness with two other females entering the Oracle's domain. The one who spotted them wasn't certain who the other females were, but one of the females had blonde hair."

There was no need to hear anymore. Terak leapt from the parapet, letting the rage and adrenaline that had been banked to come to the fore and fuel him.

It was time to meet Fallon.

# CHAPTER TWENTY-FIVE

For the first time in her life, Larissa found herself in the area known as the Wilderness. Several miles from the city, it was a mini-city in its own right, except here you could find any race, any beast, or any magic.

Too dangerous, Dad had said when he forbade her or her brothers to ever go here, with the creatures that had only become known in the last few decades mingling with the humans who didn't feel the need to separate themselves from everything new the realms offered.

The building they pulled in front of was a dark-brown brick box, but the line of beings outside of the building was a sight from Larissa's wildest imaginings – neo-hippie fairies, elves in leather corsets and collars, dwarven drag queens, and even the occasional humanoid beast in a business suit.

Fallon and Aislynn rode in the front of the car, Aislynn driving. Car, what a laugh. Tank was more like it, everything thick and dark. Safe and suffocating.

From the vantage point of the middle seat and observing in the rearview mirror, Larissa watched as Fallon's expression got progressively darker throughout the trip, until now when it was near thunderous. "Should I be scared about meeting the Oracle?" She hated that she had to ask, making her appear weaker than she already felt.

Aislynn looked back and gave a reassuring smile. "Don't mind Fallon. She has issues with this place."

Fallon's lip curled. "Oh, of all the beings in that place, I'm the one with issues?"

"We're expected," Aislynn said, pointing toward the door.

"Fine, fine." Fallon looked back. "Stay with us, don't drink anything, and roll your eyes at whatever the bitch says."

"Fallon!"

Fallon didn't respond to Aislynn. She got out of the car and waited until Aislynn and Larissa lined behind her. Once they were ready, Fallon walked across the street, aggression projecting from every line of her body.

At either side of the entrance were two giants. Literal giants. They had to be about nine feet tall, both bald with grey-tinged skin. They were big and blocky, and Larissa didn't want to be anywhere near them.

Aislynn must have seen the question in her face because she leaned down. "Stone giants," she explained. "Not full-blooded though. That's why they're so small."

Larissa nodded, not sure what she could add to that.

Beside the stone giants was a man. He was human, unless excessive greasiness was a special characteristic of one of the new races. He was in charge of admittance – allowing entrance at his whim, denying those who seemed to have a problem with him putting his hand under their skirts. Anyone who voiced disappointment was given a look by one of the giants, after which they slunk away.

As they walked toward the door, something that looked like a cherub with a mustache zoomed around them. When he saw Fallon, a small scream erupted from him and he headed for the door, waving chubby arms. "Boss, she's here!"

Fallon approached, her gaze focused entirely on the greasy man. Aislynn was on lookout, taking in their surroundings and the people around them.

They stopped in front of the giants, ignoring the loud complaints of those in line they jumped in front of. Fallon said, "Seemus, nice to see you at the door today."

The oily man's lips pressed together, his eyes giving a slow rake over Fallon's body in an obvious and distasteful show of dominance. It might have worked if he wasn't noticeably shorter than the swordswoman. "You've been summoned, I assume?"

"Would I be here otherwise?"

"You have to leave the sword," Seemus said, taking a step back between the two stone giants, getting out of Fallon's reach while allowing the giants a clear path to her.

Fallon eyed the two giants and snorted. They did not like this probably rare display of fearlessness, for both brought themselves to their full height in preparation for a fight. Fallon took a step closer.

"Tenro goes where I go, and as I've been summoned, I'm going inside."

Seemus made a small motion with his hand and stepped back even farther inside the doorway. "I'm afraid my orders are very specific. No weapons ever. You need to go now, and tell Wulver to send someone more respectful."

"Which means you are denying me?" Fallon asked, and smiled. Larissa had seen rabid dogs snarl with more warmth. "After the day I've had, that is excellent news."

The stone giants took a step forward.


Inside the club, the silvery curtains that separated the front doorway from the club entrance billowed inward as Seemus crashed between them. He landed on the edge of the dance floor, out cold. If any of the beings noticed, it didn't stop them from dancing.

Fallon came through the door, stepping on Seemus's body as she entered. Aislynn was a little gentler, stepping over the unconscious man and directing Larissa to do the same.

Aislynn kept a hand on her elbow, but that pressure was nothing in comparison to all the other stimuli. Breathing wasn't the best idea here, as thick smoke and the earthy, sharp smells of herbs and spices – even money most were of a narcotic nature – clogged her sinuses. The lights went from too bright to deepest dark and back again in seconds, not letting eyes adjust. Underneath the too-loud music were snippets of conversation in dozens of languages, with most of them not in a human dialect.

Fallon led the way, her gait steady and sure as she made a path toward the back of the club, seeming not to take in any of the sights, though how she could be immune to the sight of the tall elf in a tuxedo dancing with the short, bearded dwarf in a wedding dress was a mystery.

What kind of place was this?

Better question, what kind of woman was this Oracle?

Fallon reached the back and flung aside a set of dark silk curtains to reveal a door. Without knocking, she opened it and stepped inside

It was *1001 Nights* in live action. Everyone here wore body-baring, jewel-toned outfits right out of a harem scene.

By the heat suffusing her face, Larissa knew she was sporting a mighty blush. Their actions belonged in a harem, people all around engaging in acts of hedonism that would make the most jaded courtesan blush.

*Dear gods, I never knew a man could do that. I need to find another cuss-out when some guy makes me really mad...*

"So *why the hell* did we need to come here to you?"

Fallon's pissed-off voice knocked through Larissa's shock. It took a few moments to focus on the swordswoman, standing a few feet away from a teal blue settee that adorned the middle of the room. The settee was surrounded by men and women, all of them tall and lithe and so beautiful Larissa had to check the urge to smooth her hair and clothes in their presence. The way Fallon stood blocked the person she was talking to.

A few steps closer, and the face of the Oracle came into view.

She looked human to Larissa's eyes – and it wasn't as if she was wearing a lot of clothing to hide any parts that might not be – but her coloring could best be described as *dipped in gold*. Velvety brown skin, thick dark hair, near-black eyes, but all held a deep golden sheen that was as beautiful as it was unusual. The woman was beyond stunning.

The Oracle said nothing at Fallon's outburst. The men and women surrounding her paid no attention to the swordswoman. They kept massaging the Oracle, the oil they used smelling sickly-sweet to Larissa's overworked nasal passages. When the Oracle tilted her head back, a man took the opportunity to lean in and press his lips to the hollow of her throat.

After long moments that had Fallon growing more agitated by the second, the Oracle finally spoke. "Oh, Fallon, you're here."

It looked like Fallon was tensing to attack the woman, but before she could, Aislynn sidled alongside her and grabbed her shoulder. "Let me take over now," she said to the redhead. Fallon's eyes still blazed, but she nodded, taking a step back.

Aislynn kneeled in front of the Oracle. "Great Oracle, we have come as requested."

The Oracle's attention was still on Fallon. She smiled, a lift of her lips designed to irritate. "You see, Fallon, this is how I should be approached. Watch and learn."

Fallon ground her teeth together and bent forward, her sword hand giving a little jerk.

Without turning, Aislynn lifted her hand and motioned Fallon to stay back. This scene or some variation thereof had to be a popular one.

The Oracle turned her attention to the elf and graced her with a blinding smile. The Oracle was a beautiful woman, but when she smiled she transformed into otherworldly. "Dearest Aislynn, it is so good to see you."

"It is always an honor to be in your presence," Aislynn replied. The words were said with the perfect balance of sincerity and warmth, and what should have sounded forced and phony became a lovely sentiment.

That dark-gold gaze turned toward Larissa. "Larissa Miller," the Oracle said. She had a rich, cultured voice, and Larissa straightened at the sound of it, half-remembered lessons in manners taking over. The Oracle smiled, and damned if it didn't look like she heard Larissa's thoughts. "It is lovely to meet you. You wouldn't believe how many people have you in the center of their minds right now."

Only one male mattered, the rest could go hang. "That's lovely, though I don't know why I deserve the sentiment. Would you have any clue why I'm suddenly so popular?"

The Oracle's smile was smug and a touch superior. Fallon's reactions were making more sense. "Now, now, I didn't bring you here to talk shop. You'll find out soon enough. Besides, your popularity has brought Terak into your life. How does it feel to be under the protection of a gargoyle? Have you become friends, or perhaps something more?"

She was the Oracle, so she probably knew everything that happened and everything that was going to happen. Fine, it was another piece of crazy Larissa needed to get used to. That didn't mean the first time she spoke of her feelings aloud it was going to be to this woman. Instead Larissa said, "Terak is a good protector. He's kept me safe while still trying to let me have my life."

One of the Oracle's female attendants rubbed oil into her bare feet. The Oracle made a little hum of pleasure, but still kept on with the conversation. "And yet he didn't protect you from being taken by Fallon."

"That was my fault. I was the one stupid enough to trust *her*," Larissa finished, using her thumb to point over at Fallon. Fallon looked supremely unconcerned. "And I walked right into a trap."

"Yes, Fallon is quite adept at deceptions with the right coaching, *aren't you*?" Fallon might have tried to make a hand gesture at that statement, but if she did, Aislynn was able to hide it quite well.

The Oracle stood, a lithe, graceful movement. She reached out to Larissa. "Come here, I have a gift for you."

No, Larissa really didn't want a gift from this woman, other than the gift of telling her exactly why a bunch of undead were after her. But the way all eyes were watching her, she probably didn't have the luxury of refusing at this moment, so she stepped forward. The Oracle took her hand, the dark skin soft and the touch delicate.

"I think," began the Oracle, "you enjoy being with the gargoyle more than you are letting on. But I understand a woman does not like giving up her secrets, especially before she knows what's going within the mind of a thick-headed male. You don't need to say anymore. I wish to give you this."

The Oracle handed her a small, leather bound booklet, about as thick as a pamphlet, and said, "You are a teacher, yes?"

It was nice of the Oracle to phrase things in the form of a question and let people feel they were imparting information. "Yes, I am."

"Excellent. I know teachers value learning, and this book has very valuable information on gargoyles. If Terak remains part of your life, this you'll want to know."

Larissa weighed it in her hand. "This is a very light history."

The Oracle arched one fine brow. "Why would I bother with that? This, my dear, is about how gargoyles mate."

*Huh.* So this was what dumbfounded felt like.

"Trust me, read that book. You'll like what you learn." The Oracle stepped back, though she didn't sit on the settee again. She looked at the elf. "Oh, and Aislynn? I need you to tell Fallon something."

"Yes, Oracle?" Aislynn answered, acting like it wasn't unusual to be receiving messages for a woman not two feet away.

The Oracle smiled, full of mischief and torment. "Tell her to get her sword ready. They're coming through the door."

Fallon bared her teeth even as she reached back and grabbed her sword. In a fluid movement she turned and ran, coming within a few feet of the doorway as the walls exploded.

This time the revelers were disturbed. Screams rent the air as a mass of bodies started running away from the chaos. Aislynn grabbed Larissa's arm, and displaying more strength than such an ethereal woman should ever possess, picked her up and toward a wall in the back.

"*Protect the Oracle*," came shouts from all around. The men and women, so languid moments ago, now held the same warrior postures of Fallon and Aislynn.

In the confusion, Larissa was thrown hard against a wall. Pain radiated through her back where she was hit, but it was manageable. She put down her hands against the wall to push away, only to feel a doorknob, thank gods. One turn confirmed it wasn't locked. It opened into an alleyway. One side was blocked off, so there was only one way to go.

Once she was at the end of the alley she glanced in both directions. Several blocks down on the right was lots of traffic and wandering beings. After one last look behind her to make sure no one had followed, she took off.

After several blocks of running the sidewalks became crowded. If it weren't for the mix of races she had never seen outside of books, it could have been any night on the town, with revelers searching for the next bar or club. She still stood out a little with her casual clothing and too quick breathing, but if ever there was a moment to celebrate being on the shorter side height wise it was now.

Head down, she walked fast and straight. Find a phone and call Michael. He'd be able to get to her. Piece of cake, though it would be a little easier if her ears weren't still buzzing from the earlier club noise.

A hand wrapped around her mouth and pulled her into an alleyway.

# CHAPTER TWENTY-SIX

Larissa's nails dug into the arm holding her as she kicked backwards. Another hand closed around her middle and a low buzz of sound started near her ear, gradually turning into words. "Calm, little human. You are safe."

She relaxed. That voice, that deep baritone meant safety. She withdrew her nails. The arms loosened enough that she could move, and she turned to face Terak.

"Thank gods." She threw herself against him with such force his body rocked back. She wrapped her arms around his neck, hugging him with all the strength in her body.

There was no hesitation as he returned the gesture. He brought her tight against him, his arms steel bands as they closed around her. His mouth rained small kisses against her temple. "You are safe. I have you. You are safe and they will never touch you again."

His wings flapped, taking them up into the air.

"I was so scared." Gods, his smell was so clean, warm and heady and such an amazing contrast from inside the club. *This* was what she wanted to be surrounded with. How could any drug be more potent than Terak close and warm and all hers?

His breath puffed across her ear and his lips never quite left her skin. "I would never stop searching for you, *never*. If I had to make war with the Guild for your safety, they would all be laid before me. I will never be separated from you."

They traveled in silence then, though Terak kept her close. As they approached her apartment, Terak's mood began to change. His relief was being replaced by silence and stillness. Once they entered the apartment the transformation was complete, as anger charged through every inch of his body. He was so tight she was almost surprised he wasn't vibrating.

He let her down, folding his wings around himself with a snap. He circled her, taking her in. "You left without me and my protection."

The words and tone were flat, but they held such anger he may as well been screaming for the knot they caused in her stomach.

"Terak." She took a cautious step toward him, holding out her hand the way she would to a growling junkyard dog. He stopped circling, and that was a good-enough sign to touch him, to rub his arm, plea and apology mixed together in the gesture. "I tried contacting you several times over two hours. I swear I did. I jumped on the balcony and I used that little silver ball you gave me, but neither worked. I didn't know what else to do."

"I never received any message. The ball is foolproof, it should have reached me." He shook his head. "It does not matter. You should not have gone! It was foolishness to leave." The flatness was now gone, and the walls vibrated with his anger.

"I had to!" He could be mad, but she wasn't going to be talked to like she was eight. "They lied and said the meeting was going to be an exchange of information. I never expected to be kidnapped, and I had my brother with me, so I wasn't alone. I had to take a chance to find out if they knew anything to help."

He made a sound of dismissal, wiping away her words with the swipe of his arm as he stomped away from her. "I told you not to trust the Guild, and I told you to never leave without me. You disobeyed my instructions. It is pure luck I was able to find you as quickly as I did."

"Excuse me?" Now he was pushing it. "If you were so worried, then you shouldn't have disappeared on me. I wasn't the one who ran away after kissing someone senseless!"

"I..." He straightened, wrapping himself in his usual dignity. "I did not run away."

"Sure seemed like that to me. For weeks every time I turned around I tripped over you, and then suddenly we share a kiss and you are nowhere to be found? What would you call that if not running away?"

"It was not running away. I needed to think upon the events of the last few days."

"Yeah, including how you kissed me."

"It was...it was..." He looked defeated. "Do you regret it?"

Talk about turning it around. Now she was on the defensive, looking into eyes filled with pain and hope. She pushed her hair back, ducking her head.

"I wouldn't say I regretted it," and she really shouldn't mumble like that, because she didn't want him to ask her to repeat what she said.

"Then what would you say?" he asked, his eyes sharpening.

"I'm…not unhappy it happened."

"Does that mean you are happy it occurred?"

Wasn't this leading the witness? Oh right, they weren't in court. "I would have preferred other circumstances."

"Such as?"

"Such as you not being engaged." Ha! There, couldn't argue with that one.

"Valry and I are no longer Intended."

Back the truck up. "What? When… How? Really?" Eloquence, thy name is Larissa Miller.

He studied her for several moments, and then he smiled.

He smiled.

A full-blown grin such as she had never seen on him. Happiness *radiated* from him in a way she'd never experienced before, and how was she supposed to respond when the sight was frying the synapses in her brain?

He advanced, walking toward her with a predatory grace he'd never displayed before. "You seem pleased by that news."

Who was this gargoyle? He had always been reserved, almost courtly in his bearing before, not this magnetic, determined animal stalking his prey. And by his direct stare, there was no doubt that his prey was her.

Since he was advancing, what else could she do but back up? "I need more details before I decide how I feel."

"What type of details, little human?"

"The usual – what happened, any chance of reconciliation, are you returning the engagement gifts?" Her back hit the wall and he was leaning over her, not allowing her any more movement.

He studied her, his eyes intense, almost scary in how focused they were on her. "What do you feel, Larissa?" and gods knew, she would admit to about anything if it meant that he kept saying her name in that exact voice.

She didn't know why he was no longer engaged, whether it was because of her words or some other reason. But it was time to move forward. If these last few weeks – hell, last few hours – had taught her anything, it was life was uncertain, and you needed to grab hold of the chances you were given, all the outside forces be damned.

His alien, beautiful face was right by hers, every line and plane as familiar as her own. A face she dreamed of belonging to a male she longed for. She reached up, stroking her finger over the grey skin. "I don't regret a moment of what's happened to me, because I found you in the middle of it all."

His head reared back inches, shock and hope and gratitude mixed together in his expression. He cupped her face, tilting her head back. His lips were warm with the right pressure, demanding she open to him without bullying her on it.

This was connection, soul-deep and scary in how right it was. His wings came around her, wrapping her in an embrace more consuming than any that only consisted of arms. Those wings brought them together, sinking skin into skin, and even that wasn't nearly close enough.

"Your lips are so soft," he said, pulling back the tiniest bit, as if parting hurt him. "All of you is so soft."

He didn't take her mouth again, but pressed his lips against the underside of her chin. With exquisite leisure he made his way down the side of her throat, only moving further after every inch had been explored.

She groaned. "Terak, what are you doing to me?"

He loved her breathy voice. He loved everything about her, but he especially loved she was now in his arms. "Do not humans enjoy this?" He licked her pulse point, the texture of her skin under his tongue a wonderful sensation. "Or this? Shall I tell you what gargoyles enjoy, little human? What a male will do when he has a female in his arms that he has dreamed about since the first moment he saw her?"

Her breathless *"Show me"* almost dropped him to his knees. Instead, he stepped back and pulled her shirt from her pants, ripping the front and scattering buttons. "I hurt every time I left you. You had me wanting, and it felt as if I would never be at ease again."

Her smile had an edge. She liked the torment she had put him through. "I need to make that up to you."

His clawed fingers traced the edge of lace on her bra. It was blue, the same blue of her eyes, and it offered her up to his mouth those plump, mouth - watering mounds. "Wearing this, *Meyja*, is apology enough."

He leaned down, his tongue tracing the edge of the lace. Her head fell backwards, offering him access to what he desired. "I love your tongue. I love how warm you are." She shook her head, as though trying to clear it. "What does *Meyja* mean?"

Coward he might be, but he wasn't ready to tell her yet. He could not chance her feelings not being the same as his, or worse, that they were, but she could not go against her family to accept him. "I will tell you after we defeat our enemy. This way you will have something pleasant to obsess over in the coming days."

Her frown told him what she thought of that, but there were ways to distract her. He stroked his claws over her stomach to her waistband and pulled the pants down her long legs.

She stood before him, bare except her undergarments. He needed to bury his face between her legs, let her taste dance on his tongue. She was warm and sweet and he needed her more than the air he breathed.

He picked her up, coming to his feet and carrying her to her bedroom. "Terak?" she asked, but stopped when he put her down on the bed.

"Shh, *Meyja*. Let me do this. I need you."

He nuzzled her through her blue panties, her little coils of hair crushing beneath his nose as he breathed deep her intoxicating fragrance.

His tongue came out and pushed against her through her panties. She groaned, wrapping her hands in his hair and holding on as if it was her only source of stability. "Oh gods yes, I do love that tongue."

He pulled the underwear to the side, and swiped his tongue over her bare sex.

Her cries dimly registered in his ears. She was pink and perfect, sweet with an undercurrent of tang.

Very much how she was in all other ways.

He wanted to take his time, bring her satisfaction over and over. His tongue moved on her and brought a long, keening cry to her lips. "Terak! Please."

"Please what?"

"I want to come. I want to come when it isn't my own hand bringing me satisfaction."

The thought of her touching herself flashed through his mind and he growled. She would do that for him one day soon.

But not now. Now she would come because of his tongue.

The little nub at the top of her sex was glistening, beckoning him. He surrounded it with his mouth, giving gentle pulls that had her gasping.

"Yes, Terak. Like that."

He pulled a little harder.

"I was wrong before. Just like that."

He smiled, and then went to work. She had the most decadent taste he had ever experienced, water after having survived crossing the desert.

The muscles in her thighs jumped under his hand, giving proof to her excitement. Her groans grew in volume, begging him to finish it.

Finally she keened, her back arching as the tremors against his tongue spoke of her climax.

Her body was pulsing in aftershock, the ripples driving him insane, because he wanted his cock inside her to experience it that way. He wanted to be deep inside her. He wanted to come in her as she clenched around him, marking her with his seed. Marking her as his woman in body as she had been in mind since the first moment he had seen her.

Her fingers uncurled from his hair, and she laughed. "I hope I didn't pull out any hair."

"A small loss considering what I have been given this night."

She smiled again, her face radiant. "That was fun. Maybe we can do other things now?"

A pounding at her door forced them apart and had him on his feet.


*Worst timing in the history of man.* "Who is it?" Larissa called out.

"Michael," came her brother's voice, loud and pissed with an undercurrent of scared, enough to remind her she never called her brother after being taken away from him to let him know she was all right.

Oops.

Terak looked at the door as if the thought of punching through it to get to the man on the other side was a good idea. She should probably prevent that. Larissa rubbed her hand over his chest. "He always did have the worst timing," she murmured.

His eyes blazed with more than interrupted lust. "He took you to the Guild. He allowed you to be harmed."

Warmth seeped through her over his fear for her, but it would do no good to allow this anger at her brother. "He didn't know what was going to happen, and he would never have knowingly allowed something to happen to me."

"It does not change the fact that he lost you."

The banging on her door started again. This was an argument they were going to have to have later. "He's my brother and he's not going away, so no matter how mad you are, you need to play nice, and you need to change into your human form."

# CHAPTER TWENTY-SEVEN

As soon as the door opened Michael grabbed Larissa by the upper arms. "You couldn't be bothered to call me? I was out of my head worried over you!"

Before she could reassure him, Terak came forward and pulled her away from Michael, placing her behind his now-human form. Great. Just what she needed, another overprotective male.

Now Michael's expression was turning thunderous as he stared at the male who would dare involve himself in family business. If they started a pissing contest, she was kicking them both out. "Michael, I'm fine. I'm fine."

He paid no attention to her, all his focus on Terak. "Who the hell do you think you are?"

Terak straightened at Michael's tone. If he had been in gargoyle form, his wings would have flared out. "I am her protector, and you will not touch her in such a way again."

"Terak," Larissa whispered, placing her hand on his back. "He was worried about me, and he didn't hurt me at all, I promise. You won't find a mark on me."

Michael had to step up the tension though. "Oh yes, the oh-so-great protector my sister loves to talk about. Got a question for you – if you're such a great protector, why couldn't my sister get hold of you today?"

Terak stood his ground. "There seems to be a problem with the magic. Though it should never have come to that, in the end it matters not. I would have returned soon. You should have waited for me. It was foolish of you to take her alone to meet with Guild members."

Michael's hands came to his hips. "I'm a cop, who the hell are you to talk to me about going into danger? Besides that, I don't try to control my sister."

Larissa would have snorted at that if she wasn't trying to keep attention away from her.

"So instead you willingly lead her into danger?" Terak bit back.

"Guys!" Larissa stepped out from behind Terak to get between the two males and pushed them apart. "Stop posturing. What's done is done. All we can do is learn from this and decide if we'd do something different next time."

Michael looked like he wanted to say more. Actually, he looked like he wanted to punch Terak. Probably the only thing stopping him was the fact that even in human form, it looked like punching Terak was more likely to cause him to break his fist than cause any damage to Terak. "I need to talk to my sister, and if you don't mind, I'd like to do it privately."

Terak crossed his arms over his chest. "I will not leave her."

It was a stare-off of epic proportions. Neither was backing down, and she was the chew-toy between them.

Then Michael's eyes flickered, and he stared hard, taking them both in – her hastily donned clothes, Terak's too-small shirt, her had-to-be swollen lips and lovemarked neck. As if a light switch had flipped, Michael now appeared a little green around the edges. "Did I interrupt something?"

Why did she feel like a teenager caught necking? Oh right, maybe because that was darn close to the truth. "Michael, that is none of your business."

He scrubbed his hands over his face, reeling away from them. "Oh gods, I did."

Well, this was awkward.

Terak stiffened behind her. When she turned his eyes were closed and his brow furrowed. "Terak?"

His eyes opened then, at first unfocused before returning to awareness. After he came back to himself he gave Michael a hard stare – which her brother handily returned – before he pulled her into the doorway of her bedroom, still in Michael's sight but beyond his hearing range. He put his mouth to her ear and whispered, "Malek has called me. There is need for me."

Terak looked none-to-happy. "Is anything wrong?"

His mouth thinned. "While I was not given details, there must be. Malek would not call otherwise."

Michael had the good manners not to try to listen in to their conversation, but he didn't leave their line of sight and his glare was focused on Terak.

She didn't want Terak to leave. Selfish, yes, but after the night she had she didn't want him anywhere out of her sight.

And after what had been going on not ten minutes ago, she wanted to finish what they had started. She was wet and achy, and thoughts of his mouth on hers and his cock pounding inside her took most of the available space inside her brain.

But his people needed him, and as much as the upcoming conversation would suck, she really needed to speak with Michael. "I promise I won't leave. You need to go and learn what's happening with your people."

He shook his head. "You are not safe here alone and I will not risk you again."

"Terak, your people need you."

"I need you to be safe."

The war was clear on his face. That he placed her welfare on the same level as his Clan humbled her, enveloped her in a warmth much gentler and sweeter than the inferno he had ignited in her minutes ago. "It would hurt me to know your people did not have you near when they needed you because of me. Go."

His mouth opened and closed several times, but no sound came out. His hands reached down and enveloped her face and he brought his forehead down to hers.

She brought her hands up to cover his. "Come back to me when you can. I'll be waiting."

His head lifted a little, his eyes opening and looking into hers. His gaze was clear and he allowed her to look at everything in him, past his barriers. It hurt, this gift of himself, but it was a welcome pain. "I will always come for you, little human. Never doubt that."

She nodded. "I know. Go."

In a shaky, stilted movement so unlike him, he turned from her and went out the front door, never stopping and never looking back, not even that last moment as the door closed behind him.

Even though he would be back, having him out of her sight had her heart crumpling. They were on the verge of something, and this interruption couldn't have been timed worse.

Michael cleared his throat. His patience was admirable and unexpected, but it was time to deal with him. "Michael, I was wrong to not call you as soon as I was safe, and I'm sorry. But you have no business talking to him like that. He saved me."

He looked at her, question in his eyes. "I'm confused, Ris. Who is this guy to you? First I thought he was a boyfriend, then an acquaintance who for some reason was guarding you, and now I have no clue."

She sat on her couch, looking around her room as different ways to tell Michael about Terak formed and were discarded. Her coat was lying by the balcony door. Funny how she didn't remember taking it off, but every second of Terak tearing off her shirt was seared into her brain. When she was ninety and rocking away in a nursing home, she'd still remember that moment.

"I told you once, he is special and I'd never regret that he had been in my life. That's still the truth. As for anything further, I'm not going to talk to you about it when we haven't even discussed it."

Michael sat down next to her. "I don't like it, but that's fair."

"How did you know I was back in the apartment?"

"When you were kidnapped I brought my unit in to help get you back. I had people everywhere, including watching here. My CO called me and said you were back. It might have been nice if he warned me about the guy with you, though."

Wait, if they were watching, wouldn't they have seen Terak with her? Why wouldn't they have been more worried about the appearance of a gargoyle and given Michael all the details?

But maybe they hadn't seen her enter. Maybe they simply saw the lights in her apartment go on, and called on that alone.

And maybe the little knot in her stomach was pure nerves and this sense of uneasiness was simply a remnant of a horrible night best forgotten, nothing more.

Maybe.

# CHAPTER TWENTY-EIGHT

Nalith stood out from among the crowd who were waiting, striding toward Terak even before his feet hit stone. "What is this, you imprison the future *Meyla*?"

His council member was walking a dangerous line. "You will not question me in such a way," Terak said. "I am sure you have heard of her crimes."

Larissa did not need to know this was the reason he was called away. Malek contacted him through the same magic means as the silver ball he had given Larissa, to tell him Nalith was inciting discord and close to advocating open rebellion, placing blame on Larissa and questioning why Terak was with her.

Nalith's voice rose in contemptuous rhythm, so all the surrounding warriors could hear. "I heard no crimes, only how the future mate of our Clan Leader was fulfilling her responsibility to us, in looking to make treaty with those who can assure the future safety of our Clan. You say we should not question you? I say the time for questioning you has been left for far too long. You have abandoned our

Clan, instead concentrating all your time on a human female who is unworthy."

His people were watching this battle. None seemed to be active in their support for Nalith, but many of their faces held a shadow of doubt.

Terak had made his decision this night. His decision – *his choice* – was Larissa. His Clan would either walk with him on this path and make their way together among the New Realms, or he would forge his own path while gargoyles stayed in the shadows and hidden in their keep.

Either way, the Clan's future would be decided tonight.

That didn't mean he would give up without a fight. "You would have as my mate one who would defy the desires of Clan and Council? Valry is no longer my Intended. She lost that privilege by conspiring with vampires. So careful Nalith, or I will think you were in league with Valry in her betrayal. Do you wish to be inside the prison as well?"

Nalith straightened to his full height "Is it so wrong I wished to hear how our people could be more powerful in this realm?"

"So do you admit you contacted the vampires with Valry?"

"With pride." Nalith's eyes blazed, his lips peeled back from his teeth. "I served to the best of my ability our strong *Meyla*, not our weak *Mennak*."

"Then in front of all the warriors assembled, you admit treason and dare try to make it appear noble? Did you see treaty with the necromancers as the way for the Clan to gain power, or for *you*?"

"You would have us bare our throats to humans and the Guild. I would have us rule over all."

"Except we would not." Terak raised his voice, a whiplash against Nalith's pathetic excuses. "We would be nothing except servants to necromancers, existing at their whims. I would rather ally and learn to live in this world than be nothing but cowed in front of the necromancers and a bully to all other races."

"You are like your father before you, too weak to walk in real power."

"What you call power I call cowardice – an inability to move forward and meet this realm and its challenges. I will not ally with evil because my own fear." He nodded to Malek. "Take him away."

Before Malek could step forward, Nalith brought out a short sword. "You think you are such a great leader? You call me a coward? I call you the dog of a human. I challenge you."

"You would fight me with a magical weapon for the challenge?"

Nalith smiled, a vitriolic twist of lips. "It is not forbidden, *Mennak*." The title dripped contempt as Nalith circled him, the sword before him.

For a coward, his hold on the sword was surprisingly good. There had been practice with this weapon. "Drop the sword. You will not be forgiven for this."

"Once you are dead and the pathetic leadership you have displayed is no longer in effect, I think I will not only be forgiven, but I will lead this Clan to a new age of gargoyles."

Nalith swiped at Terak and kept moving. Terak stayed away. Nalith was not a warrior, even if he could handle this weapon. A mistake would be made soon. Terak had to keep Nalith off balance and angered. In anger, mistakes were always made. "You think to be leader? If our enemies see you charge into battle the only way they would be hurt is by falling down in laughter. Younglings have more skill in battle than you."

"Spoken like a true savage. You have no skills save for your prowess on the battlefield, and you would demean those of us who truly rule the Clan."

Nalith lunged again, but his arm was overextended. That was the opening Terak needed. He grabbed Nalith's arm and wrapped his tail around one of Nalith's ankles. Nalith pulled back but overcompensated, and with Terak's tail still around his ankle, he could not right himself Nalith fell, and Terak grabbed the sword.

Several warriors came and restrained Nalith, taking him to the dungeon even as Nalith screamed about the mistake they were making in following Terak.

Malek approached Terak. "Is the human well?"

"Yes. She is unharmed. I saw her emerge from a side door during the assault on the club and collected her." Terak placed a hand on Malek's shoulder. "The attack was executed flawlessly. You did well. Were there any problems?"

"No. There were no injuries on either side, and everything went according to plan." Malek looked uneasy then, his head dropping a few inches. "The Oracle came up behind me. She told me you had the woman and asked if I could retreat because she wished to get her nails done."

"She is indeed a being unlike any other."

"That is one way to phrase it."

*"Mennak."* Krikus's voice cut through the low rumble of the remaining crowd.

Terak looked away from Malek. Krikus was striding through the crowd in battle armaments that gave reminder to his days as a great warrior before he became a Council member.

"Yes, Councilor?"

Krikus came to stand before him, metal bracers reflecting the light around them. "Was there any truth in Nalith's words?"

His people stood silent as they witnessed the second great clash of the evening. "Let us be plain. What is it you wish to know, Krikus?"

"Your Clan deserves to know the truth of the situation regarding the human."

The crowd had grown around him, wave upon wave of his people. There could be no more subterfuge. He would be the leader that would make his father – make Larissa – proud, or he would not be leader at all.

"I have only always wished for the good of my people. It has been what has guided me from the moment I have been born. However, Nalith has spoken some truth. I am lost without my little human. She is my mate, my *Meyja*," Terak said, ignoring the gasps that surrounded him. "And I proclaim her so in front of all of you. I will live at her side, and if the Clan cannot accept her as my mate, then I will leave the Clan."

Krikus alone seemed unsurprised by Terak's proclamation. "And to accept the human is to accept living among the other races of the realms, is that not true?"

"We no longer have the luxury of isolating ourselves."

Krikus stared him down, something the older gargoyle had not done since Terak was a boy. "You have given the Clan much to consider. You must allow Council and Clan time to discuss."

Krikus's words might say *consider*, but Terak knew. He had lost his Clan this night. They would not follow Nalith or Valry, but damage had been done and they would follow him no longer. He was strong enough he could hold on through sheer force, but no, that was not the leader he wished to be. If the Clan no longer wished to follow him, he would honor that wish.

Surprising, he thought it would hurt more. But Larissa's face blazed bright in dark places, and this decision was the easiest he had ever made. Terak nodded at Krikus and watched the older gargoyle depart, leaving him alone except for Malek. There was nothing more for him here, and he spread his wings for flight.

"*Mennak.*" Malek stopped him. The younger gargoyle looked vulnerable at that moment, a rare expression from Terak's second-in-command.

Terak gripped Malek's shoulder hard. "Calm, Malek. We both know how this will play out. You are ready for this role. I would not have selected you otherwise."

"I am not capable of being half the leader you have been, Terak."

"No, you will be greater. I will always be there if you have need of me. Be a good leader for our people. Guide them well. I am sorry I am leaving you with such a heavy burden, but none I have more faith in than you." With a final squeeze, Terak opened his wings to their full span and he took flight.

Malek's voice followed him. "Is she worth the loss of the Clan?"

*She is worth everything.*

# CHAPTER TWENTY-NINE

She was sleeping, his little human, her eyelashes soft shades under closed eyelids. Her lips made a little pout as she slept, as if she was waiting for a kiss. That was one request he would always grant.

He ghosted his lips over hers, bit by bit applying more pressure with each pass, until she woke. Those eyes opened, the room too dark to see their full color, but after the focused on him they relaxed, losing the lines of confusion and settling into happiness. "I'm sorry I fell asleep. It's been a long day."

He pushed her hair back from her cheek, the petal-soft skin sensitizing the nerve endings in his fingers. "Yes, it has. I wish I had the willpower to let you sleep as you need, but I could not wait that long to hear your voice again."

"You need to be careful saying things like that. A girl could get used to them."

"I am afraid I am unable to speak anything but the truth. I hope you can forgive me my bluntness."

She pushed herself up with one hand while her other hand stroked over the contours of his human face. "I guess I'll have to learn to manage."

He gathered her into his arms and laid her head against his chest. "You are very good to me, thank you."

For several minutes she stayed still in his arms, resting against him and occasionally rubbing her cheek against the spot over his heart.

She broke the silence. "Your heartbeat is different than a human's."

"Gargoyles have two hearts. No matter my outside appearance, I am not human."

She pushed back against his arms, giving herself enough space that she could look up into his face and meet his eyes. "Even looking at you now, seeing you in your shifted form, I'm very aware you are not human. I am here with a gargoyle, and I would have it no other way."

A weight he had not been aware of broke free inside him at her words. He swallowed hard to tamp down the shout of joy that threatened to escape. "In our creation myths, it is said gargoyles began as creatures created of magic. The first of us were created by wizards to be companions to humans, to be used however the humans desired. But the wizards made us too strong, and soon we overcame our masters and created the first of the Clans."

Her eyes widened, and he saw the scholarly part of her nature come to the fore. "Is that true?"

"How can anyone know the truth when magic is involved?" He could not help but smile at her chastened look. She was adorable, and brave, and sensual, and all his.

And he would wait no longer to make her his mate.

Terak lowered his voice, and was rewarded by her eyes half closing and her breathing becoming labored. "I know not. What I do know is gargoyles and humans are *compatible*."

He covered her mouth with his, a deep invasion that gave no mercy. She would have no doubt to the meaning of his words.

She met him stroke for stroke, his little warrior. She rose up on her knees so their mouths were level and brought her arms around his shoulders as she dug her nails into his back.

She was wearing a flimsy shirt and the same underwear she wore before. Her scent, that same scent that made his mouth water in desperation, wafted around their sanctuary and held him in thrall.

She was aggressive, crawling up his body for better leverage. She pushed into him, her tongue attacking his mouth. As she dominated him from above her hips worked on him, moving in the sensual rhythm he had seen her use many times as she danced while he watched from afar.

His hands wrapped around her hips, not to stop the little movements she made, but to encourage her to bring them closer, let him feel every delicious torment her body delivered to his. She obliged, and that sweet warmth between her thighs settled over his cock. At the desired sensation his hips shot forward in instinctive reaction. Without the fabric of her panties, he would have been inside her.

This unseated her, and she fell forward, her momentum startling him enough that he fell backward on the bed while she landed atop of him.

Her head picked up, embarrassment clear in the lines of her open mouth and wide eyes. But after a few moments she started laughing.

No sound was more dear to him, save her moans and cries when she came. "What is so funny, *Meyja?*"

Still chuckling, she ducked her head, discomfiture still evident. "We're both virgins. This situation might be hopeless."

He rolled her over so she was now on her back while he loomed above her. He nuzzled her behind her ear, making small moans erupt from her throat. "I may not have done anything yet, but I have imagined you naked and beneath me too many times to count." He leaned up and took off the shirt that hid her from his view, her bare breasts now visible to him. Her shocked gasp ended on a low moan, and her lower body started moving again.

With one finger he circled her tight nipple, the skin there pebbled and rougher than other areas of her body. But would she taste the same here, at this little pink area? His tongue laved over her, dampening the peak and tightening it further.

His teeth scraped over the nipple and he was rewarded with a low wail. He rolled it in his mouth, loving her taste here as everywhere else.

The only place she tasted better was between her legs.

One hand wandered over the gentle slope of her belly to delve into those little curls. She was panting, her legs coming apart to give him complete access. "Believe me when I say this, little human – I might not be perfect this night, but I won't stop until I have you coming apart in my arms."

She was wet and warm and perfect, as she had been earlier. "Terak, take off our clothing. I need skin."

Never would he deny her anything. Her undergarments were pulled from her body, followed by his pants, pulled with such haste he heard a rip as they came off him.

What did it matter? It didn't, not when she lay bare before him. "Spread your legs, *Meyja*. Spread your legs and let me feast."


*Meyja*. There was something so intimate, so sensual about the word. It rolled off Terak's tongue in a deep rumble, and her body went hot at the sound of it.

She had been half-serious in her conversation before about their experience, but the heat and conviction radiating from Terak indicated there was nothing to worry about.

His body was stunning, almost seven feet of thick, hard male, all hers for the taking.

She ran her tongue over her bottom lip. He seemed to like that, if the bobbing of his already hard cock was any indication. Gods, he *was* huge, as big as her imagination supplied that long-ago day.

It might take a little getting used to, but she was sure she was up for the task.

He climbed onto the bed, lowering himself between her legs. "There will not be any more interruptions from your family, will there?"

Poor Terak. What he suffered for her. "No. Michael has no desire to come anywhere near this place for quite a while."

He ran his fingernails up and down her thighs, raising goosebumps in his path. "Good. Because I do not think I could stop myself from killing the next person who interrupts me, a member of your Clan or no."

"I won't stop you. If I had a gun, I'd shoot him myself."

His fingers kept up their lazy glide until he grabbed her between her thighs and spread her legs, using his shoulders to hold them apart as he settled between them. "I am glad we are in agreement. Now, I wish to put my mouth to other uses."

Her hand shot down to push back on his head. "But you've already done that. Don't you want me to return the favor and do things to you?"

Not moving from where he rested, Terak grabbed her hand and gave each finger a kiss, nipping the littlest finger when he reached it. It was a quick pain, sharp but quickly forgotten. "I wish that very much, but not tonight. Tonight I want to gorge myself on you to convince myself this is not another dream."

"Well, how can I refuse?"

His mouth gave a quick curl into one of his almost smiles, but this one was different than others, the sensual cast reserved for this intimacy. "You are most generous. I thank you."

Those stormy grey eyes locked onto hers as his head lowered, his heated breath covering the damp flesh between her legs. His tongue peeked out, broad and flat and oh-so-talented. Oh yes, she would never forget how talented he was.

He gave a long swipe over her clit, the *zing* of sensation racing up her spine with only that little movement. "I wish to drink you down, but it would be best for you to remain wet. Therefore, I will only play here to make you come."

That sounded like a reasonable plan...and then thought processes ceased as his firm lips closed over her clit and with soft, sucking motions he brought her deeper into his mouth.

Her hands found themselves in his hair again as she held on while he played with her. His tongue would press into her, only to flick away when she pushed harder into him. She wailed, "Don't tease me."

Only for him to do it again.

Amidst this teasing one finger entered her, slow and gentle, a tentative stroke that sensitized her far more than it should. "Another finger."

He did, and now she was being stretched. She licked her lips, absorbing the newness of his actions, and in response Terak moaned. She opened her eyes to see Terak fixated on her face as he worked her body.

With his monstrous control he could do this to her all night, and that wasn't the area she wanted him to exert his control in. "Terak, I love this, but I want you in me. Please."

He let her go, rising above her and bringing his lips back to hers. The kiss was firm but his lips trembled. "You have not come yet."

"I'll come with you in me."

"But I have read it is difficult for a woman to achieve satisfaction that way."

He was so unsure, her warrior, looking down at her with anxious eyes. All because he wanted to please her. How did she get so lucky? "You read up on human mating habits?" she said, only allowing the most gentle tease into her voice.

Even at that a blush graced his cheeks. "I want you never to regret this."

"I never will. Now, come into me."

He entwined his fingers with hers as he settled between her legs. His skin was warm and rough, fine sandpaper against hers, and he squeezed her fingers as his hips pushed into hers.

It was fullness more than pain, a stretching no fingers could duplicate. His pace was slow, coming into her in small degrees until he seated himself fully in her.

"Larissa?"

It was only after they opened that she realized she had closed her eyes. "I'm fine. It feels nice and strange, but nice."

"I am not sure *nice* is the word most males wish to hear at this moment."

Her laughter bubbled forth, her gargoyle's sense of humor becoming ever more prominent and showing up at the most unusual times. She squeezed his hand harder, loving that he was here with her and that he was hers.

She raised her head and brushed her mouth against his, needing connection with him in every place her body would allow it.

Terak deepened the kiss and started to move within her, the pace slow at first.

*Nice* was also falling by the wayside, forced aside by the rekindling of the fire they shared earlier, a fire that had been banked by nervousness and the interruption of reality.

His moan told her he was experiencing it too. Their entwined hands he brought to rest on the bed by her head. His other hand he used to wrap her leg around his hip, giving him leverage and providing a different angle to thrust.

"*Holy hell!*" Dear gods, what was that *spot* he was hitting now, the one that had every pleasure center in her body sit up and start singing hallelujah?

His mouth went to her neck, kissing under her ear while his hips kept a steady rhythm to her moaning pleas. Those hips bucking into her were relentless.

The pressure was building in her, the same pattern Terak forced from her earlier in the evening. "Terak, I'm coming. Move, faster, move faster by *gods* move faster."

His mouth covered hers, his hand coming to bury itself in her hair as he did as he was instructed, burying himself to the hilt in her over and over in ever-quickening thrusts.

White was all she saw behind her eyelids while her body pulsed around him. She could feel every vein of his shaft as she squeezed him with the force of her orgasm.

Terak's low, pained groans sounded in her ear as he joined her, binding them together.

# CHAPTER THIRTY

Larissa was dozing on his chest, her hair splayed over his chest in a cascade he could not stop running his fingers through.

She stirred, her eyes opening to show him that glorious blue. After taking a moment to focus, a small smile played over her lips. "Hi," she said.

"Never have I seen anything more perfect than you at this moment."

She blushed deep red at that, her eyes refusing to meet his. "I think you are beautiful as well."

"My human form or my gargoyle self?

His tone was more hesitant than he would have wished. At his words, her gaze came back to his, all signs of embarrassment gone. She clasped his face between her two small hands. Such a soft prison. "Don't you know? Both. I find both so beautiful."

He kissed her, and everything – his love, his devotion, his *soul* – was in that kiss, hers for the taking.

They strained against each other, their bodies eager for a continuation of the pleasure of the night before. He stroked over her round, firm bottom and squeezed. She broke off the kiss, laughing and blushing. "I'm a little too sore for anything right now."

Instantly he sat up. "What do you need?"

She grabbed his arm, bringing him down. "I need you to cuddle me. Unless gargoyle males have as much a problem with that as human males apparently do."

"I do not ask my fellow warriors such things, but I always wish to be surrounded with you."

She cuddled against his shoulder. "Tell me a secret."

*You are my queen, you are my love, and I gladly leave my Clan for you.* He said, "My parents loved each other."

She raised her eyes to his. "That's a secret?"

"Remember I told you that the Clan Leader does not marry for love, he marries the strongest female for the sake of the Clan?"

She nodded. "And you told me the first night that you inherited from your father your title."

"In the Magic Realm, gargoyles were not one great Clan. There were several smaller Clans who were allies but did not answer to each other. My father was a great warrior, the Clan Leader of the largest and strongest of these scattered Clans. His Intended was the strongest, as was our custom."

"And your mother?"

"My mother's Clan was one of the smallest Clans. They were also a Clan with a greedy and unjust leader. His avarice caused the downfall of that Clan and the loss of many lives. The survivors sought my father to ask for admittance into his Clan."

Larissa went up on one elbow to look down at him. "What happened?"

"My father told me he took one look at her and knew he wanted no other female. But she was not deemed suitable."

"Why not?"

"Her mother was human."

Larissa's eyes went saucer wide. "Your mother was half-human?"

"Gargoyles can mate with humans, as well you should know," he added, leaning up to kiss her where neck met shoulder.

She giggled, squirming under his mouth. "Yes, but I didn't realize that there could be children."

"Perhaps there is more to our origin myth than merely a story to tell around the fire. Any child created in such a union is born a gargoyle. While not common, it is also not unheard of for a gargoyle to take a human mate."

The last humor left her face, and she worried her lower lip between her teeth. "But are such unions frowned on?"

"No more than a gargoyle taking as mate a gargoyle from another Clan. Until they prove themselves loyal to the Clan, they are regarded with suspicion."

"But you said that your mother was not accepted as worthy."

He brushed her long hair back, the multiple hues of blonde caressing his fingers. "What is acceptable for an ordinary Clan member is not always acceptable for the Leader of all. Is it not the same for humans?"

Her gaze lowered, her generous mouth turning down. "Yeah, I guess it is."

He lifted her chin so she would meet his gaze. "My father defied his Clan and married my mother."

Her expression could not settle on one emotion and flickered between hope and trepidation. "Were there any consequences?"

"My father was too strong for anyone in the Clan to take his title, but he was never seen in the same light again. When my mother died, he lost himself, for she was his world. That led to more talk about how he had been weak to mate with her. He died not long after."

Larissa stroked his face. "I'm so sorry."

He accepted her gentle caring and pushed his face into her hand. "It was long ago. But while I planned to return to my Clan's tradition and mate with the strongest female, I never once believed when they said loving my mother made my father weak. I saw him with her. I knew better than anyone – loving her only gave him strength. I always envied that he could mate with the female he loved while I could not."

"Then why go back to the old ways?"

"After the Great Collision, the various Clans needed to band together if we were to survive in this new world. This was not an easy process. While the Clans had always been allies, this did not mean the various factions were friends. In order to bring some stability to the Clans, I needed to make clear my intention of honoring the old ways."

She stroked his cheek with the back of her fingers. "Like I said, a good leader."

He rolled her over underneath him, kissing her. "Terak-"

"You are still sore, little human. This does not mean I cannot kiss it to make it better."

She was sighing as he kissed down her body. "Tell me secrets of yours," he said, before licking a nipple.

"Mmmm," she groaned in appreciation. "Let's see. I'm allergic to peanut butter."

"I'm very sorry to hear it."

"I'm double-jointed in a lot of areas."

"This explains much of what you did last night," he said, spreading her legs and anchoring his shoulders between them.

"And I was…oh *gods,* Terak. Do that again."

"I am yours to command."

# CHAPTER THIRTY-ONE

*Terak leaned her over the bed. The sheet was cool as it slid over her nipples but behind her, he was an inferno, his thighs behind her, his cock rubbing the valley between her thighs...*

A knock sounded at the entrance of the teacher's lounge and Taneasha Jackson stuck her head in. "Miss Miller?"

Maybe fantasizing about her sex life during the school day *wasn't* the best idea ever, even if she was on a break. Larissa drew in a deep breath and hoped her voice was steady when she said, "Yes?"

Taneasha looked nervous, her eyes darting to the side before coming to meet hers again. "I was wondering if I could talk to you?"

The girl's worried tone was enough to shake off any vestiges of embarrassment. Larissa motioned with her hand. "Of course, come in."

Taneasha made sure the door was closed before walked to stand before Larissa and started talking again. "Miss Miller, I need to talk to you about something important. But before we start, I need you to promise you won't get upset with me."

*Oh no.* Was Taneasha pregnant? On drugs? Larissa took her hand. "I promise I'll never get upset. I always want you to feel like you can come to me."

Taneasha nodded, licking her lips. "Miss Miller... I'm studying magic."

It was so far from what Larissa was expecting that full comprehension took several long moments. "Excuse me?"

"My mom forbade it, but I love it so much. I have a gift for it, my Master – that's what you call your magic teacher – he told me so."

This was not good. This was very not good, and Larissa's stomach dropped as horrifying possibilities for the girl in front of her flitted through her mind. "Taneasha, this is serious. You can't practice without the proper guidance. Magic is regulated for a reason, and it is always forbidden within the city."

"I know, but I couldn't pass up this opportunity to learn. My family would never have permitted it if I asked them."

No, Larissa knew enough about Taneasha's family to know it was not even the remotest possibility. She ran her hands through her hair. She was bound by oath to report this, but if she did, this girl would be severely punished. "Taneasha-"

Before Larissa could finish, Taneasha broke in. "Miss Miller, I told you this because something bad is happening to you."

That caught Larissa's attention. "What?"

"My Master says that once you start learning magic, you begin to feel when things aren't right with the people you care about and...well..." she blushed and looked away, then brought her attention back to Larissa. "Anyway, I've been having a bad feeling about you, so I've been casting spells, on my own and with my Master's help. They are meant for your protection and your welfare. And I've discovered some things."

Taneasha looked around, and then, from her backpack, she brought forth a globe. "Don't touch this, just look into it."

Larissa did. She was looking from someone's point of view, though whose was anyone's guess.

The mystery person walked into a large grove. From the looks of the grounds it had to be sometime in summer, early autumn at the latest.

As soon as the mystery person laid eyes on the female in the distance, they stopped.

It was the Oracle. She was wearing more than what she wore at the club, but not by much. A diaphanous white gown, with a square neck but high slits running along both thighs. She wore a gold collar and large gold cuff bracelets.

"Very punctual, Clan Leader of the Gargoyles."

And Terak's voice answered, "I am grateful I can say the same for you, Oracle."

Larissa was seeing through Terak's eyes.

She wasn't going to invade Terak's mind like this. About to pick up the globe and give it back to Taneasha, she paused when she heard the Oracle say, "Her name is Larissa Miller."

"And what care I about a human woman? Gargoyles are not bodyguards, nor are we your lackeys."

"I am not asking you to watch the woman for my sake, Clan Leader, but for you and for your Clan."

"What do you mean?"

"She is connected to the future of your Clan. Guard her well." With that pronouncement, the Oracle turned to leave.

"What do you mean?" Terak called after her. "How is she important? What am I to guard her against? I demand answers."

The Oracle looked over her shoulder and smiled. "Feel free to make an appointment. I believe I'm free in a few years."

The scene shifted, and now as Terak Larissa was looking upon many arguing gargoyles. Valry stood. "Have we sunk so low as to bow before the Oracle?"

"The Oracle has never been wrong," called a voice from the back.

"How can she be, when she makes such vague pronouncements? Merely by the act of being observed, this human becomes important to our Clan as she has taken our *Mennak* away from us for long periods of time. We have no use for the outside world, especially for a woman such as this, one who lives in the confines of the *human*-only city. Think she cares about gargoyles?"

Loud agreement followed the words, with shouts and stomping of feet. Malek stood. "While I will not say I am in complete disagreement with Valry's words, I am not so eager to cast off the words of the Oracle. I would wish to observe the human for a period of time. What can that hurt?"

Larissa-as-Terak stood. "I have heard all your words. All of it wise counsel, but I must choose a path. I choose to watch the human. While I do not trust the Oracle, I will not ignore her for no reason other than pride."

The scene faded, replaced by other. Now the scenes sped up.

Her. It was Terak watching her, before they had ever met.

She saw the seasons change. How long had he been watching her – two, three months?

And then the bottom dropped out of her stomach.

The building across the street. The protective presence she sometimes wondered about, always attributing to an overactive imagination.

Stupid. Stupid woman. Why the hell didn't you ever question anything? Why did you never question Terak?

Because everything had always been going so fast. There never seemed to be time to sit still and think.

Terak hadn't shown up as some good Samaritan who happened to pass by. He'd been watching her for a long time.

"Don't cry, Miss Miller." Taneasha covered Larissa's hand with her own. With her other hand, Larissa put her fingertips to her cheek, shocked that tears covered the surface.

"I'm so sorry, but you have to see one more thing."

Again she was looking from what she assumed was Terak's point of view. This time he was looking at a man.

Red eyes. No, not a man – a vampire.

They were in a wooded area, the light dim but not yet full dark, so it had to either be at sunrise or sunset. The trees contained the full spectrum of color, which meant this hadn't happened very long ago. The vampire spoke first. "We need her and her alone. To possess her we would be willing to pay a very high price."

The vampire had to mean *her*. He was talking to Terak about her.

"How high?"

No, no. That can't be. Terak was setting him up, there was some kind of trap being planned at that exact moment. He could not be asking what this vampire would give in exchange for her.

"When we return the Magic Realm to its former state, gargoyles will rule over all, second only to the necromancers."

Any moment, a band of gargoyles would jump out and trap the vampire. Any moment.

Any moment.

"I need time to consider my options. How do I contact you to reopen negotiations?"

The little ball went white.

The heater in the school room kicked on, blowing hot air directly overhead. Outside the door the five-minute warning bell rang, indicating that class would be over soon. A couple doors opened, and a low hum of voices drifted on air currents.

All so normal. How could everything be so normal? Shouldn't this much pain be heralded by some change: a blizzard, a volcanic explosion? Shouldn't something happen in the world when her heart shriveled in her chest?

Terak had betrayed her.

He had been watching her for months, planning to give her to the vampires since the beginning.

Helping her? He probably was keeping her safe to get better terms for his Clan.

Taneasha wrapped Larissa's hand with her own. "Miss Miller, I know they're watching you right now. I can cast a spell to get you out of here without them seeing. Do you want that? I can take you to my Master and he can help."

"Yes." She'd use Taneasha's help to get away from them, then she'd go home. She'd tell Dad everything and let him figure out the next step, because she was done. She was finished being terrorized and bullied and made love to…

A sob escaped her throat, and Larissa put her face down into her cupped hands. She dug her fingers into the skin of her face and forced herself to calm down. This was not the place to fall apart.

Taneasha stroked her hair. "Right after school, meet me at the gym. I'll have everything ready, and we'll get you to safety."

# CHAPTER THIRTY-TWO

Taneasha dragged her through the back gate behind the gym. Larissa didn't ask where she got the key when only the gym teacher was supposed to have it. Wondering about that was for later, after she avoided Terak and got to Taneasha's house.

A car idled at the curb, and Taneasha got in without hesitation, her hand wrapped around Larissa's wrist in a death lock. Larissa was pulled in, the door shut behind her, and the car took off, tires squealing as they peeled away from the curb.

As they rode, Larissa's mind became a jumble. Images of Terak from last night overlapping with the conversations that little ball showed her, and always present were the eyes of that vampire, glowing red as they bartered her life the same way someone would for a piece of meat.

The car went over a bump hard enough that Larissa was jostled in her seat and her mind came back to the present. She looked out the window, unable to place where they were. "Taneasha, this isn't the way to your house."

"I couldn't take you to my house. Too many questions." Taneasha looked around as though to assure herself that they weren't being followed. "Don't worry, Miss Miller. They'll take care of the gargoyle."

Unease trickled through Larissa. "Who are *they*?"

"My Master's other students. They were told to look out for the gargoyle."

"You never mentioned anything about that."

Taneasha looked out the side window, her attention away from Larissa. "I'm getting you to safety, so don't worry about anything."

Maybe it was because she was in the *very* unfamiliar position of being out of control around a student, but Larissa's spine began to tingle, waves of warning electrifying her nerve endings and making their presence known. "Let me out at City Hall, Taneasha. There are people there I know can help me."

"None like my Master, though."

"Yes, your master is very kind to offer…his?…services, but I want out."

"We're already where you need to be."

At that the car stopped and Taneasha started to open the door. Larissa put her hand over Taneasha's arm to stop the girl from leaving. "Taneasha, where are we?"

"We're going to meet my Master."

"I want to go home."

Taneasha's face changed, and the bright, studious, shy girl Larissa knew from class was replaced with this sly creature before her. "But Miss Miller, it took so much to bring you here."

Taneasha jerked her arm away and left the car.

Stupid. Stupid, stupid, stupid, stupid, stupid. How stupid could one woman be? Gods, she never thought Taneasha could betray her, but she should have known better. She should have called her brother.

Larissa drew in a deep breath, using the exhale to center her thoughts. She looked around, but could see nothing in here that could be used as a weapon.

"Come out, Larissa Miller."

The voice was male, though not as commanding as it wanted to be. She didn't want to be in the position of having someone or something reach in and pull her out, so Larissa exited the car.

It was the vampire from the sphere, the one who offered Terak power in exchange for her. Taneasha was at his side, a little puppy awaiting praise.

Without taking his eyes from Larissa, the vampire ran his hand over Taneasha's long braids. "Excellent, Taneasha. You have done well."

Taneasha preened under his praise, her eyes almost closed and her neck arched back so now the puppy was asking for a scratch under its chin.

"Larissa Miller, I am Garof," the vampire said. "You have been a very difficult woman to find."

The driver's side car door opened, and a young man came out. Probably human, but his size and the gun at his shoulder said disregarding him would be a mistake. Larissa focused on the vampire. "Can't say I'm sorry about that."

"No, I don't suppose you are."

Breathing helped center her. She had power, meager as it might be at this moment. These *things* needed her alive for some reason. They had not gone to all this trouble and suffered all those losses to kill her now.

The vampire held up a ring. "I need you to hold out your hand, Miss Miller. I need to try something on you."

"Don't think you're coming anywhere near me with that."

"You can hold out your hand and I shall put this on you in a very simple process, or you can resist and I shall use force to make this happen. Is this truly the time to make your stand?"

When put like that, no, it wasn't. Larissa held out her hand, fingers spread wide to let him put on the damn ring.

Without touching her he slid it over her forefinger. Only when darkness hit her vision did Larissa realize she had closed her eyes against whatever this ring was supposed to do to her. She opened them and saw a plain silver band resting on her finger, comfortable and quiet and so innocuous a vampire should not have it in his possession.

But while the ring looked innocuous, the smile on the vampire's face was anything but. His sick joy radiated out from him, and a shower would be nowhere enough to make her feel clean again.

She ripped the ring off her finger and threw it at him. "There. Whatever you needed to know, you know."

"Yes, I do, Miss Miller. You are perfect for what we need."

"Shove it, I'm not helping you. I know what you are trying to do, and I will not take part in that."

The vampire sneered at her. "You think not, a pitiable excuse for a human like you?" He laughed, contempt in the sound. "You amuse me. You espouse such grandiose statements, but at the first pressure you'll break. All your kind do."

"Go fuck yourself. No matter what you do to me, I'm not helping you." Brave words, but the more he spoke, the smaller she collapsed inside. Gods, she wasn't a warrior. How was she going to stay strong?

The vampire smirked at her. "You think we'll hurt you? You are mistaken. We would not touch you. We need you. This one, though," and he grabbed Taneasha by the hair, making her cry out as he dragged her beside him. "We do not need her."

There was no sly creature here. Now all that was before her was a scared girl who had tried to break away from her family in the stupidest way possible, and was now confronted with the price.

Taneasha held out her hand toward Larissa. "Miss Miller!"

"Get away from her!"

The vampire regarded her coldly. "If you do not do as I say, I will skin this girl alive before your eyes. And if that does not make you change your mind, I will capture another of your students and do the same thing tomorrow. And the day after. And the day after. And I will continue until you agree to help."

Taneasha was screaming, spittle dripping down her mouth. Cold sweat broke out over Larissa's skin as nausea threatened with every breath she took. "I'll do it. Please don't hurt her."

"That easy?" He threw Taneasha into the arms of a waiting male. "And here I thought you weren't going to help us. So you'll sacrifice the entire realm for a few pathetic brats. Or maybe you'll sacrifice the realm to appease your own conscience, so instead of feeling like a murderer, you can cry and wail about how you were tricked." The vampire smirked. "Pathetic."

To the men, he said, "Get ready."

# CHAPTER THIRTY-THREE

Wulver strode down the corridor to the meeting room, stopping inside the doorframe as Fallon's raised voice filtered into the corridor. "Next time I see the Oracle I'm going to take one of those spiky shoes she likes to wear and nail her in the *throat*!"

Fallon and Aislynn were both present. Aislynn noticed him first, shaking her head as well as a small shrug to her shoulders, a *What can you do?* move. For her part, Fallon was standing in the middle of the room, hands on her hips and posture as aggressive and aggrieved as it got outside of a battlefield, that sword of hers looking as if it was practically vibrating on her back. He might need to order her to the sparring rooms tonight. Maybe Rorth would be brave enough to partner her.

Wulver leaned against the door. Might as well get comfy while dealing with the seething swordswoman. "Kyo's not too happy with the circumstances, either."

Fallon's gold eyes were hard behind narrowed eyelids, her mouth a compressed line so tight there was no delineation between lip and jaw. "Then he should have had the balls to deny the Oracle.

Larissa Miller was here. We had her safe, we could have figured everything out, and instead we had to play games."

In her naiveté, in her constant fight against the powers surrounding them, this was where Fallon's weakness lay. While Wulver had a few moments when he envied her fight, times like this weren't among them. "When don't we play games? When aren't we at the whims of this god or that force? You talk like this is a rare occurrence."

A muscle ticked at where her jawline met her throat, but she didn't answer. Aislynn jumped in, no doubt to calm the negative energy vibrating in the room. "What are we going to do about Larissa Miller now?"

Wulver shook his head. "We are not to go near her unless it's a direct order from Kyo."

That started Fallon up again. She threw up her hands in a violent motion and started pacing again, though this time she kept her focus fixed on him. "Fuck, Wulver! She needs to be here! I don't know how the hell she fits into their plans, but they want her bad. I don't want to be sitting here while she plays ga-ga eyes with a gargoyle!"

He'd already had enough crap dealing with Kyo this morning. He didn't feel like going through everything again because Fallon couldn't accept reality. He growled as any alpha answering a challenge would. "It's over," he said, and even to his own ears his voice was deeper, with an echo of a wild animal running through it. "And you will not touch her. Am. I. Understood?"

Fallon's jaw worked as she stared down Wulver. Something flickered behind her eyes. It reminded

Wulver of a lizard, that inner eyelid they had that would close and reopen. It was so fast it barely registered in the conscious mind, but it left him unsettled. Abruptly, Fallon relaxed her shoulders and took a step back, her arms coming to hang beside her body. "Yeah. I understand."

Wulver breathed deep, relaxing his own muscles that locked during the argument while he struggled to control the alpha roaring in his head to pin her into submission, bare her throat and feel his teeth digging into the soft flesh, taste blood on his tongue. He turned his attention to Aislynn to help gain control. "We have other problems to deal with now. Merc took the job and the spellbook is under his control."

Aislynn's calm acceptance went a long way to help him regain control. Her jaw tightened for only a moment, but her voice was even when she spoke. "This is unhappy news, but not a surprise. It was a matter of when, not if. What of Rhaum and the Dream Crafter?"

Fallon must have decided to keep a lid on any more emotional displays to keep tension levels at bay. She replied, "Inara tells me that he expects to have her in a couple weeks and to be ready for his mini-majesty's summons when the time comes."

If Rhaum said he would have her, it was as good as done. "I'll want you and Laire to meet with her and explain the situation."

Fallon's mouth quirked, but her eyes still held that unsettling flicker. "Sure. Why not? I always enjoy playing puppet master to someone's life."

Before the conversation could go any further, the building shook violently motions, which had the three of them scrambling to stay on their feet. "What the-"

The shaking stopped and deep bellows sounded from the corridors, followed by the clang of sword on sword and high-pitched screams of pain.

Wulver spun away and ran toward the sounds of fighting. Before him, orcs and goblins overran every free inch of space, their mottled green-skinned bodies blocking exits and using swords, axes, and bows to strike down anyone who came out to fight them.

As soon as he was close to the main section Wulver leapt. The shifting pain within was dim, far away, easily ignored. Bones lengthened and teeth sharpened and senses magnified. With a hungry growl he crashed into the largest of the orcs. His jaws clamped over the creature's face, tearing away skin and bone before he ripped into the thing's throat, disgusting sludge coating his tongue and sulfur clogging his nostrils.

Aislynn's arrows whizzed by his head as the archer stayed back to rain down death. Fallon took up position beside Wulver and in concert they destroyed their enemies. Orc after orc stepped close to the fighting Fallon, only to have Aislynn's arrows bring them down. Fallon twisted Tenro and plunged the sword into the chest of the creature in front of her. Before she could yank her sword back out an orc attacked from behind. She kicked back to hit the creature in the knee, bringing him down. Freeing Tenro, she sliced the orc in half and used the momentum to get the orc who came at her next.

Aislynn's arrows flew past, striking some of the orcs in the distance. Pandemonium erupted across the control room. For every enemy brought down, three more took its place.

Darkness swirled across the floor and Shadow rose to join the fight, taking out a goblin at Aislynn's back. The elf tipped Wulver a quick smile but did not stop her assault on the advancing hordes.

A ball of fire erupted in the middle of the latest group of goblins, creating piles of flame and ash and the explosion knocking down several nearby.

Fallon turned. "Dammit Laire, what took so long?"

Laire shrugged. "Had to find my shoes." Motioning with her fingers, she brought down bolts of lightning from the ceiling and fried the orcs in front of them. "The whole place is in chaos. Everywhere needs help."

Laire began to say more, but a large orc came behind her. Fallon grabbed a long dagger from her waist and threw it, piercing the orc in the eye. The dead creature would have crashed into the mage if Fallon hadn't pushed her to the side.

Undaunted, Laire looked at the dead orc and shivered. "That would have been ugly."

"That's why mages stay at a safe distance. How are you on spells?"

"Medium."

There were still large groups of enemies. Fallon hefted Tenro. "Stay back and save power for the big stuff. Tell us what happened while I'm kicking some ass here." And with that, Fallon charged back into the melee and dragged a goblin away from a young female healer who was being pulled out of a nearby room. "How the fuck did they get past the barrier?"

Laire crossed her arms and leaned against the wall as Shadow vivisected a particularly ugly specimen ten feet in front of her. "Suicide onslaught. There were so many who hit at once the barrier was overwhelmed."

Aislynn frowned before she let loose an arrow that brought down a hanging screen, killing several things that were under it. "It would have taken hundreds to do that, perhaps thousands."

Laire's expression was uncharacteristically somber. "Yeah."

Aislynn shook her head in disbelief, risking a glance away from the battle toward the mage. "What are they after? What can they expect from this?"

A fresh batch appeared in the doorway, and Laire groaned. "Gods, how many are there? Can't they stop coming? Hang on. Fallon, at the entrance!"

At Laire's scream, all eyes turned toward the gathering across the room, to see Larissa Miller in the middle of the pack of enemies. Fallon yelled, "Time to use magic. Laire, get her."

Laire created another ball in her hands that looked like an overgrown soap bubble. She aimed it and threw it at Larissa, hitting the woman dead center of her torso.

Nothing happened.

Laire stared at her hands, then at Larissa. Laire's mouth moved, though no sound came out. Then her eyes widened, and all color fled to leave nothing but a chalky residue behind. "Oh gods." Laire voice was low and terrified.

"Laire?" Aislynn's voice held uncertainty, seeing their normally unflappable mage become this upset.

"She's a null. That's why they are after her. She's a *null!*"

Fallon got knocked over and fell to the ground. Before the orc could land another blow, she flipped over in a handstand and brought Tenro up to slice the orc between his legs, from crotch to brainpan. Without pausing she pivoted to bring the sword down and cleave another orc in two.

Aislynn let loose several more arrows to take down the creatures around Larissa. The arrows struck true, but as soon as one orc fell, another took his place. Whatever Larissa was involved in was their primary goal. "Laire, what do we do about Larissa? What the hell is a *null?*"

Backing into a corner, Laire muttered to herself before crying out, "The vault! They're using her to get into the vault!"

Aislynn could see it wasn't orcs and goblins that surrounded Larissa. A necromancer and his acolyte were behind her. They made their way to the elevator that led to the vault, unconcerned with the battle that raged around them.

Laire darted across the battle scene, her focus on Larissa and the necromancer.

"Laire, *wait!*" Aislynn cried out. The mage didn't stop, so Aislynn followed. An orc appeared in front of her. Aislynn jumped onto its shoulder, aiming an arrow and firing into his forehead before catapulting over him.

A troll tore across the floor and headed straight for Laire. She turned and cast a quick barrier in front of her, but the troll threw himself against it and hurtled the mage across the floor.

Wulver jumped on him, his claws tearing a hole into the troll's chest. While the creature was trying to throw Wulver off, Aislynn drew back and shot an arrow into that hole. The troll howled in pain, and Aislynn fired off several more.

Suddenly, as one, the orcs and goblins lifted their heads. The next moment they disappeared, magic letting them escape the building faster than the speed of thought, leaving blood and chaos and the bodies of their dead behind.

Wulver turned back into his human form, blood-drenched and eyes blazing as he came to stand before Laire. "What the fuck happened?"

Aislynn helped a shaky Laire onto her feet. "Laire, what were you saying before?"

"The vault." Laire brought her hand up to her bleeding head and winced. "They wanted the vault."

Wulver and Fallon took off, while Aislynn helped Laire before they went down to the vault as well. The mage and the elf entered the vault area in time to hear Wulver yell, "*Gods damn*, how could they have done this?"

The vault door, one of the most magically protected items in the entire world, was hanging off its hinges. Items were scattered in sparse clutter while row upon row of shelving was empty. While not everything was taken, even someone with no knowledge of the contents could tell it was sacked.

Wulver hit a comm panel. "Tec, talk to me."

A posh British accent replied. "Fully half our people are damaged, over fifty confirmed casualties, which includes several of our healers. I've made the call for back-up, but that will not be a quick process. I'm compiling what has been taken from the vault and will be finished shortly."

"Get down here as soon as you have that list." Wulver turned to Laire. "How did they get into the vault? A hundred mages working together shouldn't have been able to break it open, and a lone vampire waltzes in here and does just that?"

"Larissa Miller. She's a null. Magic has no effect on her. Walking into that vault was as easy for her as walking into a grocery store." Laire began banging her knuckles into her forehead. "I should have caught it. I should have thought."

Fallon grabbed Laire's hand. "Stop the crazy. How could you have known?"

"She was born at the Great Collision. I concentrated on the fact that magical powers never materialized, but the ability to not be affected by magic is also a power. It's just so much rarer I overlooked it."

"But you put a shield on her and that worked," said Aislynn.

"No, I didn't. I put a shield *around* her. She only affects magic she comes into contact with. If I bothered to look into it, I would have found dozens of examples of how magic items broke around her."

"And she didn't know this about herself?" Aislynn asked.

"She lives in the most perfect place to *not* know it. Think about it. The least amount of magic they can get by with, no interest in pursuing magic, and while powers materializing would have made an impression, how do you figure out you cause the absence of something?"

"Yet the vampires knew about her when we didn't." Anyone who knew Wulver knew that tone of voice did not bode well for anyone in his path.

Before any response could be made the elevator opened and Tec walked out, his gingery curls sticking up at all angles. "Three-hundred and forty-seven items," he said, the list in his hands grabbed by Laire before he came to a standstill.

"Almost half gone," Wulver said, voice low. He scratched his cheek, fingers curled against the angry-red scar. He stopped and he looked up, his eyes on Laire. "They didn't spend all that effort to get her solely to break into the vault. They need *her* for something very special. Search the list. What is big enough to start the rip and specifically needs a null?"

Laire was the embodiment of concentration, her eyes flying over the list. Her eyes stopped their movements and she jerked back, her mouth forming an *O*. "What day is today?"

"Tues-" began Ais, but Laire pulled out her phone and scrolled through the calendar function. Her teeth ground together when she found what she had been searching for.

"*Well?*" demanded Wulver.

Laire's eyes were wide, horrified. "They have the Stone of the Four Souls and the Dagger of Kerith Tay. They're going to use her to release the Four Demons."

"The demons the gods themselves had to band together to trap?" Aislynn's voice shook. "There is no way a necromancer could control them. Not even to rip the realms asunder would they chance bringing them into this world."

"I might not have any love for fangboy," Laire said, her lips giving a little twist. "But I can admit how powerful he is. If any necromancer ever had the ability to control them, it would be Reign."

"And he's arrogant enough to be willing to try," Fallon finished. "When?"

"Tonight," responded Laire. "Tonight is a blue moon. It has to be tonight, when the moon is at its zenith. It's the only time."

Aislynn spoke. "It's impossible to go against them tonight. Even if we knew where they are. Our forces are decimated. The mages used most of their spells to fight the invasion, the healers are overwhelmed, and our warrior strength is cut in half."

"We can discover where the ceremony will be held." Shadow stepped through the wall and pulled someone behind him. It was an acolyte, the one who walked with Larissa and the vampire, his hands bound behind him. "I caught him on the way out. I've already blocked his link with his master."

"I do love that freaky shadow magic stuff you do," Laire said, normal smart-assy coming back into her voice. Shadow tilted his head toward her, the only concession he heard the praise.

Wulver's lips turned up. He turned to Fallon and arched his eyebrow. "That only leaves making some new friends to help us out tonight. Can you handle it?"

It was in the form of a question, but there was an undeniable order underneath that. Fallon nodded. "Of course. I'm always up for making new friends."

The acolyte watched them, a fervent gleam in his eye. "What makes you think I'll talk to you and abandon my Master?"

"Trust me. You don't have a choice," said Wulver.

"But I think I do." And the acolyte stuck out his tongue and bit clean through. The pink fleshy nub fell to the ground and spurts of blood squirted from his mouth.

Before the tongue hit the ground Fallon pulled out a knife from a sheath on the outside of her thigh. "Laire, *fire*."

Laire complied, and Fallon's knife went red-hot. Fallon grabbed the acolyte's head with her other hand and forced his mouth open, bringing the knife against his gushing tongue, burning lips and cheeks and any other skin that lay in the way and sent the smell of burning flesh wafting through the air.

The man flailed and wrenched and shrieked, but in long moments his wound was closed

Wulver watched. When it was done, he turned to the mage "You need to bring Kyo. You would be fastest."

Laire's face tightened and a hurt, almost betrayed expression crossed her features for a brief moment. But then it smoothed into a mask, and she disappeared.

Fallon still had her hand wrapped around the acolyte's jaw, and she pulled the man close, her fingers digging into his skin, making him wince. "A necromancer wannabe not able to kill himself? I'm ashamed for you." She twisted his head, studying the work of her knife. "You should have kept your tongue, because now the Psy Master is going to *rip* into your mind."

He whimpered. She loosened her grip and leaned close to whisper in his ear. "Don't worry. If you're still alive after he's through with you, I'll take pity on you and kill you. I have enough compassion that I won't let you live like that."

# CHAPTER THIRTY-FOUR

Terak searched Larissa's apartment. Each pass plucked the ever-tightening string of fear that wound around his heart.

They had her. Somehow they had used a magic even he was not immune to and could not see through and had taken her from her books and her children. He spoke to Olivia, who informed him she had not seen Larissa since lunch. Olivia called Larissa's father and brothers who also did not know Larissa's whereabouts, and reported that information back to Terak.

It was now, when his mate was in danger, Terak understood the value of Clan, the slice-cut of being alone. He had no one to turn to who could help him save her.

Larissa's door opened, and Fallon entered, cloaked with her customary assurance. Her sword hilt shone bright above her shoulder and her movements placed her where she could draw freely.

The quick-rise of anger flooded his muscles, expanding them with desire to destroy the warrior before him, but long-fought-for control held him still. "If you have her, I'll kill you."

"If I had her, I wouldn't be here." She took a step toward him, still out of reach, still with her sword at the ready. "Did you know why they wanted her?"

Assured Fallon was, but there was a harsh tension in the lines of eyes and mouth and shoulders that not even battles with orcs and wargs had engendered. Something was out of her control, something frightening, and Fallon was readying herself for a life-altering battle.

The string around his heart pulled tight in a snap and severed the organ in his chest, the destruction leaving him unable to breathe. "Where is she?"

Fallon made no comment on the weak and pitiable sound, but her head tilted as she studied him. "She's a null," the swordswoman said after long moments. "They brought her in and used her to tear through our security. Years of magic cast by the greatest of mages, and tissue paper would have given her more of a challenge."

"Nulls are beings of myth."

"Really? Maybe you should tell that to my *dead*." Fallon's body shifted in her anger, but within a moment she was back to her original stance. "There's more. They're sacrificing her tonight to raise the Four Demons."

*Sacrifice.*

*Sacrifice.*

*Sacrifice.*

He rushed at Fallon and grabbed the swordswoman by the throat. "Tell me where she *is*!"

Fallon's eyes bore into his, molten gold surrounded by fire, and under his hand a peculiar warmth, a current of power traveling over her skin. "Get your hand off me or lose it."

His hand loosened but did not let go. "*Tell* me."

"Will you fight beside us for her and for the protection of this realm? Will you order your Clan to come to our aid?"

Terak stepped back. He did not break eye contact. He would never be ashamed of his decision, though at this moment he regretted it more than he ever contemplated. "I have no Clan. I gave them up for her. There are no others that can help."

Fallon's eyes lost their fire, though her body still had the brittle tenseness that spoke of upcoming battle. "Well, hell. Looks like I owe Ais ten bucks."

*Thwup. Thwup. Thwup.*

Both looked toward the balcony to see Malek and a half-dozen other gargoyles on the landing. Malek walked in while the others waited outside. "*Mennak*, the Guild has contacted us and told us what happened."

Confusion flew through him on hummingbird wings. "Malek, why are you here?"

"To rescue our *Meyla*."

"What are you speaking of? I am no longer Clan."

"No." Malek cut him off, his wings flaring out with the strength of that word. "That is unacceptable. We have cut ourselves from the Clan as well, because we will follow none but you. The old ways are unacceptable. We trust you to lead us in a new Clan, you and your mate."

Terak shook his head as sorrow seeped into the cracks of his battered heart, the parts that broke when he flew away that last night. "I did not want this. I wanted the Clan to be strong and united."

Malek placed his hand on Terak's shoulder. "Perhaps it was inevitable. We were never a single Clan before, perhaps it is not our way. All we know," he said, gesturing to include those behind him, "is we follow none but you. We trust you with our lives and the lives of our mates and children. We go where you lead."

"And if my first order is to place you in danger to protect my mate?"

"We live and die for our *Mennak* and our *Meyla*. It has always been so."

Terak drew him close and touched their foreheads for a moment, mixing gratitude and acceptance and relief. He pulled away. "How many warriors to follow me tonight?"

"Sixty."

Terak turned to Fallon. "Will that do?"

"Is there another choice? Now let's go kill some necromancers."

# CHAPTER THIRTY-FIVE

So here was where it ended, in a maze of caves far away from her home, a sacrifice to release powerful demons who were going to destroy this world and rip the realms apart.

Larissa huddled deeper into her jacket. Earlier, above the clang of metal on metal and the screams of those hurt and dying, she had heard Laire's voice.

*She's a null!*

Before today, she'd never heard that word, the reason for all these weeks of pain and worry.

The reason Terak had come into her life.

Larissa glanced through the bars to where Taneasha lay in the other cage. The girl was quiet now, curled in on herself, but earlier she had been alternating between screaming at the vampire to let her out and begging Larissa to forgive her, swearing that what had been shown her was real, Terak really said those things.

It didn't make sense. Nothing made sense. Had it all been a lie? Everything they had talked about those long evenings, the battles they had fought together?

Making love?

How could that have been a lie?

Shivering, she stuffed her hands into her pockets. Stiff leather brushed against her fingers, and she grabbed the unfamiliar object, pulling it out.

This was the book the Oracle had given her. *The Mating Habits of Gargoyles.*

The Oracle. The woman who had started it all, if those images were indeed true.

*Guard her well.*

He did do that. He held her and protected her and he was so warm. If he were here right now, she could be curled up against that chest that could double as a furnace.

She pushed the confusion over Terak away and flipped the pages open. Knowing what she knew of the Oracle, this book promised to be...interesting. But it wasn't like she had anything else to do while waiting to be sacrificed.

It was written in English, which was good. But instead of salacious, wonderfully purple prose, it was written in academic speak. Well, that took some of the fun out of it.

Still, she kept reading, until one passage knocked in her chest and pushed all breath from her body.

*"The ultimate physical expression of love for a gargoyle is the wrapping of their wings around their 'mate'. It is an instinctive gesture and one that the paranoid and isolated gargoyle cannot force and cannot compel, as it leaves the gargoyle's only true vulnerable spot on their body accessible to the one who is enveloped. Even couples who have been mated for years – decades – sometimes have not reached this level of trust."*

Terak wrapped her in his wings that first night as she had sobbed against the castle floor. She was the one who forced him to let her go.

A photo album of memories flipped open through her mind, and time after time Terak stood with her, his wings either completely enveloping her or half around her as they stood together. He blocked out the world and let them remain in their own little world together with those wings. He hugged her tight to him that last night. It had been the most exquisite feeling of safety of love when he enveloped her, a feeling not even the embraces of her father and brothers had ever touched.

She felt loved.

And it was because he loved her.

None of it had been a lie, and she had been an emotional *idiot* to believe otherwise for even a moment. She knew Terak. She *knew* him. He was good and honorable to the point of being a stick-in-the-mud. That she could doubt him was ridiculous.

There was a reason he had been speaking to that vampire. It didn't matter what it looked like, she was a jerk to have lost faith as she did.

Gods, she had made a real mess of things.

Revelation sparked through her body and demanded movement. She stood, regaining her fight and her momentum.

Terak loved her, and he would be here for her. Of course, that didn't mean she should wait to be rescued, but knowing back-up was fighting like hell to get to her, well, that pumped the spirits up.

She had a student to save, necromancers to thwart, and a gargoyle to make amends to. It was going to be a busy night.

# CHAPTER THIRTY-SIX

The magical shield around the mountain pulsed in bright arcs underneath the hand of the Battle Mage, the glow illuminating her almond-shaped eyes and small, straight nose as she talked to Fallon, Terak, and assorted other warriors. "We can create a pocket in the shield for a short time. If everything goes well, the pocket will stay open long enough to allow eight to twelve people to get through before the barrier seals itself again. Then we'll have to recast the spells, which will take at least ten minutes per casting. The first waves are going to be deep in the shit and sans back-up. First wave should be ready to go in three minutes."

Fallon nodded, her calm expression telling all that the mage's words were exactly what she expected to hear. "How many waves can we get in before the start of the ceremony?"

Laire looked up at the moon. "Three at most, and that's if the casting is perfect with no problems." She waved her hand toward a group of haggard beings chanting in front of the wall. "As you can tell, perfect might be hard to achieve."

Fallon looked over at Aislynn who stood at the edges of the group. The elf was on lookout, her bow at the ready. "Any signs someone has seen us?"

"None so far. The invisibility spell the wizards cast seems to be working."

The shield started to flicker and break. It wouldn't be much longer. Fallon turned back to Laire. "What about inside? Any clues what's going on there?"

"I can give guesses, nothing more," said Laire. "They suffered major casualties today, but they know they did damage to us. Even if they suspect we're here to attack them, I wouldn't be expecting huge numbers of guards, but the guards they do have will be fresh and ready to fight. As for the mages, a lot of spell power has been used today to get ready for the ceremony. They won't be at full power any more than we are. But there will be at least one vampire in there, and a half-tapped vampire is still a powerful enemy."

Terak clenched his jaw, keeping his snarls behind teeth instead of roaring out his displeasure. It was of no matter how many stood guard or fought tonight. They were dead, and he would get his mate back.

"Gargoyles." With a snap of her fingers the mage brought before them a glowing map in the sky, pointing at a little $x$ marked far away from the squares and circles that dominated the bottom. "This is where you guys are being teleported. The cave has an entrance that is high in the mountains and goes down. Impossible for anyone not winged or otherwise flying-abled, which is probably why they didn't put a barrier there. Bad news is we don't know exactly how easy it will be to travel that path. No dwarves we know had anything to do with the construction of these caves. At best, you're going to arrive T-minus fifteen minutes, putting you somewhere between the second and third wave. At best."

Terak shook his head. "I will be in the first wave through the barrier. The rest of my warriors are to be transported."

Malek came, putting his hand on Terak's shoulder. "We will retrieve our *Meyla*. Do not fear."

Terak placed his hand on Malek's shoulder, returning the gesture. He looked over at the warriors who stood ready to fight. "No matter the end of this night, we will teach the vampires to fear the gargoyle."

Laire flicked her fingers with clear impatience. "As heartwarming as this all is, gargoyles who are going to be flying need to gather together. Teleporting this many beings is not easy, and I'd like to get you somewhere close to the entrance and not Siberia."

Malek let go and stood at the head of the group of gargoyles. With a wave, the mage made the gargoyles disappear.

The mage swayed after they disappeared, and Fallon went over in front of her. "Laire?"

The Asian woman waved her off. "Long day. We all have to push past, right?"

Fallon smiled, and for the first time Terak could see friendship in the expression. "Right."

"Thirty seconds," called one of the wizards working on the barrier.

Laire clapped her hands and motioned toward the entrance. "If you're stupid or suicidal, please step up to become the first wave."

Fallon gave her a slit-eyed glare as she hefted her sword free. "That wasn't directed at me, was it?"

"If the heavy-ass sword fits."

"Ten seconds."

Terak walked to the barrier behind only Fallon. Fallon gave a quick glance towards him. "Well, Gargoyle, let's do this."

The barrier opened.

# CHAPTER THIRTY-SEVEN

The door opened to Larissa's cell, and Garof walked into the room, followed by two human men. Their eyes were lowered so no clue if they were red or not, but based on their demeanor they didn't seem much above garden-variety whipping boys.

Taneasha was crying in the corner. She stood, only to moments later fall on her knees before the vampire. "Master, please," she begged.

The vampire crouched down in front of Taneasha, taking her chin in his hand. "Hush, girl. Think of the glorious part you will play in the ascension of the necromancers to their true position in a reborn Magic Realm. Your death will have so much more meaning than a child like you deserves." He motioned to his followers. "Grab the child. I will transport the null."

The men each grabbed one of Taneasha's arms and dragged her out of the cell.

Garof turned to Larissa. "I have no need to drag you, do I?"

"No." Larissa stood. "I would prefer you didn't. I am capable of walking myself."

"Good. I prefer when things are kept dignified, do you agree?"

They walked for several minutes until they came to a room where two stone altars stood next to each other, about ten feet apart with a fire pit between them. Floating above the fire was an ornate dagger and a large red stone, both items she had grabbed from the vault.

Taneasha was already chained to the altar on the left. Garof grabbed her upper arm, but Larissa pulled away. "I said I wouldn't make a scene. Don't touch me." She walked to the other altar.

Manacles. The stupid bastards were going to chain her down. She bit the inside of her cheek to keep the relief that pulsed through her from showing on her face. The cuffs were older but in good condition. They also glowed red, which meant they were enchanted.

Which meant the vampires probably placed most of their trust in the magic of the chains and not the physical strength of the chains themselves. That seemed to be the theme of the day.

And there were no manacles for the feet, which meant she had a chance of making at least step one of her plan succeeding.

Too bad she hadn't formulated step two yet.

Larissa lay on the altar and put her arms up. Garof shackled her. "I am impressed, human. It is rare to see such a display of obedience."

"Hate to break it to you, but compliments from you don't really do it for me, so I wouldn't bother."

The vampire inclined his head. "As you wish." He stood between the two altars and motioned for the two followers to kneel at the foot. "Start the casting."

Not even a minute after the two men began to chant, a shrill scream filled the room. The two acolytes stopped chanting, only to have Garof say, "Do not stop, no matter what!"

Another human in a robe ran up to the vampire. "Master, we are being attacked."

Garof stepped away, though not before Larissa saw his lips form a snarl. As he walked from the room, she heard him say, "They must be delayed until the spell can be completed." Garof and the robed human left.

The only bad guys left in the room were the two chanting.

No time like the present. The cuffs were tight but nothing compared to what her brothers put her through. She freed her hands with barely a scrape.

The rhythmic chanting was rising in volume, and the cave walls started to not so much shake as *undulate.* Both the dagger and the jewel were glowing, the dagger red and the stone blue.

The commotion outside the cavern was growing louder as well, echoes of multitudes of footsteps intermixed with the clanging of metal on metal and screams – which abruptly stopped.

And then came the call. *"Meyja!"*

*Terak!* He was here, yes, he was and no way was she going to be some sort of sacrifice for these idiot vampires. She had a gargoyle waiting who she was going to kiss until her lips fell off and then mate with him and live wherever they could be together – her world, his world, or a world they would create on their own.

Dumb and Dumber down there on the floor were oblivious to everything outside their chants. And in front of her, right beside the fire pit, was a decent-sized and solid-looking cauldron.

Never had she been quieter than she was at that moment, not even when she had been taking pictures of her brother Christopher getting to second base on their sofa with his high-school girlfriend.

A couple of well-aimed conks later, both men were unconscious. If they got brain damage, oh well.

Taneasha rattled her chains, her eyes pleading when Larissa looked at her. "Please, Miss Miller, don't leave me here. I'm so sorry. I never thought anything like this would happen. They said they wanted to talk to you about helping with a spell. I'm so sorry."

Maybe she was. And maybe Larissa understood how this could happen with a girl as shy and sensitive as Taneasha was. That didn't change the fact this was Taneasha's fault and there would be consequences for her actions. "I'm going to free you and get us out of here. Everything else can wait until we're safe."

Knocked-out acolyte number one had the key, and Larissa freed the girl from the altar. Now, where to go? Terak's voice had come from the main door, but that was where the necromancer had gone. To run out there would be to run straight into them.

Looking around the cave, there was one small side door behind the altars. It could lead anywhere, or it could lead nowhere at all, but it was the only other door. "We're going through there. The front door would be too dangerous with that battle going on."

Taneasha nodded, staying close to her.

"I need you to stay a bit away from me."

Taneasha looked at her with hurt eyes, but understanding dawned moments later when Larissa grabbed the stone and dagger. "I don't know what these things would do to anyone not magically immune, and I don't want to find out by watching what happens to you."

Taneasha nodded, staying a small distance away as they ran through the doors.

# CHAPTER THIRTY-EIGHT

Terak clawed through another orc, dismembering the beast before throwing the carcass to the side.

There were fewer enemies than expected. The earlier attack on the Guild must have taken most of their resources. The first wave made good progress as they tore through the underlings, but it was too soon to gloat over easy triumph – the necromancers still awaited them.

"Doing okay over there, Gargoyle?" Fallon's voice could be heard above the cacophony. Her sword clanged as metal struck metal in her own battles.

He didn't bother to answer. Instead, he threw his head back and yelled, *"Meyja!"*

A blast of power hit Terak in the chest and threw him back into the wall, the stone jabbing into his body.

"Pity gargoyles are resistant to magic. That would have made a satisfying spectacle of carnage." Garof's voice penetrated the daze Terak was shaking off. He rose to see the damned vampire standing before him. "Originally created by necromancers, at least that is what the myths say about your kind. My brethren did perhaps *too* good of a job."

"Where's my *mate*?"

"You should have taken me up on my offer. It would have worked out much better for you."

The vampire raised his hand and cast another blasting spell, but Terak rolled out of the path and only dealt with the flying debris behind him.

Out of the corner of his eye, Terak saw Fallon finish her fight and rush toward the vampire. The vampire saw it as well, for he waved in Fallon's direction and a wall of rock shot up between them and the rest of the battle. "I'll deal with Fallon later. I want to finish killing you first."

Terak growled and lunged for the vampire, dropping them both to the ground. But the vampire twisted his body, using momentum and a strength Terak was not expecting to throw Terak into the opposite cave wall.

Terak regained his feet to see Garof already on his. "Don't underestimate me, Gargoyle. You are indeed a warrior beyond compare, but I am Vampire. You are nothing to me." The vampire stilled then, his head cocked to the side and his eyes wide in alarm.

Terak used the chance to run into the vampire again, slicing into his neck with his claws.

Flesh parted, but no blood came out. Instead in a blink the skin knitted itself together, and Garof punched Terak in the chest so hard he couldn't breathe for a second. The vampire kicked the side of his knee, and Terak fell before him. Garof kicked Terak in the face and he crumpled into the ground. "As entertaining as this has been, Gargoyle, I believe I will finish this after the Magic Realm has been returned to us. You will be a fitting sacrifice."

A thread of worry was buried in the vampire's tone, and hope pulsed through Terak's muscles, granting strength and pushing him to his feet. If the vampire was worried, it meant his little human was well and was causing problems for the damned necromancers. Of course she was. His mate was more than a match for a legion of undead.

Garof was not quick enough this time to throw Terak when the gargoyle landed on his back. They wrestled as Terak landed blow after blow.

The blows had little effect and the vampire freed himself. He grabbed Terak by the throat and repeatedly punched him in the chest. Terak's bones fractured under the prolonged force, and his entire torso became a mass of pain.

Garof dropped him and grabbed a sword from the ground, an evil-looking blade with serrated edges. "I've heard of the gargoyles' formidable healing abilities, so I best end this now." He raised the sword high...

...and *screamed.*

Frantically, Garof tried to reach behind him. Terak stared as the vampire twisted, revealing an ornate dagger hilt protruding from his back. Larissa stood behind the vampire, her arm lowering from driving the blade into the undead. Terak reached for her, but his wounds were not healed enough yet that he could move much.

Larissa stepped back from the vampire as he fell to the ground. The wound was smoking, and his skin was starting to crackle and blacken.

The vampire was a repulsive sight. Larissa's face held a sick horror as she watched the disintegration of the creature. "Larissa," Terak called, to break through her fascination as much as for help.

It worked. The most beautiful smile lit her face and she moved toward him.

Tremors rocked the mountain, knocking her to the ground, as well as a young girl behind her that only now Terak noticed. The tremors stopped, and Laire's voice magically echoed through the caverns the way a PA system would. "Attention, good guys. You did great because I'm getting readings the ceremony was stopped. But bad news anyway. This mountain is magically booby-trapped so if the ceremony doesn't go through, the mountain will implode. We're holding it together the best we can, but we suggest getting your tushies out here ASAP if not faster."

Larissa turned to the girl behind her. "Run out now!" The girl did not have to be told twice and escaped, and though he would have told a child the same thing, a momentary shiver of loathing hit his gut on how easily the girl ran from those who had helped her and left them to their fates.

His bones were already knitting together, so he pushed himself up. Since he could yell at Larissa to run all he desired and she would never leave, he needed to push past the pain and get them out of here.

He took a step forward and hit a shimmery blue wall. A force cage. Terak punched into it, but he could not get through. Larissa stood on the other side, her eyes wide.

The vampire still lay on the ground, black smoke still rising from his all-but-decomposed corpse. A rusty laugh escaped from a now-lipless skull. "It was a good fight, Gargoyle. I think it only fitting we die together. It's not a very strong cage. The weight of the mountain bearing down will pierce it, and you'll be crushed to death. I'd say this battle is a draw."

No. This couldn't be happening, this couldn't be real. She had been the target, and now she was safe and sound. This was supposed to be the end of it. She was *not* supposed to see the male she loved trapped in front of her, waiting for a mountain to crush him to death.

"Leave me!" He was bloody and bleeding in the cage, his arm hanging at an odd angle. "This place will soon be destroyed. Go!"

He was trapped. She could travel through the force field, but she could do nothing to free him. This power that had necromancers hunting her was worthless when it mattered.

"*Meyja-*"

"What does that mean?" she interrupted, her eyes clear on his. "You swore you would tell me once this was over. What does it mean?"

His eyes were intense on hers. "It means *Beloved above all, even above the Clan.*"

And if there was any question of what her choice would be – which there wasn't – that decided her beyond any doubts. She pushed inside the force field.

His arms and wings came around her as if he could not help himself, even as he said, "*Meyja*, I don't want you here. Think of your father, your brothers. They need you. I need you to live. I need you to leave."

She snuggled into his embrace. "For once, I'm only going to think about what I want and not consider them. I'm not going to ever leave you, Terak. If this is where it ends, I'll face the end with you."

He sunk to the floor, keeping her in his arms, kissing her face, her hair. "Love you, *Meyja*. I have always loved you. Forgive me for not telling you before this day."

She nuzzled into him. "You did. I didn't understand." The rumbling was louder now, the heat building. She curled into Terak's arms. "Love you, my Gargoyle. My warrior."

*Love you.*

Shadowy arms wrapped around her, and Larissa was pulled down through the floor.

# CHAPTER THIRTY-NINE

"Hi there, Sleeping Beauty."

*So I've died and gone to hell.* It was unmistakably Fallon's voice, and the swordswoman wasn't on her favorite persons list. Considering Fallon's general attitude, there was no way she was on anyone's favorite persons list.

But Fallon had come to free her. And she had fought with Terak. And she did look cool carrying around such a big sword.

*Okay, maybe purgatory.*

"Take your time waking up. It's fine. It's not like we have anything else to do except sit around and stare at you."

Awareness came in short spurts. Grass scratched her cheek and arms, and the earth was solid underneath, solid and cool, but warmer than it had been when she had been forced through it like a ghost, insubstantial, weightless, *wrongness.* Her skin prickled at the sense memory, and she shuddered with the renewed cold. Did Terak feel...

*Terak.*

"Terak?"

"Here," and strong, rough fingers grazed her chin. She forced her eyes open to see his beloved face. He was sitting to her left, looking as if had just risen from beside her.

"What happened?" Because last she checked, she and Terak were about to get crushed under a mountain.

"Shadow," Fallon answered as Terak helped Larissa into a sitting position.

The world's rotation was observable, but Larissa took a few deep breaths to get the dizziness under control. Once that was accomplished, she looked to the area where Fallon pointed, to see the dark warrior on the ground, a healer above him. Shadow looked greyer, like a faded copy instead of the original.

"Is he okay?"

"He will be. Mostly," Fallon said. "Don't overthink it. It's what we do."

Larissa looked at the various Guild members. No, they weren't nice and they weren't good, but while she would happily live her life if she never met up with them again, that didn't mean they weren't needed in these days. Days that would only get darker during this period that the necromancers could destroy all.

She reached for Terak, needing skin contact. He meshed his fingers with hers, his eyes dark and bright. "Thank you all for saving Terak and saving me."

From out of a giant purse Laire pulled out a small, black velvet bag. "I'll tell you how you can show your thanks – hand over that little bauble you've got with you."

Terak's fingers tightened on hers. At his nod Larissa fished the jewel from her pocket. "What would this have done?"

"Pray you never find out," Laire said. She held out the opened bag. "Drop it in there, please."

Larissa did as asked, and Laire spoke a few words in an unidentified language before tying the bag off and tucking it back in her purse. Laire looked her over, and the term *X-ray vision* floated through Larissa's brain. The mage asked, "The dagger?"

"Buried in Garof's back, if you want to go back for it."

For one moment, fear flickered over Laire's face, but the Asian woman closed her eyes and turned away, heading back for her companions. Fallon exhaled in an explosive blast, and Larissa decided to not ask any questions.

And now to the other problem of the night. "Taneasha?"

"We have her, and we know her part in this."

Fallon's tone might have warned against asking any questions, but Larissa couldn't let it go at that, no matter what the girl did. "What's going to happen to her?"

"We're not going to kill her, if that's what you're worried about." Never let it be said Fallon tried to soften news. "But you're not going to see her in class again."

Before Larissa could even begin to process her conflicted feelings about her former student, from the sky dropped several gargoyles. Terak rose but kept her in his arms, beneath his wings. She curled into him.

Terak called out, "All have survived?"

"Yes. We looked for you, but the mountain was crumbling too quickly and we had no choice except to leave."

"I would have it no other way, Malek."

Larissa squirmed a little. When Terak looked at her she arched her eyebrow and tilted her head a tiny amount. They really were a couple because Terak read her wants perfectly and set her down, though he kept her close. She spoke to the assembled gargoyles. "Thank you for coming to my aid. I am grateful to all of you beyond what I can say."

Malek shook his head, his arm casting aside her words. "You are ours to protect, *Meyla*. It is duty and honor to come to your side when we are needed. We made that promise when we followed your mate away from the Clan."

*Away from the Clan.* Larissa looked up at Terak. He stared straight ahead as if he had no idea she was looking at him, but the tick in his jaw gave him away. "What do they mean, *away from the Clan*?"

He took a long breath before he gazed down at her. "I made a choice."

"No." There was no way she was going to let this happen. Not his Clan. "I'm not worth it."

His gaze became fierce and he brought himself to his full height. "You are worth everything," he said, the tone brooking no argument. "I would give this realm for you, so do not talk to me of leaving the Clan. They cannot accept you, so I will have no more dealings with them."

"Your people-"

"My *Meyja*."

Before she could continue, noises above made everyone turn their attention to the sky, in time to see a contingent of gargoyles descending in front of them.

An older gargoyle stepped forward, and Terak moved to meet him while keeping her behind him. "Krikus, how did you know of this place?"

"The Guild transported us here once the danger was past. I informed them the need to see you was urgent." The old councilor looked past Terak and straight at Larissa. When their eyes met, he gave a bow. "Forgive me for not introducing myself earlier, *Meyla*. I am Krikus."

Terak went still at the title. "You call her *Meyla*?"

"Why would we not? She is the mate of our *Mennak*."

With those words, as one, the gargoyles dropped to their knees in front of Terak. Malek smiled, and he and the warriors joined in the display.

The wondrous confusion on Terak's face cracked Larissa's heart. Her beloved gargoyle was so exposed for all to see – his desire for what they were offering warring with the disbelief it could be happening.

Krikus waited for Terak's attention to return to him before he spoke again. "It will not be easy. We still have doubts, and some will never be convinced. But you are right – our Clan must be united to survive. We choose the path behind you. We will follow as you create this new place."

Terak was still speechless, so Larissa came up and placed her hand in his. "I hope," she began, and gave Krikus the smile she had perfected when she convinced her father to let her go on her first date, "This means you will help me in learning how to best serve my Clan."

Surprise lit the old gargoyle's face before a wide smile split his face. "I would be honored, *Meyla*."

Terak's eyes were soft on her, adoring, and Larissa basked in the force of that gaze. Her gargoyle, her mate, her *love*. Still, a little tease wouldn't hurt. "There is one last thing to conquer."

Terak's visage turned wary, and he glanced around. "What is that?"

"You need to meet *my* family."

# CHAPTER FORTY

He heard her coming toward him, the *clack-clack* of her shoes heralding her arrival on the stone embankment long before her words reached his ears. "Why are you in that form?"

Terak turned to face his mate as she approached him, wearing a long coat belted at her waist. "I thought you would prefer me to meet your family while I was in my human guise."

Her mouth was tight, little frown lines between her eyebrows. "As you told me, no matter what you look like, you are a gargoyle. I didn't fall in love with a human, I don't want a human with me as I introduce the male I love to my family. I want the Clan Leader of the Gargoyles, my mate, by my side tonight."

His heart became more hers at those words, if that were even possible. Still, he shook his head. "They will only see me as a monster and try to take you away. I do not wish to fight the family of my mate, but I will not let them keep you from me."

"Terak," she sighed, coming over to take his face between her hands. "That won't happen. They already know everything and know what to expect when they meet you."

"Are you saying your Clan is happy with your mate?"

"I'm saying they don't have a choice in the matter."

He brought up one hand to cover hers as it lay against his face, warm and soft. "Why would you believe that? Your father is anything but weak-willed. He will not accept so easily any mating of yours, but especially to one who is connected to the New Realms."

"My dad has to accept it, because I told him I love you the same way he loved my mother, and I asked him if anything in this world would have kept him from her side. When he admitted nothing would, I asked him what lengths he thought I would go or what I would give up to stay with you. I can't say he's completely happy, I won't lie about that. But you left the Clan to be with me. Do you think you mated with someone who does not have the same level of commitment as you do?"

"Never, little human. You awe me with all you have given up already to be at my side."

"Then prove your faith in me, and turn into your true form." With a naughty smile, she started to remove the long coat. "I'll make it worth your while."

Her reveal was a punch to his chest, stealing his breath away as he took her in. Her dress emphasized the soft swell of her breasts, the skirt was very tight and very short, and on her feet were shoes with spikes that made the lines of her legs into works of art.

He reached out to touch her, but she backed away and waggled a finger at him. "*Tsk tsk*, I don't see your gargoyle form yet."

Putting aside his own fears, he took a deep breath, closed his eyes, and changed into his true form.

When he opened his eyes again, he saw her gaze moving over his body, taking in every inch. "Now this is what I want."

"Then give me my reward, mate."

She smiled then, walking toward him with her hips swaying, the sight of it making his body hard. Once she was before him again she lifted herself onto her toes and took his bottom lip between her teeth, giving a soft bite she knew would drive him insane. "Out of the two of us, I'm the one who should be worried."

"Oh?" he said, enjoying the feel of her.

She licked the spot she had just bitten. "After all, I'm only a puny, insubstantial human. I can't defend myself."

He moved his mouth to graze over hers. "A gargoyle who is not strong enough to defend his mate does not deserve to live."

She lowered her mouth to nuzzle under his chin. "I have no claws."

"I disagree. I feel your claws when you rake them down my back," and he groaned as she proceed to show him how good her claws felt as they traveled his front.

She nipped the underside of his jaw. "I can't fly."

His hands cupped her face, locking their gazes. "I will always carry you."

That beautiful smile that defined his world lit her face. "Show me."

He was undone. He lifted her into his arms and jumped into the air before them, taking flight.

He thought he loved flying before, but holding Larissa in his arms remade the experience. She kissed his earlobe, worrying the flesh between her teeth before she bit down. He struggled to keep his eyes open against the sensual assault, but when she licked the shell of his ear he shuddered, losing momentum and dropping a few feet.

She giggled. "Am I having an effect on the mighty Clan Leader," she teased, blowing into his ear now.

"Larissa," he growled, but she paid him no mind. Putting her mouth to his ear, she whispered, "Wrap my legs around your waist."

He groaned. "What are you doing to me?"

"Me? I'm enjoying the flight. You concentrate on keeping us in the air, I'll take care of the rest."

She slid her leg down his torso. He should stop her, yet somehow, he found himself settling her as she wished.

Once she was secure, her hand reached down between her legs to the fastening of his pants. "Larissa," he tried again, but even as he spoke her name her hand curled around his aching shaft, freeing him from the fabric. "Gods, I love the feel of you," she breathed, stroking as far down as she could. "I want you all the time. I think of you inside me all the time." She wiggled down his body, bringing them into intimate contact.

It took all his willpower to stay aloft. He had no reserves for speech, so he could not tell her to stop.

Otherwise he would...and then she stroked him against the wet warmth of her pussy, laid bare to him.

"Where...are your undergarments?" Sweat ran down his spine, pillowing in the hollow of his back as his hips instinctively flexed toward her.

"Oops, guess I forgot something." Nothing in her voice suggested she was sorry for this.

She would pay. She would pay for doing this to him, for robbing him of all sanity right as he was going to meet her Clan. As soon as he could think again, she would pay.

Larissa gave him a quick, hard kiss, her eyes hazy with lust. "I wish I could taste this right now, but I've learned adaptability is key to survival. I'll get back to that later." Using her legs, she worked herself on him, but without leverage there was little friction, only the delicious feel of her wetness over his tip. Her nails dug into his back right above where his wings attached while the pointy spikes of her heels speared into his thighs in the most pleasurable pain he had ever known.

"Terak," she cried. She was pink and tousled, her pouty lips parted in frustration that she was not able to take him deeper and bring them both the pleasure they craved.

Below them was a deserted park. He needed to end this or he would lose his sanity.

He landed with a hard thud, his usual grace absent as he stumbled. Wasting no time he fell to his knees, placing her with gentle care on the ground on her back before he fell above her, his wings flaring out behind them.

Larissa's breaths were jagged as she watched him. He plunged into her, the tightening of her body against the sudden invasion bringing him to near climax.

No, not without her. He fought against every nerve in his body begging him to plunge again, to race toward climax. Instead he stroked inside her with small, even movements, movements that made her breath labored and her back arch.

"Yes, yes, yes," she chanted, her hips squirming against his, pushing him harder inside her. Using her heels, she pulled him in. "Deeper, Terak. Get as deep as you can in me and make me come."

Her words broke any restraint and now he only knew her, to pound inside her and pour himself into his mate, to mark her so deeply no one who beheld her would ever doubt to whom she belonged, and her cry of satisfaction while her body clenched around him signaled her acceptance of that claim.

His head fell back as he came inside her, growling and cursing at one of the strongest orgasms of his life came over him.

Long moments later when their breathing normalized, she looked up at him. Her eyes were dreamy. She lifted her hands, delicate human fingers stroking over brow bone and pointed ears, pulling strands of his much thicker hair. "Why would I want to be with anyone but you?"

He leaned down, kissing her mouth, letting her sureness overcome his doubts. "We are supposed to meet with your father soon. I doubt he will be happy if I bring you to him in this condition."

"We'll stop at my apartment to get cleaned up." She smiled, a light teasing cast to her mouth. "Don't be overworried about making a bad impression. No matter what you do, Dad's going to hate you on sight."

Terak reared back. "I thought you said that he would accept me."

"Oh yes, he's going to accept you. He has no choice on that. But that doesn't mean he's going to like you. You are taking away his baby girl, after all."

"Is it always like this with humans?"

"Welcome to the family."

# CHAPTER FORTY-ONE

Zemar waited outside, silent and still, a living statue hidden in the ragged shadows cast by the building.

The acolyte arrived, oblivious to his presence. The boy's focus was on the pouch he carried. He stroked the pouch with a hand that trembled with the slightest touch, the way others would caress a lover. The boy was laughable in his overt desire for power, a power he could no more wield than a toddler rule a nation.

Would the boy be foolish enough to run with the dagger? It was a powerful temptation, promising untold power to one who could master it.

No, no running for this one. The sheen of sweat coating his face even on this cold autumn night, the wide eyes and shallow breaths answered the question as the boy approached the door. He coveted, but he would obey.

The boy was right to let his fear triumph over any ambitions he might harbor. The dagger would only destroy him.

Zemar melted from the shadows to enjoy the panic of the boy before he registered who stood before him. The boy bowed, holding forth the weapon for Zemar to take. "Master," was all he said.

Zemar spoke no words to him. The blade now in his hands, he went into the building, taking the elevator to the penthouse.

The apartment was an expansive space, leather and chrome shaping the interior. The far wall was made of glass, and from this dizzying height the effect was the city laid bare, showing its soft underbelly in submission.

A couch was situated in front of the window and Zemar approached it. Reign sat in the middle, his arms draped over the back of the couch, the drained body of a young woman on the ground, her red hair a blanket over his feet.

Reign did not bother to take the dagger, merely continued his observation of the city. "Fallon?"

"She is still alive, my Lord."

Reign's rich laugh filled the air. "As if she were ever in any danger from the fools that were present." His eyes darkened to black-red. He murmured, "The only one who will take Fallon is me."

Zemar watched his Master stroke his hand over his lips while his gaze stayed on the window. With a negligent movement, Reign reached out his hand. Zemar obeyed, handing the dagger over.

Reign studied the blade, twisting it in his hand to go over every inch with his gaze. "How many did she kill?"

"Dozens, my Lord, until her sword was dull with the blood of her enemies."

Reign stroked the edge of the dagger with his forefinger until a drop of blood was drawn. The blood absorbed into the blade. "Only that? I will see her bathed in blood before me."

*"And what of the Oracle's prophecy?"*

Fallon snorted. "The usual crap she pulls. Of course Larissa was important to the Gargoyle Clan, she's going to be the wife of the Clan Leader and make future heirs to the throne. Is it me, or is using untold powers to play matchmaker a little beneath her?"

*"The young enjoy getting into mischief. She will grow out of it."*

"That's an interesting statement. Tell me, how old is she, and how much younger is she than you?"

*"Nice try. Back to the gargoyle. Do you truly believe you can trust him?"*

Fallon was resting her head on the back of the chair, her eyes closed in tiredness. "I believe we can. Strange to think of gargoyles as allies, but he truly does love her, and the other side wants her dead. As long as that's the case, he'll fight like hell for us."

*"Any male fights like hell for his mate."*

"Oh? And what would you know about that?"

"Fallon, who are you talking to?"

Aislynn's voice cut through the air, startling Fallon so she jerked upright in her seat. "Ais, I didn't hear you come in." Fallon rose, bending her neck to the side in a deep stretch. "Talking to myself, as usual. Just trying to come down from the last few weeks. What do you need?"

Aislynn shifted, motioning behind her with her thumb. "Wulver has called us. No rest for the wicked and all that."

"What's up?"

"Tec is giving us a complete list of missing items, with Laire providing commentary on how much chaos and destruction each can cause. We need to strategize about Merc and the spellbook, and it seems as though the Master of Monsters will be returning."

"Great, I can't wait to see Wulver start humping the furniture again. Something to look forward to. Anything else?"

Aislynn pretended to think for a moment, pressing her forefinger against her chin. "Don't expect to use your vacation benefits anytime soon?"

"Figures." Fallon made an *after you* gesture with her hand, and the two females left the room.

*"What do I know of mates? Wouldn't you like to know..."*

## The End

# NOTE FROM
# DANIELLE MONSCH

Peoples! Thanks for purchasing **Stone Guardian**, book 1 in the *Entwined Realms* series. I appreciate you giving a new author a chance, and hope you enjoyed.

More will be coming to the *Entwined Realms.* If you want to know as soon as they are released, please sign up for my newsletter! Newsletters are sent out only when a book is released or I'm giving stuff away, and your email is never used for any other purpose or sold/distributed to anyone else! http://www.daniellemonsch.com/dani/signup/

# ABOUT THE AUTHOR

Born to the pothole-ridden streets of Pittsburgh, PA, Danielle Monsch started writing in a time long ago, a time when there were not enough vampire stories to read and she had to write her own to fill the void. Yes, such a time of darkness did indeed exist.

Danielle writes stories full of fantastical goodness and plenty of action, but always with lots of romance (and a bit of woo-hoo!) mixed in. Vampires and Werewolves and Demons and Angels, Sword & Sorcery, Fairy Tales, Updated Mythologies and the like – if it's out of the ordinary, it's fair game for her stories.

Go to www.DanielleMonsch.com for one-stop shopping with everything to do with Danielle - there you can join her newsletter (*highly* encouraged as it contains all info about upcoming books, plus lots of random surprises) follow her on twitter, and like her on facebook. Just want to send Danielle a quick email? Easy enough, that's Dani@DanielleMonsch.com.